W9-AXZ-319

The Cottage On Lighthouse Lane

The Cottage On Lighthouse Lane

DAVIS BUNN

KENSINGTON
PUBLISHING CORP.
www.kensingtonbooks.com

KENSINGTON BOOKS are published by

Kensington Publishing Corp.
119 West 40th Street
New York, NY 10018

All Kensington titles, imprints and distributed lines are available at special quantity discounts for bulk purchases for sales promotion, premiums, fund-raising, educational or institutional use. Special book excerpts or customized printings can also be created to fit specific needs. For details, write or phone the office of the Kensington Special Sales Manager: Kensington Publishing Corp., 119 West 40th Street, New York, NY 10018. Attn. Special Sales Department. Phone: 1-800-221-2647.

Library of Congress Control Number: 2020952334

ISBN-13: 978-1-4967-2502-8
ISBN-10: 1-4967-2502-6

First Kensington Hardcover Edition: May 2021

ISBN-13: 978-1-4967-2504-2 (ebook)
ISBN-10: 1-4967-2504-2 (ebook)

10 9 8 7 6 5 4 3 2 1

Printed in the United States of America

FOR URSULA

A True Visionary

and

Our Dearest Friend

ACKNOWLEDGMENTS

Writing this story has been dependent upon the advice, wisdom, and input of so many great people. Great, as in, nice and helpful and kind in how they guided me through the acting life. And great, as in, actually being great stars in the entertainment galaxy. I have never acted, and almost all my film/streaming experience has been on the other side of the camera. To write about this version of events has been a very daunting task. These wonderful people are the only reason that I even decided to try. All the good bits are due to them. All the failings are my own.

David Lipman is the producer of the Shrek film series and co-producer of *Iron Man*. Ileen Maisel produced *The Golden Compass* among many many others. Jamie Wolpert has been a VP with both Simon Pegg's Stolen Pictures and Elton John's Rocket Films. Chris Sharpe is the former head of Liberty Media Europe. Mark Pinkosh is a star of stage and screen, whose credits include *Charlie's Angels* and *Eight is Enough*.

There are almost as many books on acting as there are on how to write a novel–authors are by nature voracious consumers of the written word, which makes them more ready and willing buyers. As far as sheer difficulty in mastering a craft, my money has to go on those people who dare to stand in front of the camera. It has been a delight, and a very real challenge, to join their company at the front of the stage, even temporarily.

My editor, Wendy McClurdy, has been a true friend and great teacher. It has meant a great deal to see that this story, perhaps of all those I have written with and for her, hit the mark. Thanks also to my agent, he of infinite patience, Chip MacGregor.

My wife, Isabella, remains the single most important element and guide to this writer's life.

The following books became my daily companions, and in some cases my true friends. For anyone wishing to delve further into this most mysterious of crafts, I cannot recommend these too highly:

Making Movies, Sidney Lumet, Vintage Books

Which Lie Did I Tell, William Goldman, Bloomsbury

On Acting, Sanford Meisner and Dennis Longwell, Vintage Books

In Pieces, Sally Fields, Grand Central Publishing

An Actor Prepares, Constantin Stanislavsky, Aristophanes Press

Audition, Michael Shurtleff and Bob Fosse, Bloomsbury

Acting in Film, Michael Caine, Applause Books

The Art of Acting, Stella Adler, Applause Books

So, Anyway, John Cleese, Cornerstone Books

CHAPTER 1

The best day and the worst day of Billy Rose Walker's life began the hour before dawn. When his mother entered Billy's dream and sang to him.

In his younger days, such dreams about his mother had haunted any number of Billy's nights. His grandmother, Ada Rose, used to call night's close the loneliest hour. It was when spirits became restless, and not just those laid in God's green earth. A body burdened with illness, Ada used to say, was most threatened in the dark hour before dawn. Bonds holding body and spirit together were weakest then. The temptation to just slip away and leave behind all the hardship and the hurt was too much for some.

Billy rose from his bed and washed his face and stood waiting for his mother's voice to go silent. The last time he'd suffered from dreams of his mother had been in the months after Ada passed. But that was almost ten years ago. Billy told himself it was the result of too many hard-fought days, working for a man who hated the sight of him, and decided to go for a daybreak run.

Eleven years ago, Billy graduated from the UNC-Asheville theater program. He followed this with two and a half years in local theater and modeling around the Southeast. When he had six months' living expenses saved, he packed up his dreams and his meager belongings and set out for LA. Eight and a half tough years later, he was still clawing his way up the Hollywood ladder's lower rungs.

They were shooting a romantic drama in El Paso. Billy's character was the only son of an oil and cattle baron. The lady was a distinctly Latina beauty, and a US citizen. And a lawyer fighting for the rights of local undocumented workers. Which brought her into direct conflict with Billy's family and all their interests. The drama was heightened by corrupt cops bribed by the Juárez cartels. There were some solid action sequences, enough humor to make the jaded crew laugh, and a jalapeño-spiced love story. Every day on set, Billy heard somebody predict the film might have legs.

Billy returned to his room, showered, dressed, had a smoothie for breakfast, and was downstairs in time to watch the crew bus arrive.

Billy slipped into his customary seat next to Trevor, the assistant director. He slid his pack under the seat and nodded hellos to a few of the crew. He liked the team for the most part. Seven weeks into an eight-week shoot, four days off for Christmas, there were clear patterns of camaraderie and friction. Most of the crew members welcomed Billy and made room for him in their conversations. That wasn't usually the way between principal actors and the others on set. A lot of the time, stars kept to the LA attitude, talking exclusively to their publicist and their agent and the director and their stylist and the rest of their tight little clique.

Just as often, though, union guys living on the clock created the hostility. At the end of every shoot, the crew accepted their paychecks and were off to the next gig, if they were lucky. Their attitude went something like, the only reason those jokers standing in the lights take home the big bucks was because the behind-camera team spent fourteen or sixteen hours each day busting their humps. Billy knew for a fact this attitude was well justified. So he went out of his way to learn their names and show appreciation for all they did.

Billy saw how Trevor remained slumped back, eyes closed, wincing at the light flashing through the side window. "Rough night?"

Trevor drank from his go-cup without lifting his head from the seat or opening his eyes. "I'm so hungover, I don't know if I'm gonna make it."

"You don't drink."

"Crying shame how I've got to feel this way without regretting the night before." Another sip. "How far did you run?"

"Five miles. Not far, not fast."

Trevor took another sip. "Big scene today. You ready to fall in love?"

"I been head over heels for the lady since our first day on set."

Trevor's assistant and a young intern were seated across from Billy. They had the day's sequencing sheets spread out across both their laps. They were long accustomed to Trevor's slow and sullen start to every day. Both of them laughed without lifting their gazes from the time grid. Even Trevor cracked a smile. Billy's love interest and co-star was a Latina beauty named Consuela Adler. Connie had proven herself to be a monumental pain.

Billy assumed that was it for the morning chatter. He settled back and enjoyed the late January morning's crisp desert quality. El Paso was not a pretty city, but Billy found himself fascinated by the region. He had used his free days to drive one of the set's rental cars into the hill country and hike. The hotel's deputy manager was a bearded local in his twenties. He was a fanatic about his homeland, a proud Texan who hunted in season and knew all the region's trails by name. He kitted Billy out with detailed cartographic maps and took genuine pleasure in talking Billy through the arroyos and the vegetation and the legends. The highway connecting their hotel to the day's shoot rounded the city's downtown section, bringing them close enough to the neighboring hills for Billy to almost taste the sage and creosote and heat.

Billy was mentally working on his next trail day when Trevor said quietly, "There's been talk."

"Good or bad?"

Trevor balanced a ham-sized hand. "Could go either way."

Trevor was not a man known for dealing in rumors. Billy slipped farther down in his seat, as far as his six-two frame allowed. When his knees dug into the seat ahead of him and his head was almost lined with Trevor's, he said softly, "Tell me."

Trevor Culley was a massive African American whose voice could stop traffic in the next county. This morning, however, Trevor said quietly, "Got a call from a buddy late last night. Senior exec at the studio. Claims *Harrowgate* is in trouble and sinking fast."

Harrowgate was what the industry called a tentpole feature, a major project with a production budget topping seventy million dollars. Tentpole films anchored the summer and Christmas seasons, and basically drove the studio's bottom line. A failure of this size could push the studio into the red for the year. "This is real?"

"My pal says so."

"Two questions," Billy said. "Why does he think this is important enough to call you in the middle of the night? And what does that have to do with us?"

"Those are good questions," Trevor said.

Billy gave his friend a couple of minutes, then elbowed the well-padded ribs. "Talk."

"Seems a number of senior execs have started dropping by and watching our dailies."

That pushed Billy straighter in his seat. "Whoa."

"They've got to find something to fill that vacuum. There's talk we just might be what they're looking for." Trevor opened one eye. "You do understand what something like this could do to your career."

Billy opened his mouth, but no sound came.

Since coming to LA, Billy reckoned he had gone up for somewhere around four hundred auditions. Four hundred times he'd amped up his hopes and his drive, burnished his image, smiled his best, sounded bright and excited, and worked his hardest to win the prize. Four hundred auditions had netted him eighty-one parts. Thirty-nine of them in commercials. Most of the rest were walk-on roles, a few lines of dialogue. The bigger the budget, the smaller his face time. This was just his seventh film where he'd had a starring role, and the very first which had more than a TV-sized budget. Eleven million dollars. Small potatoes for a studio feature. But still.

It actually caused Billy a pain in his gut to think this might truly mark a real chance.

Trevor showed Billy a gentle smile. The way Billy had seen him watch his twin girls. Knowing a lot more than he would ever be able to put into words. Trevor then addressed him by his stage name. "You're going to be just fine, Billy Rose."

Billy's throat was suddenly so tight it was hard to breathe. Much less swallow. "What are you going on about?"

Trevor turned back to the road ahead. "You'll see soon enough."

CHAPTER 2

～⁕～

Mimi Janic dreamed of the burning house.

She had not been woken by that dream for years. Certainly not since she had arrived in the United States at age nine. During her final months in eastern Ukraine, however, she had smelled those flames at least a couple of times every week. These days, when she thought of it at all, the dream was part of the long, lonely months after they separated Mimi from her sister. The last living member of her immediate family. Gone forever.

Sometimes in the fire dream, Mimi was a child of five or perhaps six. Tonight, though, she was an infant standing in her crib. She grasped the railings with her small hands and watched as burning cinders flickered and fell all around her. There was a distinct beauty to the moment, and a mystery, like she watched a fairy tale come to life. But there was no fear. Somewhere in the distance she heard faint shouts and screams. But they could not touch her there in her crib.

The cinders flickered as they fell, surrounding her in an elven glow that illuminated her crib and nothing else. She heard herself laugh and saw her hand reach out to try and catch one.

Then she looked up and saw flames rushing across the ceiling. Suddenly the room was filled with a hungry roar and . . .

Mimi opened her eyes and lifted her hands, checking for burns from the cinders. It was a gesture from her childhood, as much as the lonely aching void that surrounded her racing heart.

She rose from the bed and checked the time. She was not due at the school where she taught for another three hours. She used the bathroom and made a cup of tea and packed her day clothes into a canvas shoulder bag. Then she dressed in tights and a sweatshirt and set out.

The dawn street outside her little apartment was breathless and still. As she crossed the park with the children's playground, a lone bird woke up and chirped sleepily. Mimi loved these moments, when the town of Miramar was almost hers to claim.

She let herself into the studio where she taught three Pilates classes each week. She hoped someday to teach dance as well, when her schedule permitted. Mimi had discovered Pilates and dance and yoga her first year in university. They had framed happy time in her life. She had used them almost daily to build a temporary shelter from such things as dreams. She still did.

Mimi had never actually witnessed the burning house. It had taken place while she was asleep. She had woken up the next morning, walked into the kitchen, and joined her mother and younger sister at the back window, staring at the smoldering ruins of their neighbors' home.

Back then, the Russians had not yet started their invasion into eastern Ukraine. Instead, they supplied local paramilitaries with weapons and training. Her father was a surgeon who had treated wounds on both sides of the clandestine war. That was probably why he had been made to vanish. Despite three years of searching, Mimi's mother had never discovered what had happened to her husband. Some of Mimi's worst dreams involved finding her father in one of the mass forest graves.

She entered the studio, turned on all the lights, and crossed the floor to the music system set into the wall alcove. She slipped the thumb drive from her pocket and inserted it into the USB port. She had been introduced to fusion jazz by the family who had brought her to America. George Benson's rendition of "On Broadway" filled the room. She turned up the volume loud enough to banish the dark thoughts. She walked to the bar running the length of the mirrored side-wall and stretched slowly, pushing away the dream's last lingering tendrils.

When she was ready, she danced.

Mimi had attended Cal Poly in San Luis Obispo, because they were the only school outside Los Angeles that had offered her a full ride. She stayed on for a master's and might have gone further, but her student loans were piling up and the system did not offer even a partial scholarship for doctoral students in education. She did not mind nearly as much as she might have expected. By then, Mimi had politely severed her ties to the family in Los Angeles, and she was ready to strike out on her own.

California required those studying education on state scholarships to work a couple of years at some assigned location. The graduating student could apply for a particular post, but it was very rarely granted. Mimi had spent two semesters as a student teacher and another doing graduate research in Miramar. She had fallen in love with the region and the locals. She had written the town's name in the appropriate blank space on her application, knowing there was no chance of it happening. If her life had taught her anything, it was that dreams came true for other people. Never for her.

But the recent COVID crisis had left the state's education system in disarray. And when her assignment came through, Mimi found herself being directed to move the seventy or so miles north, where she was to teach middle school.

That first year, Mimi kept waiting for the ax to fall. Even now, two years later, she still occasionally feared some official in a gray suit might step forward and inform her that a terrible mistake had been made. That she had actually been assigned to the Lompoc state prison.

Two years was a long enough period to reveal any number of flaws and hidden fissures in the region. Even so, the reasons to love Miramar just kept mounting.

Like today.

In the midst of the COVID crisis, the school counselor had taken early retirement. Mimi had minored in counseling through both her undergraduate and graduate days, so she requested the job. She found the prospect of helping students with personal problems both appealing and terrifying. Especially since she had so many unresolved issues of her own. Two years on, Mimi had come to love the balance of teaching and this more intimate connection to some students. And to her constant surprise, they seemed to love it as well.

This year she taught fifteen hours each week and spent the remaining periods counseling. Her sign-up sheet was usually filled a week or so in advance. After lunch that day she entered the school's administrative offices and found her first student already waiting. The name on her sign-up sheet was Linh Nguyen. As Mimi walked over, the principal stepped into her open doorway. Mimi waited to see if she was being summoned, but the older woman just watched her. As did

Yolinda, the assistant principal. When no one spoke, Mimi said, "Linh? Good morning. Won't you come inside?"

Her office was a tiny afterthought positioned at the back of the administrative section. Mimi suspected it had originally served as a closet. Her first day, Mimi had pushed the battered desk under the tiny window, opening up the central space as much as possible. A small side table held a box of tissues and a vase of daffodils. A number of her repeat students brought flowers. "How can I help you?"

Linh Nguyen was an awkward thirteen, small for her age, but growing into what Mimi thought would soon become a delicate beauty. "My brother died."

"When was this, Linh?"

"Over two years ago, almost three."

"How are you and your family holding up?"

"My father is gone, too. Six years now. My mother, she is so sad. And some days . . ."

Mimi lifted the box of tissues and offered them to the student. "Sometimes it feels like your mother isn't there, is that what you mean?"

"Like she can't see me."

"Like she is too busy searching for her son who is gone."

"She turns away from the lights, like it hurts her eyes." Linh's voice was a musical whisper now. "She won't look at me."

"It hurts her to see you alive and well," Mimi said, remembering.

"I hear stories," Linh said. "About how you see things."

Mimi hesitated. This was the first time her other activities had come up during school hours. She knew from numerous comments that many of the other teachers knew. Perhaps all of them. She had to be very careful here. "What do you mean by that, Linh?"

"I work in my uncle's café. I hear other women say how

you can see what is not there." Linh began shredding her tissue. "I am hoping you will speak with my mother."

"Is that your mother asking, or you?"

"I tell her what I hear." Linh's accent grew more pronounced. "She looks at me. Truly looks."

"I need to be certain that your mother actually wants this to take place. Not you."

"She wants. She *needs.* I know this."

"Where is your uncle's café?"

"On the Coastal Road."

"I know it. If she agrees, we can meet there Saturday afternoon at two. Wait, I'm not done. I don't speak with the dead, Linh." Mimi spoke firmly, but softly. "Your mother needs to accept this before we meet."

Linh's expression was unreadable. Mimi could not tell whether she accepted the statement as truth, or if perhaps she simply decided that further pressing would not help. Or if it mattered one way or the other.

Mimi asked, "Does your mother speak English?"

"Some. A little. Not so good."

"Then another adult must be there to interpret. No student can participate. This means you should not be present. I must maintain a complete separation between my work here in the school and this other element of my life."

"My aunt, she will do this. She is as worried as me." Linh started to add something more, then stopped.

"Was there something else you wanted to speak with me about?"

"I hear you take the sad walk with some students. To the point."

"I have never heard it called that before," Mimi said. " 'The sad walk.' I think it's lovely."

"It is true, yes?"

When Mimi first settled in Miramar, a number of students

returned to school with new and aching voids in their families. California's central coast had seen more than its share of COVID-related deaths. In those early therapy sessions, Mimi had found herself confronting young hearts broken and lives shattered by loss and fear. In the midst of another sleepless night, she had recalled her own early distress. How hard it was to have no grave to visit. These people had the grave, and yet it did not fill the void.

Which was when she had the idea.

The next day she had spoken with the four students who worried her the most. And suggested they take a walk together. She had decided not to call it a pilgrimage. The word was too alien to the California spirit. To her utter astonishment, all had agreed immediately. As if they all had just been waiting for her to come up with the idea.

That next Saturday the five of them had walked the long lane leading out to Lighthouse Point. They had stood together on the rocky promontory, and at Mimi's urging each of the students had spoken a few words, addressing the wind and the ocean and the empty air, offering a soft and tearful good-bye to the dearly departed.

By that following Friday eight other students had approached her, asking if they might come. Assuming she would take another such walk. Which she did, of course. And when they gathered in the parking lot, she found all of the original students there as well.

The second astonishment was how good it made her feel. Not just for getting it right with these young people, but for herself. As if she had finally found a release of her own. After all these years.

Two years later, Mimi still took those walks once each month. The act had cemented her place in the community. Families often stopped her on the street or in stores, wanting to thank her for the difference she made in young lives. Sorrow, she discovered, was the great leveler.

It was in one such conversation that she first heard how Lighthouse Point had become renamed. The first few times she heard it, she had no idea what they were talking about. Nowadays the people who stopped her used its new name, Cape Farewell.

Mimi told the student, "We go this coming Saturday."

"I can come?"

"You would be most welcome."

"My mother too?"

"This walk is only for students. It helps them feel free to speak what is on their hearts." When she was certain Linh had accepted this, she said, "I ask these students to meet with me for another three sessions of counseling after their first walk. But this is not required. Would you be willing?"

Linh nodded. "I am so sad when I think about Tranh."

"Tranh was your late brother's name? Sometimes feeling sad is a necessary part of the healing process. It becomes a question of how to move beyond the sorrow. Perhaps I can help you make that transition." When the student did not object, Mimi said, "Tell me, what is your most vivid memory of your brother?"

CHAPTER 3

⚓

That day they were shooting a protest gathering, a pivotal moment in the romance between Billy and his co-star. Connie Adler was a big name throughout much of South America, both as a model and as the star of a massively successful telenovela. This was her first Hollywood role. Connie spoke English with a distinctly Latina flavor. She was, in a word, stunning. The day she arrived, all the males on set and some of the women had been positively arrested by the sight of her. Just the same, Billy was not certain she would make it in Hollywood. Her actions were too theatrical, big gestures and fake emotions and all the other traits learned during six years of doing Mexican soaps. She argued and she resisted whenever the director instructed her to tamp things down. She threw monumental tantrums over being required to repeat takes.

Billy suspected the tirades had a second motive. They kept the director and visiting studio execs focused on her. Everyone worked to soothe her. They shifted things around to suit her every whim. They did their best to make her feel like the entire project, if not the whole world, revolved around her. Most actors in Billy's position would have thrown a fit of their own, being sidelined like that. But he was more than content with how things were. Billy had two reasons of his own for playing like he was just another supporting actor.

For one thing, everybody on set knew he was doing his best to keep things running on schedule. Billy had cut his teeth standing just one notch outside the shadows. Being nearly forgotten, except when he was in front of the camera.

And then there was the other reason.

On most sets the work atmosphere and the emotional mood were both established by the director. Nowadays a growing proportion of directors thrived on harmony. They were the ones who tended to get hired again. Investors preferred to visit a set and see a happy team, humming along in synch, everyone certain they were making a great film.

But this was not always the case.

Vince Edwards thrived on tension. Billy had studied several of his films and considered him a near genius. Even so, Vince had never managed to reach the highest levels. Which Vince clearly thought he deserved.

Vince's tactics were the stuff of legends. At the start of every shoot, Vince took aim at someone. Actor, set designer, sound technician, it didn't matter. Sometimes it was because of a mistake; other times Vince detected a bad attitude only he could see. These victims were instantly sent packing. Because his habits were so well known, agents insisted on full payment if their client became Vince's target.

Despite his infamous flaws, Vince remained in fairly constant demand. He got value for dollars invested. His films held the look of more expensive projects. He delivered on time and under budget. And, most important of all, his films made money.

But this particular project went differently. From the very first day.

Right from the start, the entire crew was aware that Vince had taken aim at Billy Rose. He might as well have had a target painted on his back.

Billy had no idea how he had angered the director. He was equally at a loss over how he had won the coveted lead role. Billy seldom did. It had all started with just another audition. Three people had been seated behind a trestle table. Billy had been handed a script and told to read the lead's part. A young male assistant had fed him Connie's lines in a slightly nasal voice. Five minutes into the read, perhaps less, they thanked Billy, said they'd be in touch, yada yada.

Four days later, he had been called back for a second read.

Two days after that, he had been brought in for a screen test.

And the next day his agent had received the contract. For a shoot starting in three weeks.

This had made his third starring role in two years. A major step up, even though the others had been low-*low*-budget indies. Even so. Because the first film had been a surprise hit overseas, or so Billy had heard. Not from his agent, of course, who considered Billy a journeyman actor a few months away from the bus ride home. Billy had heard this from a couple of pals in the industry. All of them saying there was a faint buzz in the LA film world that perhaps, just perhaps, Billy Rose was a guy to watch.

At long, long last.

Of course none of this explained what Billy was doing here. Starring in his most expensive production ever. For a director who clearly would like nothing more than to chop Billy Rose off at the knees.

Connie Adler had insisted on the cosmetician's exclusive attention that morning. A handwritten *Do Not Disturb* sign was taped to the makeup door. Billy minded, but not as much as might be the case. He had been doing his own face for years. The key was to match his hair and gear to the previous scene, when they had shot a breakfast confrontation between Billy and his father that supposedly took place earlier the same morning as today's protest. He waited until Gayle, the senior makeup lady, appeared in the doorway. Billy asked for the still photo they would have used to match him up.

Gayle retreated inside, then returned and handed him the eight-by-ten. "Sorry."

"No problem."

"You want my assistant to do you up?"

"*No!*" The voice from inside the makeup booth was one notch off fury. "I *need* her for my *hair!*"

The makeup lady sighed. Shook her head.

Billy shrugged. "You can check out my work before I go under the lights."

She leaned forward and kissed his cheek. "You're a star, Billy Rose."

He stopped by the wardrobe trailer, where the seamstress looked up from her machine long enough to snap, "You're not allowed to have a problem today. All problem appointments are taken."

"I need a new hat. Mine got stepped on by the—"

"I know all about your hat. I spent half the night getting it back to where it will sit like yesterday. It's in your trailer with your clothes." She waved him off. "Go, go. If you have another problem, I can maybe fit you in next week."

By the time he was dressed and satisfied with his face, the AD had marked four spots where he wanted Billy to stand. Trevor Culley was a master when it came to crowd scenes. An outdoor concert, political speech, flash gathering, street party, or ten seconds before a bomb goes off—Trevor could shoot it so the viewer was drawn in tight, so the audience was *right there*.

The script had Billy fall in love with Connie during today's protest. Billy thought it was a brilliant way to use Connie's strengths to the film's favor. Her big gestures and theatrical emotions would play almost natural. Billy was checking out his positions when Trevor came rushing over. "You know what I'm going to say."

"I start here at the back of the crowd. Gradually I'm drawn forward."

"From one mark to the next."

"Right. As Connie gets further into her speech, I become caught up. Not in what she's saying. In her. The woman."

Trevor almost managed to hide his grin. "Go on."

"Connie reveals herself to be everything I'm not. She is freewheeling with her passion. She cares about these people, even when it means she's risking her life to try and protect them. She makes me feel like a coward. Which I am, really. Down deep, I've spent my entire life being afraid of my father and his rage. Which has meant I've been hiding from my own emotions as well. Passion is an alien concept to me. I see it in Connie, and it shames me almost as much as it draws me forward."

"You make my job easy." Trevor pointed to picnic tables set up by the canteen wagon, where the on-set publicist was chatting with an older woman dressed entirely in black. "Some reporter lady wants a word."

The location publicist was accompanied by a rail-thin woman in her late thirties, dressed in what looked like black canvas—trousers, top, and cork-soled sandals—with oversized round spectacles in a startling shade of purple. "Billy Rose, meet Kari Simmons from *Variety*."

The reporter's gaze carried a laser intensity. "How do you do, William?"

"My birth certificate reads 'Billy.' The name has always worked well enough for me."

When the location publicist fielded a call and excused herself, Kari gestured at an outlying picnic table. "Why don't we sit down."

Billy followed her over, watched Kari Simmons open her pad and place the recorder down between them. She asked, "Small-town Carolina kid comes to the big city. You've been in LA how long?"

"Eight and a half very long years."

"What's your impression? Say you have to describe life in Hollywood to a newcomer. What would you tell them?"

He found himself intrigued by her question. It was probably a softball toss, nothing more than an attempt to put him at ease. Open him up. Even so, he gave her honesty. "I'd say the folks who move to Los Angeles are defined by restless courage. They're looking for something new and different, and they have the guts to try and find it. Everybody else stays home."

She studied him with what might have been a tight smile. Or maybe she was just squinting against the sun. "Does that describe you, Billy Rose?"

"It does. Yes."

"Same question, sort of. Quick summary of where you come from?"

Most interviews were an exhaustive, boring process. The same questions were asked half-a-dozen different ways. The interviewers often seemed mindless to Billy. Bloggers were the worst. Commercial magazines and television types all had bosses who kept them in line, more or less.

Kari Simmons was different.

For one thing, she was attractive in a hard-edged LA sort of way. Kari was neat, precise, alert. Her style might not appeal to him, but at least she took time over how she appeared. She broke in with, "We're waiting here."

"I'm from Appalachia Country," he replied. "Nowhere town by the name of Dellwood, deep in the Blue Ridge Mountains, west of Asheville."

"Carolina, right?"

"*North* Carolina."

This time her smile was visible. "From the Carolina hill country to Hollywood."

"So I could become another journeyman actor. One of thousands."

"Looking for the big break."

"There you go." He shared her smile. "Wondering why this big-time journalist is sitting here with me."

"How did you get into acting?"

"There are a hundred different answers to that question."

She nodded. "There usually are."

"I was raised by my grandmother, a true earthbound angel. She said I inherited my parents' restless spirit. They died when I was six. Ada Rose took whatever life handed her and made the best of it. A lot of the Appalachia folks are like that." The woman's intensity seemed to amplify his own memories. Make it easier to release them. Which he would no doubt regret, once this was done. Even so, he went on speaking. "A trip to the big city meant going to the cinema. Ada could park me there all day if need be. I'd watch the same film three, four times, and stay happy as a clam. Same for settling down in front of the TV and watching my favorite show. For Ada, film and TV simply became my way out. But for me, it was always more than that. I can't remember a time when I didn't want to do what I'm doing now."

"Acting for the big screen."

"Big or little makes no difference as far as I'm concerned. Acting for the camera. That's the key."

"No interest in starring onstage?"

"You're talking like I have a choice in the matter." Billy

shrugged. "I got a scholarship to UNC Asheville. The acting department there was all about theater."

"And you've been a member of the LA Theater Ensemble for three years."

The lady had certainly done her research. "I've learned a lot. And sure, I'd probably take a theater gig if it was offered. But my heart is out there. In front of the cameras." Billy held up his hand, halting her next question. "Same question. Why are we having this conversation at all?"

She seemed to like that. "I was sent out here to do a standard piece on a small-budget feature. Three paragraphs, four if it's a slow week. One photograph my editor would probably cut down to thumbnail size. Or maybe just leave for the digital version. I actually tried to get out of coming. But the studio offered to pay my way, and there wasn't much else going on, and then I got assigned to cover an NBC pilot they're shooting in Las Vegas. I'm slated to stop there on the way back. But all that was yesterday. Now it looks like I just might have a scoop."

Billy decided he liked her and her soft way of speaking. Which was probably a terrible idea. There was every chance her article would reveal her to be just another LA acid drone. "Go ahead and ask the rest of your questions."

"Don't you want to know what's changed?"

"Whatever rumors you're carrying—"

"They're not rumors."

"Just the same, I should probably hear them from the folks in charge here."

Kari studied him a long moment, then spotted something behind him and cut off the recorder. "Looks like our time is up. Thanks for talking with me, Billy Rose. I actually enjoyed that."

Billy rose, shook her hand, and waved at where Trevor was gesturing for him to come on set. "Truth be told, Ms. Simmons, so did I."

CHAPTER 4

Trevor's assistant led Billy over to where the AD was placing central figures among the crowd. It was like watching a grand master set up chess pieces. These characters included the family attorney, two corrupt and three honest cops who would get into a serious tangle in tomorrow's scenes, four of the ranch hands from the family spread, and so on. Everyone who had a speaking role in the greater film was carefully positioned. One single glimpse would then be enough to flash the character into the viewer's consciousness. A lot of stars would have been doubly upset by the process—first, because they were being made to stand and wait while lesser mortals were set in place, and next, because the AD was handling this and not the director. Billy could not have cared less.

Vince was up on the makeshift stage talking softly to Connie. Even from this distance Billy could see his love interest was borderline frantic. Connie's eyes kept darting back to someone or something out beyond the crowd. Billy wondered if she was frightened by being next up with the *Variety* reporter. He gave a mental nod of agreement. If he'd known in advance what was coming, he might have freaked out right alongside her.

For such a big man, Trevor was astonishingly light on his feet. He threaded through the crowd he'd just set in place, stopped in front of Billy, and said, "Looks like it's you and me again."

"I've got no problem with that."

Trevor pointed to the two ladies standing to his left. "This is Miriam and her daughter, Sandrine."

"Hi."

"We just love your work, Mr. Rose." Miriam was in her late fifties, and her voice was at complete odds to her appearance. She was dressed to look like an itinerant farm worker, with tired sun-darkened features and limp graying hair and clothes to match. But the lady sounded like a radio host. Clear American English with a distinct Texas twang, bright and chipper and ready to burst into song. "Don't we, hon."

"I've seen *Palm Island,* like, ten times." Her daughter was aged somewhere north of thirty and sounded like she was twelve. Excitement would do that.

"You ladies are from El Paso?"

"Born and raised." Miriam reached for her daughter's hand. "We're both dental hygienists. We use our days off to do bit parts whenever we can."

"Today is really special, though," her daughter said. "After we got the callback last night, I couldn't sleep a wink."

Trevor said, "If the ladies will stop sounding like they're waiting for autographs on Sunset, I thought I'd play the camera on them. Have you in the background."

"Until Connie draws me forward," Billy said, nodding.

"The first clear sight we have of your face is when you get caught up in what Connie is saying," Trevor agreed. He pointed at the pavement by their feet. "You step from here to your second halt. The camera tracks you, drawing you gradually into a close-up."

"Sounds like a plan."

Trevor turned to the ladies. "You're taking time off from a very hard life picking fruit. Leaving the farm means a day without pay. Being here means the world. You watch the stage with burning hope."

"I could just faint away," Miriam declared.

"Focus all that excitement of yours at the lady on the stage," Trevor said. Then to Billy, "We good?"

"Raring to go."

Trevor took two steps back, allowing the cameraman to step forward. The Steadicam operator was typical of the breed, built low to the ground and strong as a bull. Along with the camera itself, he wore a battery belt and a hydraulic system to steady the shoot. Call it sixty pounds of gear. Nine o'clock on a January morning and he had already sweated through his T-shirt.

Billy waited while Trevor positioned the cameraman for the first upward-looking shot. Trevor then tracked him backward as Billy moved to his next mark. By the time Trevor started toward the stage, the two women were quivering with what Billy figured were equal parts excitement and dread.

Miriam asked him, "What if we mess it all up?"

"The camera already loves you," Billy said. He figured it really didn't matter what he said, so much as just letting them hear a friendly voice. "Don't look at it. You can trust the cameraman to do his job perfectly. You focus out there."

Billy directed their attention to the stage. Vince and Trevor talked while a cosmetician dabbed at the sweat beading Connie's face. "The lady up there is having some trouble with her lines today." Billy ignored how the cameraman lifted his head from the viewfinder long enough to smirk. "Whatever she does, however many mistakes she makes, it doesn't change your job down here."

Sandrine said, "Standing here next to you about has me ready to scream."

"Just take that excitement you feel, and let it shine."

The cameraman said, "Hope you ladies were paying attention. That's the word of a pro."

Sandrine looked at Billy, dark eyes liquid with the thrill of standing in a baking-hot parking lot. "The first time I saw you on the screen, I knew you were somebody special."

Vince chose that moment to shout, "Places, everyone! This is a take!"

Periods between takes were as close to suspended animation as Billy Rose Walker ever cared to come. He was required to remain split from what he considered his outside life until the day's shoot was over. He had learned the hard way that he could not repeatedly enter the character's emotional phase and then leave it, and return again. Such splits resulted in an emotional falseness. Even if the director and the film's editor did not catch it, Billy always knew. On several occasions he had watched a completed film and known in his gut when they had used a shot from after he had stepped away from the role. The sight had left him so nauseous he had feared he would be sick all over his shoes.

He had developed methods to maintain the character's state of mind. Billy hated being confined in his trailer. Within a few minutes of entering, he felt the walls starting to close in. He also did not like talking. The crew and their good-natured chatter were off-limits. If he was hungry, Billy always sat alone. He ate only enough to still the pangs. Sometimes he found a shady spot and listened to music. Or read. But his favorite action was to work out with free weights. Nothing anchored him to the character's world so well as the mindless repetition of lifting and sweating and letting time pass him by.

As usual, the gaffers had set up a weight room beneath an open-sided canvas awning. Billy walked over, stripped down to his boxers, pulled on a tank top and gym shorts, and began his routine. Low weights, high reps. Very slow, very calm, concentrating on his breathing. Not even counting the number of times he completed each maneuver. Going until his muscles burned. Waiting through a rest period, staring out at the empty parking lot beyond their set.

By now, his actions were well known to the crew. If people passed through his field of vision, he did his best not to see them at all. It used to bother him, how a lot of the women and some of the men would scope him out. Back in his early teens, when he was still trying to fathom the man he was becoming, the invitations there in so many gazes were both alluring and a little frightening. But in time he had learned to live with it, just as he had his looks. He knew he was attractive. But Billy had also seen how so many great-looking actors identify themselves by how others saw them. By how others *wanted* them. He loathed how they treated other people as little more than living mirrors, mostly there to burnish their image. So Billy did his best to remain clinical about his looks. Just another attribute. Like his voice. Or his dark blond hair. Or his grayish-blue eyes. Or how he photographed well.

Almost every male actor who commanded leading roles today had what in the industry was known as clinically balanced features. The distance from chin to nose, nose to hairline, eyes level with ears . . . the list was two pages long. Included were all the aesthetically pleasing elements, such as sculpted jawline, high cheekbones, piercing gaze, and so forth. Any number of actors struggling for roles went in for plastic surgery, hoping to improve their chances by forcing their looks into these computer-generated molds. Billy considered himself lucky. Nothing more, nothing less. His face and his build and his voice, these were tools of the trade. Working out between takes was just another part of staying prepped.

Billy shifted to arm curls, small weights, taking his time, thirty reps, forty, fifty. When he needed, he stopped and stretched. Then he returned to the next series. He could keep this up all day, and often did.

Twice a guy in a suit walked over and observed him. A small part of Billy's brain recognized him as some senior executive from the studio's Century City offices. Trevor's words flashed through his brain, and he momentarily wondered if this was why Connie had freaked on the podium before the first take, seeing the guy watching her. But the thoughts threatened to pull him away from the day's real task. Billy took the sweat-drenched towel from around his shoulders and draped it over his head like a prayer shawl. He sat like that, staring at the ground by his feet, until he was ready for working his triceps. When he stood and walked to the weight rack, the suit was gone.

Twenty minutes later, Trevor's assistant came for him. Billy toweled off, reworked his makeup, dressed, and allowed the two continuity staffers to check him over. Then he walked to where the assistant stood by his first station. Trevor was directing the cameraman from the side of the podium, which meant they intended to shoot Billy with a long lens. The director called for places, checked off the cameramen and sound, and then Billy was on. The character's emotions came flooding back, taking over.

Connie flubbed her lines.

The director rolled his finger and said, "Okay, we're still rolling. From the top."

Billy's consciousness only spared a tiny fragment for Connie as she stumbled through another take. This was far from the hardest trial he had known on set. Toughest for him were the close-ups when the person he was acting against was not even in the room. Small-budget features could only afford major names by limiting their days on set. Such stars loathed standing around, saying their lines and playing their roles for the sake of somebody else being in the camera's eye. Sometimes a stand-in actor spoke the lines, but usually it was one of the assistants. They read the words off the page, love story or vicious argument or confession or betrayal, their voices flat as any amateur's. And Billy had to go for it. All in. The emotions fresh and raw and there for the camera to see.

So he walked through the crowd, hitting his marks just so, maintaining the growing emotional bond between himself and the woman who was not actually up there on the stage. But she was. There. In his mind and heart. Where it mattered.

He was approaching his fourth and final mark when it happened.

Trevor's cameraman had shifted over to where he could shoot Billy's approach while keeping Connie's silhouette in the frame. Connie followed the camera's direction, usually a terrible mistake, but in this case . . .

She and Billy *linked*.

Billy felt the connection in his gut. Despite the day's rising heat, he shivered.

Connie froze, only for a moment, but when she restarted her lines, a change had come over her. She was no longer speaking to the crowd. She was talking to him. The speech became something real, a passion that flamed in them both.

Then the director called, "Cut! Okay, I think we've got something there. Everybody, take a break."

And it was over.

When he came off set, Billy spotted Kari Simmons direct her photographer over to shoot a few of him stripped down and doing weights. But his favorite gaffer, a Latino named

JoJo, noticed the guy's approach. JoJo competed statewide in bodybuilding contests. He was known around the set as Subzero, and not because of the superhero. JoJo was only a fraction smaller than a double-wide fridge. Billy had seen him single-handedly lift a Volkswagen's front end and shift it into the proper position for the shoot. The photographer took one look at the brute headed in his direction and veered away. JoJo untied the side awning and let it drop down to mask them from the watching eyes. When Billy thanked him, JoJo said, "I'm heading for the canteen. You want I should bring you something?"

"Gatorade would be nice. Maybe a smoothie."

"You got it."

Billy sighed his way down onto the bench. Waited until the world drifted back out of focus. When it was just him and the heat and the weights and his character, he started the next routine.

CHAPTER 5

❧

When Mimi first arrived in Miramar, the locals' casual attitudes confused her. She wondered if perhaps they took the area's beauty for granted. Now she knew differently. They might show the world a very California offhand manner, but down deep where it mattered, locals viewed the central coast region with a reverential respect. She saw it in the way they shared sunset walks, or stood in collective mirth as children and dogs chased butterflies, or held little ones up so they could watch hummingbirds quarrel over feeders. Their love of Miramar was everywhere. She had to live here awhile to understand how deep these waters ran.

On Wednesday morning Mimi entered the admin offices to find the principal standing in her open doorway, waiting. Soon as the outer door clicked shut, Adela said, "Can I have a word?"

Mimi reviewed her life and work from the previous few days. As far as she could tell, everything seemed to be running smoothly, no lines crossed. Even so, she could not help but worry when Yolinda followed Mimi inside the principal's office and shut the door. Mimi found herself thinking back to the fears she had brought with her to Miramar. The threat of losing another home was a barely covered wound. Silently Mimi begged, *Please don't send me to Lompoc.*

Adela Perez was a pinch-faced woman with an energy that almost crackled around her small frame. She was aged somewhere in her sixties, no one knew for certain. Her iron-gray hair was always pulled back so tightly it added to her natural squint. Dark eyes glittered with a wrath that terrified wayward students. "Your meeting with Linh Nguyen yesterday. What did she want?"

"She is having difficulty dealing with the loss of her brother."

"I knew it." Adela crossed her arms. "Linh's mother is in my support group. The lady is barely keeping things together."

Yolinda Baisey was both the principal's trusted aide and Mimi's best friend among the staff. She was a tall dark-skinned lady in her fifties, with a warmth that balanced Adela's constant tension. Yolinda said, "Linh's uncle and aunt live down the street from me. Everybody in that family is concerned."

"Basically, Linh runs the household," Adela said. "She shops. She cooks the meals. She makes sure her younger sister has clean clothes. The works."

"What do you want me to do?"

Yolinda stepped up alongside their boss. "Linh's mother needs to learn how to say good-bye and let go."

Mimi looked from one face to the other. "I've already told Linh no adults are allowed to join us for the farewell walks."

The two other women showed surprise. "Linh asked you?"

"That is good news," Adela said. "It makes our job all the easier."

"I'll speak with Linh's aunt tonight," Yolinda said.

Mimi looked from one woman to the other. "About what?"

Yolinda said, "You know we've both recently lost family."

"Of course." Yolinda's mother had passed a few months back. Earlier that winter Mimi had attended the funeral of Adela's late husband.

Adela asked, "How often do you go out with the students?"

"It used to be every other week. Now we've cut it back to once a month."

"The students come more than once?"

"Some do. I suppose a majority come at least twice. A few have been coming almost every time since this started."

"Will you do one for adults?"

"Certainly." She chose her words very carefully. "We follow a certain pattern. Each person says a few words, then makes an offering of some sort. We end by holding hands and saying farewell. As we start back, I tell them to see the path as a walk into a new future. The loss is still there, but it does not dominate their lives or the days ahead."

The two women exchanged a glance. Yolinda said, "I wish we'd had this conversation weeks ago."

Mimi asked, "Why don't you do this yourselves?"

"Same reason as the students, I expect," Yolinda replied. "We need a guiding hand."

Adela asked, "When can you do one for adults?"

Mimi did not need to think that through. "How about a week from Saturday?"

The next afternoon Yolinda sent Mimi a text asking her to stop by after her last class. The halls emptied fast and Mimi walked the corridor to a show tune being played badly by the orchestra. The administrative office's outer door was open, and soon as Mimi came into view, Yolinda rose from her desk. The assistant principal had competed at state level in ballroom and Latin dance, and taught the occasional class at the same studio as Mimi. Yolinda took hold of Mimi's arm and guided her away from the school offices.

Mimi asked, "What's the matter?"

"Nothing I need Adela to hear." When they were down by the school's wall display and trophy cases, Yolinda stopped and asked, "You still doing that thing?"

Mimi hesitated. "I'm not sure what you're asking."

"Don't give me that. You know exactly what I'm talking about. That thing of yours. I want to know if you're still working that magic."

"Please don't call it that. 'Magic.' That word doesn't fit what happens. At all."

"Well, what is it, then?"

"I actually have no idea."

Yolinda was too wound up to smile. "You need to name it, girl. How else are you going to claim it as yours?"

"I don't *claim* anything."

"Now you're just dancing around it." When Mimi did not respond, Yolinda continued, "You've got yourself a gift. You have any idea how many people would like to do what you can?"

"Why are we talking about this?"

"My sister-in-law, Cloethe. You've seen her at the studio."

"Yes." Mimi recalled a lovely older woman with striking almond-shaped eyes who carried herself with a tragic air. She did not dance so much as drift through the sessions, like the music could not fully reach her. "She's your sister?"

"In-law. My brother, Delon, we've always been real close. He's been having health problems. They've spent five months going to doctors, specialists, having tests, getting poked and prodded, you name it. Will you help?"

Mimi said what she always did. "I don't always hear any-thing."

"You *hear*."

"You're the one who needs to be listening. Maybe this isn't a good idea."

"How can you say such a thing?"

"Because I don't want you turning away from me when what I say isn't what you and your sister-in-law want to hear."

To her credit, Yolinda didn't come back with some kind of false assurance. "I've heard you tell it like it is."

Mimi started to ask who had told Yolinda, then decided it didn't matter. "If I hear something, I have to say it."

"You don't have any choice in the matter?"

"None. If I hear, it has to be spoken out loud."

Yolinda stared at her. "Girl, you are giving me a serious case of the shivers."

"Your sister-in-law needs to understand this. The truth is often very hard to bear. Sometimes it is better not knowing."

"The woman is beyond desperate."

"If you really think . . ." When Yolinda remained as she was, the entreaty clear in her gaze, Mimi conceded. "All right. Yes."

Yolinda pursed her lips. Breathed a single tight line. "Do you want to hear more about Delon's problem?"

"It's best if I don't know anything in advance." Mimi felt an electric thrill. Because despite everything this gift had cost her, it still was a pleasure. In an odd and sometimes-painful manner, but still. "Of course I'll try and help."

CHAPTER 6

The first time it happened, Mimi was fourteen years old.

She was dining with the family, as usual. The mother did not like having Mimi at the family table, but Gregor, Mimi's distant uncle, insisted. This discord had dominated Mimi's home life since her arrival in Los Angeles. The mother was pure LA, born and raised, and shrugged off her Polish heritage with comments like, "Everybody has to come from somewhere." The father had been brought to the United States as an infant. Gregor's only recollections of Kiev, his birthplace, came from visits he made as an adult. But the traditions of his motherland were deeply embedded. He wanted to adopt Mimi, but his wife adamantly refused. Their two children—a daughter three years older than Mimi and a son two years younger—absorbed the discord from their parents and treated Mimi as the outsider she was forced to remain.

That particular evening there had been guests, a fairly regular occurrence. Two business associates and their wives had been invited home as a means of sealing a major deal, one of Gregor's largest. Mimi sat in her customary corner position, closest to the hall leading to the front door. She did not speak. She seldom did in such family gatherings. Whenever Gregor addressed her directly, his wife responded with a frown, disliking this reminder of the stranger in their midst.

Only, this evening had been different.

Toward the end of the meal, Mimi had become enveloped in a distinct sense of wrongness. It did not come from inside herself, nor was it the result of the usual underlying friction. This was something else entirely. Something new. For Mimi, it was as though her vision had become split. On the one hand, she observed the six adults continue their pleasant chatter. On the other, she *saw*. The guests' secret motives, their intent and their menace, became as clear to her as the conversation, as the food she could no longer eat.

She sat and waited for the sensations to pass. But the longer she remained silent, the stronger the feelings grew. Toward the end of the evening, the pressure inside her became explosive. As if the effort it required not to speak threatened to blast her apart.

Mimi's strongest impression was that her father had spoken to her. Stepped up close and whispered, not to her ears, but straight to her heart. For the first time since her beloved father had left for the hospital and never returned. He was there. With her. Shattering the loneliness that characterized her life in LA.

That night she did not sleep at all.

Mimi ran through the experience over and over. And she decided that it actually might not have been her father at all. Instead, the experience reminded her of how it had felt as a child, when her father returned from one of his long sojourns to village clinics, and all of a sudden everything was right in her world. That was how it had been at the table. Like all the disjointed components of her life fit together again. For that one extremely intense moment.

* * *

Mimi attended Saint Bernard Catholic School. The next morning in chapel, the priest's lesson had been about John 14:26, which says: *"But the Comforter, the Holy Spirit, whom the Father will send in my name, he shall teach you all things."* It was the first time in a long while that Mimi had listened to any sermon with all her being.

The concept suited Mimi's experience, especially how the priest described it: What he said was, the words did not come with any promise of ending the crisis or whatever the individual faced. Instead, the Comforter would be there with her. Granting a new vision, a clear understanding, of each step that was to come.

Mimi left the chapel knowing with utter certainty that she had to tell Gregor what had happened. If what she had experienced was real, and not just a powerful sensation, Gregor and his company were in great danger. She owed it to him to reveal what she had experienced.

By the time he returned from work that evening, Mimi was consumed by a very real dread. She had maintained her small tight space in this family by going unnoticed. She lived on the periphery. Five years of ingrained habit were about to be thrown out the window. And for what?

Even so, she knew she had to do this. The reason why did not matter so much as the absolute conviction it was right. No matter what the cost.

She waited until after dinner, when Gregor retreated to the den and turned on the evening business report. Gregor watched her enter and close the door behind her, soft as she could. When she stood there by the exit, tying her fingers in nervous knots, he asked, "Has someone been bothering you?"

Something about the way he spoke, quietly concerned and very aware, gave her the strength to say, "I know something about your business. And the people that were here for dinner. Something bad."

He cut off the television. "How is this possible?"

It seemed too silly, standing there talking to the man who had stubbornly remained her guardian, despite his wife's desire to see her gone and forgotten. When she remained silent, he patted the chair next to his. "Come sit down, Mimi. We are friends, yes? Good. I know things are not easy for you. But you are doing well in school, and your teachers are pleased with you, though they wish you would speak out more." He smiled at her surprise. "Of course I keep up with you. You are part of our family, no matter what . . ." He let the rest of his thought go unspoken.

Even so, the warmth in his gaze and words gave her the strength to say, "I think I have had a vision."

"Have you now."

"Or something."

"And it told you that our guests from the other evening were not good people?" When she nodded her response, he asked, "Did you hear anything else?"

"They are going to sign the papers," she said. "They will accept your payment. But they will never give you what they promised."

"Of course they will. They are legally required—"

"Not if they go out of business."

Her words pushed him back in his seat. "They are going to declare bankruptcy?"

"They have already met with the lawyers."

His voice sounded strangled now. "What?"

"In secret. Because they know if you found out, you could say something. I forgot the word . . ."

" 'Breach of fiduciary trust,' is that it?"

"Yes."

"Tell me everything, Mimi. Please."

CHAPTER 7

❦

Three days later, Mimi and Gregor met his mother outside the Ukrainian Orthodox Saint Volodymyr Church in Hollywood. Gregor's mother was an opinionated, upbeat woman who dressed in loud and often clashing colors. Mimi had liked her from the very first time they met. Anastasia preferred to speak Polish, and often sniffed at how her son insisted on replying in English, though he understood the language perfectly well. Like so many citizens of western Ukraine, Anastasia was of Polish heritage. She approved of how Mimi spoke to her in their native tongue, and insisted Mimi call her Aunt Anastasia. Which was perhaps true, in the most elongated sense of the word. But Mimi always considered it a reward for maintaining a diplomatic peace with Gregor's wife.

Anastasia was an inch taller than her only son and had a big laugh and opinions to match. She and Gregor's wife argued every time they met, and as a result Mimi seldom saw her. Mimi had always suspected Anastasia was why Mimi had been taken in. She secretly wished she lived with Anastasia, but the older woman had never offered.

She embraced her son, kissed Mimi on both cheeks, then looked up at the church's grand edifice. "Twenty-six years I have lived in this city, and never have I been inside this place."

Gregor asked, "Why are we here today, Mama?"

"Because of this young lady." She fitted a brilliantly colored silk scarf over her hair, drew a second from her purse, and offered it to Mimi. "You know what to do, yes?" She watched Mimi cover her hair and knot the scarf under her chin, then continued, "These ladies might look like the three scariest crows you have ever seen, but they cannot harm you. I am ordering you not to be frightened. Do you understand?"

"Yes, Aunt Anastasia."

"Good girl."

Gregor protested, "Mama, please let's—"

"My son, your job is to witness and remain silent." She shouldered her purse. "Now let's get this over with."

The church's interior was dark and filled with fragrances from Mimi's earliest memories. Her family had attended the Polish Catholic church in Donetsk, but her father had often taken her to services in such a place as this, Communions and weddings and festivals celebrated by his Russian-Ukrainian colleagues. She had always enjoyed her times inside the Orthodox churches. They all smelled like this, the incense cold and clinging to her long after she returned to the light of day.

The walls of Saint Volodymyr's were lined with icons, most of them depicting the slanted eyes and pointed beards of traditional Russian saints. The Ukrainian Orthodox church was fiercely independent of its Russian neighbor, though to an outsider like Mimi there was little to distinguish the two.

Anastasia took Mimi's hand and led her up the central aisle. A priest stood in the nave and watched their approach, but he neither greeted them nor showed any sign of welcome. One aisle from the front, Anastasia dropped to one knee and made the broad sign of the Orthodox cross, forehead to shoulders and down to midthigh. She rose and bowed and repeated the cross. Mimi followed suit, remembering how her father had taught her the motions soon after she had learned to walk. It was strange how he seemed so close, here in this place, nine thousand miles from his unmarked grave.

Anastasia directed her to an empty wooden chair facing the front aisle. Three women sat so close together they seemed to clutch at each other. They were dressed in the black of ancient mourners, with matching head coverings of mantilla lace. Mimi might have expected a moment of fear, had she known this was why they came, to sit facing these dark-clad crones. But there was no room for fear here.

The central figure inspected her with a rheumy gaze, then spoke in Ukrainian. "Tell the child to give me her hand."

"I understand you." Mimi reached out and felt her wrist taken in a remarkably strong grip. The old woman's hand held no temperature, neither hot nor cold. To Mimi, it felt like she was seized by old bones.

The woman bent over Mimi's open palm, then looked deep into Mimi's eyes. "Tell me what you experienced."

"What I heard was not meant for you," Mimi replied.

The crones seated to either side lifted their heads. The one to Mimi's left said, "What you *heard*?"

The central woman said, "The hearing, then. Tell us that."

"The night came together. Or the candles on the table, I don't know which. But there was a power in the room. It spoke to me." She found it remarkably easy to talk with them. As if they were joined together at some visceral level, far beneath that of mere words, in a space where the shadows of time and distance held no sway. Where the reality of visions and portents and whispered truths dwelled.

"This was the first time you listened to the unspoken?" When Mimi nodded, she demanded, "And yet you did not flee."

"The feeling was . . ." Mimi stopped. "'Feeling' is not strong enough."

"'Presence,'" the woman to her left suggested.

The woman opposite complained, "This one must find the way forward alone."

"She knew. She simply did not know the word."

"'Presence' is correct," Mimi said. "It reminded me of my father."

The women seemed to draw closer together. Like they joined into one shadow of mantilla lace and ancient grief. "The doctor," one said.

"The one who protested against injustice," the one to Mimi's left said.

"He sought to heal all who were brought to him," the central crone said. "Their heritage meant nothing. Only the need."

"His is a good soul," the one to her right said. "His compassion burns strong in this one."

Mimi found herself fighting sudden tears. Not over how they offered this strange compliment. Rather how they spoke of her father. To them, the doctor was still with them. Here in this church. The great man still lived.

And then it was over. The three women unclutched, and the central figure lifted her gaze so as to tell Anastasia, "This one's gift is real."

"And strong," another said. Mimi could no longer tell which, for her vision had blurred. "She holds fast to her father's heart-flame."

Anastasia thanked the ladies, waited until Mimi stood beside her, and together they repeated the genuflections.

Once they were outside, Anastasia asked her son, "Tell me again what this one said."

"That our new partners were going to steal from us." Gregor looked mildly shell-shocked. "If what she says is true, we face ruin."

"There is no 'if.'" Anastasia turned to Mimi. "Is there still time for him to save the company?"

"Yes." The answer was there in the still, dry California heat. As if it had waited outside for her to return to the daylight and the rushing traffic. "But only today. Not tomorrow."

"Go. Hurry," Anastasia told her son. "I will see to the young lady and get her home."

Gregor rushed off. Anastasia watched him go, then asked, "You will speak with others who have questions they cannot answer?"

"I . . . Yes."

"They will, of course, pay you. I will see to that."

"No." On this, Mimi was certain. "I will not take money."

"But . . ." The vehemence in Mimi's response clearly shocked the older woman. "Child, you have nothing of your own."

"I don't care. If they insist on paying, I won't talk with them."

Anastasia looked ready to object, then thought better of it. She drove Mimi home in silence.

Only when Anastasia pulled into the drive did she speak again. "You have heard of the Sisters of Pity?"

Mimi thought a moment. "No."

"There is no reason why you should. I will find the book where I read about them and give it to Gregor. Theirs is not a happy story, so I cannot say for certain. But I think you should read it."

Mimi saw Gregor's wife appear in the front window. She

stood there a long moment, staring at the car and the two people. Finally she turned and walked away. Mimi had no desire to leave Anastasia's company and enter that house and resume the solitude that awaited her. She asked, "Will you tell me?"

"If you wish." Anastasia cut off the motor. "In the 1600s, the citizens of Venice established a House of Mercy where children of prostitutes were raised. Until that time, these babies were often dropped into the canals at night, their little bodies left to be found at sunrise. The House of Mercy possessed a *scaffetta*, an opening cut into the exterior wall. If the baby was small enough to fit inside this metal drawer, the House would accept the child and raise it as their own. All these children, most of whom were girls, were given the same last name. *Della Pietà.*

"The hospital was officially secular, but it was joined to one of Venice's main churches and run according to monastic rules. Children learned to read and write and do arithmetic, a rare achievement for women of this time. Dowries were raised, and many of them married into Venetian society. But some chose to remain."

"The Sisters of Pity," Mimi said.

"Those with talent were taught to play musical instruments. Many became virtuosos. Their fame spread, and soon they played all over the city. Mind you, this was the first time in history that women were allowed to play in orchestras, much less rise to the level of soloists. As their renown spread to other nations, the city refused to allow them to travel. Instead, people journeyed from all over Europe, drawn by the legend of these Sisters of Pity. Their music left the king of Sweden in awe. The Venetian composer Antonio Vivaldi wrote several of his most difficult pieces with these women in mind. Haydn created symphonies specifically for them. They dominated the city's musical scene for over a hundred years."

Mimi swiveled in her seat so as to face the older woman. And waited.

"I know your life here is difficult." Anastasia pointed at the empty window. "That woman refuses to see you for the gentle and wounded bird that you are."

Though Mimi's eyes burned at the sympathy and anger in those words, she refused to give in to tears. "I don't want to talk about her."

"That makes two of us." She let her hand drop. "Twice I have asked Gregor to let you move in with me. But he fears my health issues might worsen with the strain of caring for another."

"I didn't know you were sick."

"We all carry our secret burdens." Anastasia smiled at her. "Some better than others."

Mimi swallowed. "I wish . . ."

Her gaze hardened. "There is no room in such lives as ours for impossible wishes." When Mimi did not respond, she said, "I wish my husband had not suffered his second heart attack. I wish he and I could have enjoyed our autumn years together. I wish I could hear his laughter once more. I wish I had been blessed with more than one child. You understand?"

"I like you very much," Mimi said.

"You are a remarkable young woman, and I am glad to play this small role in the uncovering of your gift." She reached across the central console and hugged Mimi. It was the first time they had touched. "We shall see more of each other going forward, which is a blessing to us both."

Later that night, when she was safe in her little room under the eaves, it finally became clear to Mimi why she had been so repulsed by the idea of taking money.

The three crones held the answer.

Those old women were ruled by their gift. They were only safe in those dark shadows, surrounded by old incense and the cold gazes of dead icons. In the world of light and action and people and laughter, they were outcasts. They were laughed at, three old ladies who limped on canes and mumbled to themselves. People came when they were desperate, but afterward the trio were shunned. Mimi wanted none of that. She had not endured so many impossible events to become trapped inside a cave of shadows and candles and whispered secrets.

She might have a gift. Even so, she would use it in a way that did not dominate her existence.

She wanted to *live*.

CHAPTER 8

Midway through Billy's next take, Connie blew her lines again. But Trevor's cameraman continued to track him, so Billy shifted from mark to mark, falling in love as he approached the stage. This was the defining difference between screen and theater. Right here. Billy's part could not be dictated by his co-star or her troubles. There was no audience on hand to judge his every move. He did what he had to do, in order to bring his character to the fore.

Billy had learned through trial and error how to maintain his role and hold fast to this internal state, even when dealing with the external vacuum. Up there on the stage, where he locked his gaze as he moved, stood not Connie but rather the woman he was coming to love. *She was there.* She *called* to him. Billy *lived* this second reality. And in the time it took to walk through the crowd and reach the edge of the stage, *he fell in love.*

When Billy returned to the shaded weight area, three more gaffers and two female staffers had joined him and JoJo. Waiting was a normal process of any shoot. Finding a way to vent was crucial to maintaining a steady mental state. Billy found an ice-cold Gatorade and a fresh smoothie next to where he left his clothes. Billy waved his thanks to JoJo and restarted his bench presses.

Midway through his second routine, Connie Adler walked over and seated herself on the next workout bench. Billy finished his set, placed the bar back in the handles, and wondered if he should say something. But Connie just sat there, staring out over the empty parking lot. So he breathed in and out, giving his muscles a chance to recover, then lifted the bar and started again.

Even though he remained silent, Billy felt the gray separation between reality and his role begin to fragment. He was worried about being pulled away from his character. It felt like he watched a soft January mist become shredded by a rising wind. Gradually Connie's tension and fear infected him as well.

Then Trevor drifted over to where he could glance around the canvas wall and catch Billy's eye. The AD's furtive movement suggested he didn't want Connie to notice him. Trevor gave Billy a thumbs-up and slipped back out of sight.

Trevor was well aware of Billy's habits. He knew Billy retreated here to maintain his role between sets. Billy assumed Trevor showed himself to let Billy know his part was in the can. He could shift back into reality. Dismiss his role for the afternoon. Talk to Connie, person to person.

Billy wiped his face with the towel and asked, "You doing okay?"

"You know I'm not. Everybody does." Connie waved at the world beyond the blank canvas wall. "You saw Peter Veer, the studio executive, yes?"

He nodded. "I saw."

"He's watching me all the time." Now that the lights were off, her accent was stronger. Like a Latina version of smoky molasses. "Maybe he's here to fire me."

"Not a chance." He could be certain of that, if nothing else. They were too close to a final wrap. "More likely, they're sizing you up for a new role."

The prospect caused her to release tears. Billy rose, walked to the pile of fresh towels, and brought one back. "Try not to streak your makeup. The exec is bound to notice if the ladies have to start all over on your face."

"I hate being so weak." Her hands shook as she dabbed her face. "I don't know what to do. Vince, he is . . ."

Billy seated himself and softly replied, "Even though nobody can hear us, it's probably best not to go there."

She took a deep breath. Another. And forced herself to settle. "Vince scares me."

"And that makes you nervous." His voice was scarcely a whisper. "So you try harder. And you focus on him, tight as you can. And then you forget your lines."

She pressed the towel to her eyes with both hands. Billy reached out and set a hand on her shoulder. It felt like he touched the flank of a terrified horse. Eventually she managed, "What am I to do?"

"Start with your strengths." He thought back to his favorite teacher, the lessons that had meant the most in those awful moments before his first big role. "You are stunningly beautiful. Your image on camera is electric. Your voice is almost too sexy."

"But all this means nothing . . ." She went quiet when he increased the pressure on her shoulder.

"Your strengths," he repeated. "Roles in telenovelas require you to project. Like you're acting in theater. Vince may be hard to follow, but his intent is real. You need to shift to the big screen. You have to go tight. Small. Make every gesture, every emotion, a fraction of what you've built up inside yourself."

"All this, Vince is telling me." She was growing quiet now. "I could hear him better if he wasn't so . . ."

"I have a technique I've used for tough roles." He let his hand drop. "But I have no idea if it would work for you."

"Tell me. Please."

"Go for the opposite of what comes natural. Start by naming the exact reverse of what Vince says."

She turned and stared at him. "Vince will kill me."

"Not if you give him what he wants. You can't tell him what you're thinking. He's the director. So accept these emotions, the pressure, and remember your core objective. Go tight." This close, Connie's emerald gaze was so big, so inviting, Billy felt tempted to dive in and lose himself.

"I don't understand. But just the same it calls to me, what you say."

"How is Vince telling you to play this scene?"

"With fire. And pain for my friends. And fury at your father."

"What is the opposite of this?"

"Calm."

"Try again. We're after a different approach."

She watched him. Finally, "Selfish."

"There you go."

"Self-absorbed. Conceited. Only think about me. Only *do* for me."

He leaned back, caught up now in glimpsing the change in her. "Do you feel it?"

"It is the part of me I fight against. All my life I fight. It shames me."

"You're good at suppressing what you don't want to show, right?"

"The best." She smiled. The first time in several long days. "Every beautiful Mexican woman has to be."

"For this next take, release both these sentiments and also how you feel about working with Vince. Let it all boil up inside."

"But . . ." She stopped when he raised one finger.

"Then struggle against it," Billy went on. "Focus on this struggle. Let the conflict dominate." Billy gave her a chance to object, complain, something. Instead, she offered nothing save another blast of those heart-melting eyes. "You're falling in love. That's the underlying core to this scene. You're addressing the crowd, but you're . . ."

"Wanting you," she said.

"Wanting my character. So you're terribly conflicted. Be that way. Forget everything else. That's my advice. Focus on the energies inside you, keep it all locked in tight. That becomes the emotion you carry from take to take. Go for what creates the conflict."

"Between me and Vince," she said, then offered him a molten look. "And between me and you."

"Between you and my character," he repeated, only this time they were both smiling.

She studied him a long moment, until a voice from the set called for the next take. They stood together. Connie said, "If the whole world was not watching, I would hug you."

Billy grinned. "Save it for our big love scene."

Vince called a time-out after two more takes. The crew needed a meal and the lights needed adjusting. As the afternoon settled into stronger shadows, lights had to be cranked up and aimed once more to maintain the sense of temporal continuity. This was a cost of shooting on location. One of many.

There were two canteen trucks, one for the extras and another for the crew. Trevor was known to be very picky when it came to who dished out their meals. The crew's truck was from Baton Rouge and the chef spiced her dishes too heavily for some. Billy liked the food just fine.

Old Town contained seventeen blocks of Spanish-style structures and winding lanes and hitching posts and shaded front porches and handblown glass windows. All the shop signs were painted in the original style, bright orange or red lettering on polished cedar planks. Crossroads and parks were anchored by clutches of mesquite and cottonwood trees. Birds were everywhere.

When Billy joined the line, some of the crew shuffled aside, making way for him to move to the front. Billy chatted with JoJo and remained where he was. The afternoon wind had picked up, hot as a blow-dryer. Billy wore a towel around his neck and used it to wipe away the makeup that slipped off with his sweat. JoJo murmured, "Here comes the brass."

Trevor stepped up beside Billy and said, "Let's talk."

So Billy walked forward and accepted his plate and followed the assistant director to the empty table farthest from the food truck. He passed where the *Variety* reporter was seated with the location publicist and the studio executive. Kari Simmons lifted her gaze and inspected Billy until the exec reached out and tapped her hand, drawing her back around.

Which was when he noticed so many of the crew pretending not to watch him settle in place, facing the director. "What's going on?"

Trevor unfurled his napkin, took out his fork, and said, "What did you tell Connie?"

Billy tried his best not to sound defensive as he described their conversation. The assistant director ate steadily, his gaze on his food. Billy finished with, "Did I do wrong?"

Trevor wiped his mouth and hands, and asked, "What did you think of these last takes?"

"She looked . . ." He searched for a word that wouldn't spark the director's ire. "Settled."

"We got what we needed. But you took a risk. We both did."

"The last thing I want is to get on Vince's bad side."

Trevor pushed his plate to one side. "Little late for that."

"Tell me." Billy worked his way through a couple more bites. "Vince hasn't spoken ten words to me since we started the shoot. I'm terrified he's going to shred me in the editing room. Shorten my on-screen role, make the story all about Connie, play me as second fiddle. It keeps me up nights."

"The truth is, I don't know why things are like they are. All I can tell you is, Vince sent me over to lay down the law."

Billy pushed his plate aside. "I'm all ears."

"Don't."

"That's it?"

"That was the long and short of what he said." Trevor leaned across the table. "Now you want to hear what I think?"

Billy swallowed hard. "Go ahead."

"You remember what I said this morning about the studio's problem child?"

"This summer's disaster. I remember."

"The exec seated across from the *Variety* reporter—no, don't turn around. Peter Veer has just been named to the studio's executive board. You understand what that means?"

"Sure. He's the newest member of the green-light team." In every studio, streaming service, and television network, there was always a core group responsible for deciding which project moved from concept to the screen. "What's he doing here?"

"The million-dollar question." Trevor's face was so close, Billy could see the flecks of dark in his gray eyes, like someone had flicked a paintbrush at his face. "The word from my friend is, Vince wanted somebody else for your current role. Peter Veer insisted on you, or the film didn't get made."

"What?"

Trevor shrugged. "So now that their summer tentpole is in trouble, more and more senior execs have been gathering in the screening room, watching our dailies." Trevor smiled at Billy's silence. "Thought that might brighten your day."

"What does this have to do with my talking to Connie?"

"No idea." Trevor glanced over Billy's shoulder, then moved in closer still. "I sent her over because she needs what Vince is clearly not giving her. It was a make-or-break moment for this project. And you helped her turn the corner."

"Did I shoot my own career in the process?"

"Maybe. But I don't think so." Trevor showed him a smile that was only possible from a man working sixteen-hour days, seven days a week, month on month. Tight and happy and exhausted and hopeful. "You keep giving your finest, you might find out how the world looks from high-altitude orbit."

Billy tried to fashion a response as Trevor rose from his seat. But just then, nothing came to mind.

Trevor seemed genuinely pleased with Billy's silence. "Finish your meal. We go again in five."

CHAPTER 9

By the time they finished the last crowd scene, the wind had died to almost nothing. The trees remained poised in the afternoon light, their dry leaves silenced by the January dusk. Vince dismissed about two-thirds of the extras and half the crew. Their director was determined to complete two more takes. He insisted that Connie's exhaustion would play well. As usual, he did not even glance Billy's way.

The first take went well enough. Billy was stationed by the stairs as Connie emerged from the excited group of protest leaders. He walked her through the last remnants of the crowd. They talked in weary snatches as they approached her pickup. Billy's task was to show in his gaze, his step, his every word, that he was smitten. Connie simply had to play it exactly as she was—weary, stressed, not really in the mood to make peace with the son of her enemy.

They paused for Trevor to reset the extras and Vince to have a word with Connie. Billy returned to the canteen wagon for a jolt of old overbrewed coffee. The excitement of Trevor's news had worn off now, replaced by a sweat-stained weariness he felt in his bones.

Trevor called his name and pointed to his mark by the stairs. Billy set his cup back on the counter, thanked the cook, and headed back.

Vince stood by the close-up cameraman, staring at Connie through a viewfinder. He looked up to where a gaffer stood on a ladder and said, "Shift the central light a fraction more to my left."

Billy heard the light gaffer use a rubber mallet to pound the side of the klieg light. A second time. On the third strike there was a snap like a bullwhip.

The gaffer actually screamed.

The air was so still, Billy heard the approaching hiss. Like a snake striking. Then the cable slammed into his right shoulder, fifty pounds of rubber-encased metal wiring.

Billy heard Trevor roar his name. He had no idea why. But whenever Trevor used that voice, something bad was going down.

Then the cable's exposed tip struck Billy at the point where his neck met his shoulder.

Billy had heard of mountain men who survived a lightning strike. Appalachia summer storms carried fierce power, sometimes the strikes coming so close together it sounded like one great enormous roar. Like the sky overhead was being torn apart. Billy did not hear the storm's apex through his ears. The electric explosion ripped *inside* him.

His life was blown to pieces.

The force held him upright and rigid, stretched out on a rack, for what seemed like eons. A time beyond time.

When he was finally released, Billy did not feel himself crash to the earth. But he knew he fell because his vision tilted, and lowered, until he looked sideways at a dozen feet rushing toward him. A hundred.

Billy actually felt his heart seize up.

Then he died.

CHAPTER 10

Consciousness returned in tight flashes, like when lightning illuminated a dark and scary landscape. Pain dragged him back the first time, a raw wound at the core of his being, made worse by how the film's medic knelt on him and pounded his chest with both fists. Billy opened his eyes in time to watch the bearded guy lean over and fasten his lips to Billy's, breathing with him.

Then he was gone.

The next flash, and three guys, maybe four, gripped him in various places, ready to heft him onto a gurney. The lead ambulance technician was a woman almost as big as JoJo. "Okay, on my three. One, two . . ."

The next moment Billy stared up at the ambo's metal roof. Trevor leaned in so close, Billy could see the freckles hidden in the caramel skin. "Come on, Billy. Stay with me, brother."

He liked that word and all the concern it held. *Brother.* His passage back into blackness was easier.

The siren drew him back, or maybe it was how the ambulance jerked hard as it stopped. A new person in surgical blues crawled into the ambulance, shouldering Trevor aside. The woman's face was Asian and sharp and ready. She flashed a light in his eyes and spoke in staccato bursts that Billy could not be bothered to catch. She backed out, and hands gripped his gurney and hustled it from the ambulance. Billy wanted to tell them everything hurt, but he was already on his way out again.

Billy could have drifted there in nowhere land for days. Every now and then, he floated up toward the surface. Close enough to know he had been given some heavy meds. They coursed through his body like a liquid one degree off ice. Not quite able to congeal his veins, but close. They were that strong.

He almost reached the surface when several people lifted him onto a hard table and ran him through an incredibly noisy machine. The metal racket pounded at him for a few seconds, but not even that clamor was enough to hold him for long.

The next time Billy swam up, he lay in a bed where the mattress had been cranked up under his knees and behind his back, keeping him from straightening out fully. The freedom from pain was so exquisite he actually didn't want to go back to sleep. He floated there in a soft bliss, knowing it was a risk to feel this good.

Back in western Carolina, a number of the moonshining clans had switched over to grass. Many of Billy's childhood buddies saw growing weed as their only alternative to the unemployment line. That or leaving the hills—which for most Blue Ridge boys was little more than a life sentence. But grass made him sleepy, alcohol brought out a latent rage he rarely let himself feel, and coke did nasty things to his brain. Since his mind and his body were all he had going, Billy had found it easy enough to keep such temptations at arm's length.

Whatever they had given him was something else entirely.

When Billy finally opened his eyes, he lay in a regular bed, not the ICU unit, which he took as a very good sign. He had gotten to know the intensive care system during Ada's last long decline. Such rooms all had glass walls facing the nurses' central station. Privacy was another word for pulling the drapes shut. All the patients' vitals were on constant display via screens along the nurses' station.

Billy was in a room all his very own. The door was shut. The IV was hooked into a machine the size of a sewing box, probably what fed him his cocktail. On the bed's other side was an electronic monitor that blinked in time to his heart. It appeared to be beating at a constant rate. A very good sign. The window was dark, the hospital very quiet. He sighed with the pleasure of having made it through another close call.

Billy heard heavy breathing and turned his head ever so slightly toward the door, just a fraction of movement. Enough to see a shadow figure slumbering in the chair beside his bed. He could not bring the person into focus, but was pretty certain it was Trevor. For the moment, though, who it was mattered less than knowing the team had insisted on keeping him company.

A heavyset nurse opened Billy's door and turned on the light. She showed surprise to find his eyes open and tracking her. "My goodness, you gave me half a start. How're you feeling, hon?"

Billy smiled at the woman's Texas twang. Close enough to his home country's accent to make him feel welcome. But the effort required to open his mouth and shape a reply forced him back under. Billy shut his eyes and swam away.

When Billy next opened his eyes, dawn formed a golden wash upon his side window. He blinked slowly, taking in the fact that he was genuinely back. Slowly he surveyed his body, like running a mental tongue over an ailing tooth. The entire left side of his body ached something awful, but at a drug-induced distance. The dosage of whatever they were giving him had been reduced to where his aches and pains formed a muted chorus.

There was a snuffling noise from his other side. Billy slowly turned his head, inch by inch, enough to discover the person in his bedside chair was none other than Kari Simmons. The *Variety* reporter had the blanket tucked up close to her chin. There was no reason to be so touched by her presence. No reason to feel emotions swell up like they did. Billy lay there and studied her a long moment, until slumber rose up like a blanket all his very own.

When he next woke, the clarity was strong enough that he lay there with his eyes still closed, savoring the fact that he was both alive and getting better.

Specific noises carried an exquisite flavor, like music of a celestial order. The squeak of a trolley wheel being pushed down the corridor beyond his door. The soft murmur of nurses. Even the beep of his heart monitor. Each sound carried a sibilant rush of pleasure.

It was then that his last dream came back to him. The realization was enough to cause him to open his eyes.

Sunlight streamed through his window, marking a substantial passage of time. He turned his head and found Kari Simmons watching him, a faint smile creasing her features. "Well, hey, sailor."

Billy lifted his right hand and rubbed his face. At least half his body seemed to be in working order.

"The others spelled you through the night," Kari said. "I volunteered so they could get back to work. You want me to ring the nurse?"

He ungummed both tongue and lips, then croaked, "In a minute."

She lifted the cup from his bedside table and fit the straw between his lips. The iced water tasted exquisite.

"More?" When Billy shook his head, she plied the pitcher and refilled the cup. "Shame on you. You gave everybody such a bad scare."

"Was that a joke?"

"Half of one."

"Not even. Maybe a fifth. But nice, just the same," Billy said.

He watched her settle back into the chair. She was a strange one, this Hollywood reporter. Beneath the cynical hard edges and the probing gaze and the strangely awful fashion sense, beat what Billy suspected was a decent and caring heart. He could scarcely believe his own ears when he heard himself say, "I was dreaming about my mother."

She took her time folding up her blanket and tucking it into the shelf below his cup and pitcher. "She died, right?"

"When I was six. She and my dad went off on some gig and never came back." Billy turned his head back so as to stare at the ceiling. It felt good talking about this, which was beyond odd. Normally, he did his best to cram such memories back inside their cast-iron lockbox. "She had a beautiful voice. Whenever they were home, she'd be singing all the time. Early sixties was her era. She loved the Rat Pack. Sinatra, Martin, Sammy Davis, she could do them all."

Billy went quiet then. Thinking about earlier times, when the dream used to wake him in the wee dark hours. Lying there in his grandmother's home, helpless in the knowledge that his parents had finally left him for good. Coming to terms, or trying to, with the new word that so many people used to describe him: orphan. Seeing it in the faces of adults in his school, his neighborhood, his grandmother's church. Poor little orphan Billy Rose Walker. The dreams had been awful then. The worst nightmares of all. Hearing the voice that would never sing for him again.

A secret rage against the parents who abandoned him had carried Billy through some very hard days. They had loved their music and their band and their travels more than they had loved him. Why hadn't they taken him along? Wasn't he a good kid? Much as he screamed and begged not to be left behind, they always hugged him and waved as they drove off. The fury had helped seal the hurt down where no one else could see. Where it didn't rake those burning talons over his lonely life. Except when the dream came, and he had no choice but to cry himself back to sleep.

Billy blinked and drew the world back into focus. The hospital, the day, even the pain, played a welcome role. He said, "Sorry. I guess . . ."

"Terrible thing, memories," Kari said. For once, her gaze was gentle.

Billy smiled, glad that she was there with him. "Maybe you better ring for the nurse."

CHAPTER 11

The day nurse was a small woman, scarcely reaching Billy's chest. But she was strong as steel cord, able to take most of his weight and support him across the room and into the bathroom. Which was good, because the journey would have been impossible without her. She was there when he came out and let him set the pace back to his bed. She fed him his morning meds, shooed Kari from the room, and brought him a breakfast he didn't want.

Kari must have phoned the set, because by the time he finished pushing his eggs around the plate, Trevor and the studio executive were standing there in the doorway. But before they could say more than hello and how was he doing, the doctor arrived and ordered them out.

Dr. Ming was a beautiful Asian woman with pianist's hands, her long fingers holding both dexterity and strength. She fitted the electrodes to his chest and forehead, then spent a considerable amount of time scrolling through the EKG tape. She peeled off the bandage covering his left shoulder, pulled back the covers, and inspected his left side from hairline to ankle. Billy didn't like seeing the blue-black streaks running down his body. It brought the incident back in living color, close and intense enough to make him nauseous. He shut his eyes and let the doctor probe away.

Finally she readjusted his covers, applied a salve and new bandage to his shoulder, and opened the door. "Please join us." When Trevor and Peter Veer entered the room, she said, "Tell me what happened."

"We're doing a location shoot in Old Town," Trevor began.

Dr. Ming shook her head. "Skip the windup and get to the accident."

Peter smiled at Billy from behind the doctor's back. Trevor said, "We were adjusting the kliegs. A cable popped loose and fell on Billy."

"Kliegs are big lights, correct?"

"The most intense lights on set." Trevor looked almost as nauseous as Billy felt. "That particular cable fed power to six kliegs."

"What happened then?"

Peter spoke for the first time. "There was a crack like gunfire."

"Or lightning," Trevor said.

"Sparks flashed all around Billy," Peter said.

"For what seemed like hours," Trevor said.

"Five seconds," Peter corrected. "Less. And the sparks were all on his left side."

"Our staff medic was one of the team adjusting the lights," Trevor said. "He was on Billy almost before he hit the ground. Working his chest, doing the mouth-to-mouth thing."

"All right, that explains a lot." She addressed Billy. "Your injuries are more symptomatic of a lightning strike. That is something we see quite a lot in these parts. Direct strikes, side splash, contact with the strike object, ground current.

Those are the major types. America has a quarter of a million such incidents each year, and one in ten is fatal. In your case it sounds like you probably suffered both heart asystole and respiratory arrest. If that is correct, the medic's rapid response saved your life."

By this point Peter had stopped smiling. Trevor looked as green as his dark skin allowed. The doctor pointed to Billy's shoulder. "You suffered typical third-degree burns where the cable made contact. These striations along your left side are known as Lichtenberg figures, and are formed when capillaries beneath the skin rupture, due to the electrical discharge. They shouldn't last more than about three weeks. If they remain much longer than that, you need to come see me."

Peter asked, "You're saying he can go?"

She turned and glared him into silence, then resumed. "The scans show no actual fractures, which means you were very fortunate. Broken bones often result from a direct strike, due to the severe contraction of muscles. But your joints are so swollen I can't tell if there has been any cartilage damage."

"Everything hurts," Billy confessed.

"Which is hardly a surprise. You will suffer that discomfort for at least a couple of weeks, probably longer. Stiffness and restricted movement may last months." She touched his rib cage. "Does it hurt to breathe?"

"Not shallow breaths. Which is all I'm taking."

She fit the stethoscope to her ears. "Deep breath. Much as you can."

He did and groaned, causing her to pull back. "Again. Try to stay quiet."

Billy breathed until the pain halted him.

"All right, that's enough." She stuffed the scope back in her pocket. "Basically, you have sprained every joint along that side of your body. Which means movement will be severely limited."

This time Billy was the one who asked, "I can go?"

"Actually, some movement at this stage will help your recovery. But you need to be very careful not to strain yourself further." She turned and addressed the pair. "You want him to resume work?"

Peter replied, "We are in the final week of a film shoot."

"Every remaining scene has Billy front and center," Trevor said.

"Each additional day costs us over four hundred thousand dollars," Peter said.

"They need me," Billy said. "It's as simple as that."

The doctor asked them, "You can have medical personnel on hand?"

"We're bringing out a physician's assistant on the studio's payroll. His flight is due to land in ninety minutes," Peter replied.

"The patient will need constant monitoring," the doctor cautioned. "His schedule of meds must be maintained. We'll supply you with a wheelchair and walker."

"No walker," Billy said.

"You'll take it and be grateful," Trevor ordered. "Now thank the doctor."

"I'll look like an old man," Billy complained.

The doctor actually smiled. "You're welcome."

Chapter 12

An hour or so later, they finished the paperwork and released Billy. While they waited, Trevor said, "Kari said to tell you good luck."

"She's gone?"

"Off to her next assignment." Trevor and Peter just smiled. "Look at the man. He's sorry to see the back of a reporter."

"Definitely one for the books," Peter said.

"The man breaks hearts wherever he goes," Trevor said.

A nurse helped him into the hospital chair and pushed him down the corridor. Trevor pulled up in one of the set's rented SUVs, and together with Peter he helped settle Billy in the passenger seat. The nurse had fed Billy his meds just prior to setting off. They began to kick in just as Trevor pulled from the curb. Billy asked, "You mind if I roll down my window?"

"Not too far," Peter said from the backseat. "The wind feels like a blow-dryer on full heat."

Those were the last words anyone spoke as they drove around downtown. The freeway was relatively calm at midday. Heat shimmered off the pavement and turned the concrete ribbon into something almost beautiful. Windows in the high-rise buildings glimmered like molten mirrors. Billy kept the window cracked just enough for the outside air to wash over his face. The sky was a dusty blue, pale as dirty porcelain. It felt better than good to ride in this silent vehicle. Alive.

The set came to a complete halt as they pulled up. Everyone watched as Billy eased from the ride and settled into his wheelchair. JoJo was the first to approach and solemnly welcome him back. He was followed by so many others. But not Vince. Or Connie. It tired Billy out, responding to all the greetings. Even so, their solemn relief at his appearance was all part of the afternoon's warm goodness.

The physician's assistant was Kyle, a tall, rangy man in his early thirties. Kyle didn't like the trailer any more than Billy. He had JoJo shift some of the weight stations and then set up his treatment table under the canvas awning. Kyle had short brown hair with frosted tips, and an easy professional manner. "Tell me how you want this to go."

"The doctor said I needed to work my joints."

"I know all that. The good Doctor Ming and I are new besties. What I want to know is, how do *you* want this to play out?"

Billy looked over to where the set was slowly gearing back up. "Everything needs to be timed around my takes."

"Correction, dearie. Just two takes per day, a third only allowed if a close-up is required. Any more and the powers that be will have words."

"Says who?"

"The elephant in the room is who."

"Peter Veer said I only make two takes?"

"None other. And yon director did not like hearing it, not one teeny bit. Which side is the one we need to work on?"

"Left. But both sides are hurting."

"That's to be expected, seeing as how the ear bone is connected to the toe bone. Or something like that. I forget exactly. It's been ever such a long time since school." He shifted around to Billy's other side. "On a scale of one to ten, what's your pain level?"

"It was about a nine, until you pulled me out of the chair. Now it's closer to fifteen."

"We need to get you comfortable so we can work. And that can't happen if you're all stressed." He settled Billy on the table's edge and checked his watch. "We're still forty minutes from your next meds, but who's to say my watch isn't slow. Can you stay there without toppling over?"

"If you hurry."

"I'm quite fleet of foot, especially when meds are involved." He brought a plastic Baggie and a bottle of iced water. "They really loaded you down with some good stuff. I'm ever so tempted to sample."

Billy found himself liking Kyle just fine. He swallowed one at a time, then, "You don't mind working in this heat?"

"Lift your arms so I can pull off that T-shirt. Oh, my dear sweet word, would you look at what they've done to your lovely body." His frosted hair flickered as he bent in close and probed Billy's ribs. "Can you breathe for me?"

"A little."

"All right. We'll start with some gentle motions, a bit of realigning your spine, nothing that should have you screaming overmuch. Which is probably a good thing, since I'm already getting the stink eye from that mobile launchpad over there. Let's start you on your front."

Billy eased himself down in groaning stages. Once he settled into the curved face pillow, Kyle began a gentle probing down the length of Billy's spine. Pushing gently here and there, working a bit in the spaces between vertebrae. Billy murmured, "That feels good."

"Of course it does. The sort of meds you're on, I could

probably attack you with a hammer and chisel and you'd enjoy it." Kyle moved up to the neck. "To answer your question, I've never minded the heat. Those horrid refrigerated meat lockers they call trailers are another thing entirely. Reminds me of Rochester. Dreadful place. Full of bullies and beer bellies and hairy everything. I couldn't get out of there fast enough."

Billy found himself drifting off, carried by Kyle's murmured nonsense. He wondered if the man actually heard what he was saying, or if his singsong cadence was intended all along to carry him away.

The afternoon take was simple enough. A first-date dinner where Connie's character had all the good lines. Billy's job was basically to feed her questions and play the captivated male. Whenever Connie posed a question of her own, Billy deflected, because that was what his character had been doing all his life. Not allowing himself to see how totally his world was dominated by his father's constant aggressive ire. Which gave Connie's character the choice, the one that framed her willingness to give Billy's guy a romantic chance. Either she pushed and prodded, and risked forcing him away, or she accepted Billy's character as possessing both a sensitive and wounded nature. Which she did. But it was done with a calculated wisdom. Connie's character wanted him to accept that here was a lady he could trust.

In the next day's scene, Billy's character was meant to open up. They were scheduled to share a lovers' sunset, when Connie's character shows Billy a way out of his impossible life. If he dares.

In less than a week they would shoot their love scene.

Him with the halfway purple body. Not exactly the way Billy had envisioned showing off his almost-naked form.

Forty-five minutes before Billy was scheduled to appear

under the lights, Trevor came over with the makeup ladies. Kyle fed Billy another dose, then helped steady him while the ladies fit him into his date costume. That done, Billy shifted into the makeup chair. Trevor walked Billy through his lines while the ladies did his face and hair. Billy could see Vince over by the restaurant's table with Connie, pointing at elements on the script, heads together. When they finished, Vince did not even glance in Billy's direction. Not once. Billy knew he should probably be worried about the director's attitude. How the film's boss had not so much as asked how Billy was doing, or welcomed him back with more than a nod. But the meds were working on him, and Trevor was a big source of much-needed strength and solace. Billy decided he had room either to give the take his best, or worry about the director's cold shoulder. But not both.

What was more interesting, at least as far as Billy was concerned, was Peter Veer. The studio's senior executive remained close at hand. He spent most of his time talking on the phone, or seated at one of the shaded tables texting, or pacing around the parking lot, gesticulating while one of his two aides took frantic notes. As the ladies worked on his face and hair, Billy found himself calmed by the executive's presence. This was the exact opposite from his normal response to a front-office guy tracking his moves on set.

Vince called, "Places, everyone."

Billy pushed himself out of the makeup chair in stages. "Give me the walker."

Kyle said, "The wheelchair is better."

"Then you use it."

"Attitude. You must be feeling better." Kyle unfolded the walker and steadied it as Billy transferred his weight. "Have you ever used one of these before?"

"I'm a fast learner." He gritted his teeth and moved forward. *Shift the frame, hands tight on the padded handles, step. Again.* Billy expected some snickers, probably a few snide murmurs. As in, *Get a load of Billy Rose Walker living up to his name.*

Instead, the entire crew came to a standstill.

As Billy slowly made his way to his mark by the restaurant's entrance, it seemed that they not only watched, but held their breath.

The take began with Billy standing by the passenger door of his daddy's hand-me-down Cadillac, there to take Connie's hand, play the gentleman. Billy's stand-in moved away, Kyle took the walker and stepped out of the lights, Trevor hovered, and Vince asked, "We ready?"

"Good as gold." Trevor's gaze never left Billy's face.

"Connie?"

"Yes."

"All right, everyone. This is a take."

CHAPTER 13

Peter Veer, the studio executive, remained well removed from the set. As they lined up the shot, he lowered his phone and watched intensely. Billy had the feeling his attention was mostly on Vince. The meds kicked in about the time Vince checked through the camera's viewfinder a final time and said, "Sound check."

"One, two," Billy said.

"Good luck, Billy," Connie said.

"Ready," the soundman said.

"Quiet on set, this is a take," Vince said. Then, "Action."

Billy's greatest fear had been playing the parrot. Giving back the words with nothing behind them. Being unable to connect with his character or the story. But under the lights he entered a foggy netherworld. Or rather, part of him did. Billy watched the scene unfold, and his character hit the marks and responded to Connie and gradually gave in to the woman's passion and magnetic fire. Up close and romantically personal.

Unlike every other day, though, a part of him drifted. Maybe it was the meds, maybe the closeness of what almost happened. But he did not fully integrate with the moment. He was able to capture glimpses of the set and the people, the behind-camera world that normally vanished the instant he started acting.

But like the guy said, there was nothing normal about this particular day.

Vince called a pause while the lights were adjusted for the table shot. Instantly Kyle was there with the chair, a cup of iced water, and a helping hand. Trevor offered him the script, which Billy waved away. The lines of dialogue sparked behind his open eyes. At least his retention seemed intact.

Everybody moved at double speed. When the set was ready, however, Connie flubbed her lines. They continued on through the scene, then Vince ordered, "Keep rolling. Do it again."

Peter Veer stepped forward. Billy met the executive's gaze for the first time since rising from his hospital bed and gave a fraction of a head shake. He said, "It's okay."

The director noticed the exchange. That was the director's job, to notice everything that happened on set. Billy had no idea why Vince would get so worked up over Billy saying he wanted to keep to Vince's schedule. But the director's response was unmistakable. Vince's face pinched tight, and his voice grated with a very real burn as he said, "And, Action."

Connie missed one cue and then skipped over a crucial line of dialogue. Billy did his job: played it straight, smiled, and responded in the places marked on his script. They could shoot around, redub, add close-ups, whatever.

When the scene was done, Vince remained crouched directly beside the first camera, his face maybe two feet from Connie's. Close enough to whisper, "Keep rolling. Again."

Billy nodded once to Connie, calm and ready. He knew

what Vince was doing. Not going directly against Peter's orders. But getting his way, just the same.

"Keep rolling. Again."

Billy had worked like this on many other occasions. Low-budget films made for TV were often shot with multiple takes played out together, struggling to meet impossible deadlines and air dates that were put in place months before the shoot even began.

After five takes, though, his energy just vanished. Or maybe the meds were finally taking full hold. Whatever. Vince remained crouched and close and intense enough to grip Connie with his fierce determination to get this right and in the can. She delivered her best take yet. But when it came time for Billy to grip her hand with both of his and deliver his final line . . .

He fainted dead away.

CHAPTER 14

~❧~

Like most California coastal towns, Miramar was made up of many distinct communities. Even a place this small had its own internal boundaries. There were actually two commercial hubs to Miramar. One extended outward from Ocean Avenue, mostly on the northern side. Mimi's condominium faced Ocean Park, which actually was four and a half blocks from the shore, and marked the end of the business district. From there to the Pacific, winding lanes held vastly more expensive homes. Ocean Avenue ended at an L-junction with the Coastal Road, which wrapped its slow and winding way around Miramar Bay.

When Mimi left her condo that Sunday, the pearl light of early daybreak was only visible if she looked straight up. Away from the shore, Ocean Avenue climbed a slow and gentle hill. The town was wrapped in a morning fog, draping every surface in liquid gemstones that captured the growing light. She loved having the town to herself at moments like this. Mimi often thought if she could just listen more intently, the town might whisper its hidden secrets.

She attended the first Mass, something she did a couple of times every week. Whenever possible she also stopped here before using her gift. Mimi had heard others refer to such events as readings. She disliked the term almost as much as she did the word she had found in the Bible: "prophecy." They both carried baggage that left her feeling the permanent outsider.

She had no idea how to describe her relationship with the divine. It troubled her sometimes, this mystery at the heart of her existence. But she had learned to live with the unanswered while still a child. Mimi had long since decided that most of life's questions were not meant to be resolved.

She had started attending Mass with Gregor's mother. His own family had no interest in religion of any kind. They treated Anastasia's almost-daily church attendance as just another part of her old-world character. Mimi had liked the reverence and the calm and the music from her very first visit. It linked her to vague memories of such times back in Donetsk, when she was part of a family, with a sister and two parents and a hint of normalcy, even when they lived surrounded by civil rage and bitter strife. Nowadays she tried very hard to be reverential. But she strived equally hard to be honest. And these two aims, reverence and honesty, often seemed to be in direct conflict.

When Mass ended, she descended Ocean Avenue to where it joined with the Coastal Road. Miramar Bay was three and a quarter miles wide, bound at both ends by tall cliff-edged headlands. The Coastal Road was lined by numerous hotels dating from the 1920s. All of them were small—thirty rooms at the most—and none were part of any major chain. The entire beach was deeded as public, with hotel properties ending at the road.

The parking lots below the northern cliffs were already full. Within another hour the Sunday traffic would be backed up almost to her home. A number of people walked the coastal path that ran between the road and the shore. Dogs and families with young children raced around the low-tide sands, chasing gulls that rose lazily at the very last moment. The air was spiced with salt and seaweed and frigid ocean winds. The sun sent golden lances over the eastern hills.

Most of the hotels remained as they had begun, two-star establishments where inland families could enjoy a few inexpensive days by the beach. Two of the original establishments, however, were now elegant guesthouses with Oriental-style bridges crossing koi ponds and suites fronting broad slate-tiled verandas with thatched roofs. Mimi's destination was the café situated between these two inns. The octagonal building was surrounded by willows and rock-rimmed Japanese gardens. The café frequently was Mimi's destination after such lazy Sunday walks. Exterior and interior tables alike were formed from pieces of driftwood that had been molded together and sanded down to a golden-gray finish.

As soon as Mimi stepped through the entrance, Linh's uncle walked around the counter and approached her. "Mimi Janic, yes? This way."

Mimi followed him across the main room. She did not think his brusque manner was simply due to the Sunday-morning rush. He pulled back curtains masking a passage with a PRIVATE sign attached to the wall overhead. The small rear alcove was made bright by a side window that overlooked miniature pines. As soon as Mimi saw just two older women seated at the table, she knew her suspicions were correct.

The uncle said, "She's here."

But when he started to leave, the younger of the two women spoke sharply in Vietnamese, then said to Mimi, "Please to forgive my husband's bad manners, Ms. Janic."

"Call me Mimi."

"I am Bian, and this is Linh's mother, Chau. My husband is Dinh. Please sit. You will take tea?"

She would have liked something to drink, but the tension in the room was very pervasive. "No, thank you."

The aunt spoke again, drawing her husband over. But he refused to seat himself. Bian glowered at him when he took up station by the rear wall. She addressed him a third time. Dinh stonily ignored her.

The two sisters were seated with their backs against the rear wall. Both were small and spare in every way possible. Their clothes were almost identical; they both wore long-sleeved white cotton tops, with cloth buttons done up to the neck, and black trousers. They shared pale unlined faces, sharp features, and clear gazes in their dark eyes. But there the similarities ended.

Linh's mother was delicate in the manner of someone recovering from a long illness. Or perhaps not recovering at all. Her dark hair was thinning and hung untended around her downcast face, utterly unlike Linh's lush black cascade. She had still not glanced once in Mimi's direction.

The aunt was something else entirely. Mimi was fairly certain Bian's delicate manner was a deception. The air around Bian's spare frame seemed to vibrate with barely suppressed energy. She spoke in heavily accented English, "Linh, she say you her favorite teacher."

"I am honored." Unseen currents and tensions swept around the four of them. "Linh is a sweet person. And so very intelligent."

"Yes, is so." Bian indicated her sister with the downcast gaze. "My sister does not want to ask any question."

Mimi nodded. "I understand."

"Is this true?" Bian shot her sister an angry look. "You understand when I do not?"

"To ask means to accept a future that contains neither interest or concern." Mimi addressed Linh's mother directly.

"What holds you is the past. The absences that no future can change."

The mother shuddered, just the faintest of tremors, but confirmation enough that she both understood and agreed in her own fashion.

Bian's gaze sparked with something new, a different level of intensity. "You know this how?"

Mimi glanced at the uncle, and saw the raw fear in his gaze. "It happens more often than you might expect."

Then she waited.

Bian cleared her throat. "I have a question."

Mimi did not need to look at Dinh again. His tension was a palpable force now, so strong she could almost taste it. This was something she had endured any number of times. "I don't promise answers. If nothing comes, I will tell you only that."

It was hard to tell if Bian even heard her. She was already rushing ahead, desperate now. She reached for her purse. "How much I pay you? Linh did not say."

"I do not accept payment."

"No, no, you cannot do this for Linh." She clutched her purse with both hands. "For her mother, yes, perhaps. But I pay."

"I don't take money *ever*." Mimi could sense the uncle's desperate fear rise with every word she spoke. "I do this as a service. For free."

Bian wrestled with that, her fingers kneading the leather purse. Finally she said, "My older son. He is gone. Four years now, almost five. We argued. All the time we argue. Then he leave. Now I worry. So very much."

Mimi felt the familiar pressing transition, like her entire body was abruptly captured by unseen winds. "Give me your hand, please."

But when Bian set her right hand on the table and Mimi reached out . . .

She froze.

To touch the proffered hand would have meant speaking. And Mimi could not do that.

Normally such awareness came after she made contact. Today, however, it was enough to reach out. She realized that Bian's son was gay. He lived in Los Angeles with his partner of four and a half years.

His mother would never accept this. She treated her son's orientation as a flaw to be fought over. For her to regain contact and continue their lifetime quarrel would have meant breaking her son's heart.

Only then did she understand the husband's tension. Mimi had naturally assumed the man resented her becoming inserted into a very private matter. Or perhaps he disbelieved Mimi's ability, or felt it was wrong for them to even ask questions of this foreign woman. In the past some family members had shouted that Mimi was both an outsider and unwelcome. They yelled that she should leave and never return.

Not today.

Mimi saw that Dinh was in regular contact with his son. They spoke by phone several times a week. At least once each month, father and son met. Most often in San Luis Obispo, sometimes in Santa Barbara, a few times he made the journey to the big city. Dinh was friends with the partner, a good-hearted Puerto Rican artist named Julio. The affection between the three men was deep and strong.

All this came in the time it took to breathe once and withdraw her hand. For if they had touched, Mimi would have felt compelled to tell the woman everything. And that could not happen.

Mimi said, "I'm sorry. I cannot give you very much."

"But I need to know."

"Your son is well. He is happy. I can tell you nothing else." As Mimi rose from the table, Linh's mother lifted her gaze and looked at her. There was a flicker of something in those placid features, perhaps relief. Or maybe gratitude.

Linh's uncle followed her back through the café. When he opened the door, he leaned in close and asked, "You saw?"

"About your son and Julio," she replied. "Yes, I saw."

He bowed low. "Please to return, Miss Mimi. You are most welcome here anytime."

CHAPTER 15

Billy woke after night had settled beyond his window. He felt a surge of relief over not being back in the hospital. Kyle was taking his pulse and making notes in a leather-bound pad. It must have been his touch that woke Billy. When the PA noticed Billy had opened his eyes, he said, "Welcome back, stranger."

The room was similar, but not his own. "Where am I?"

"Vince kindly offered you his suite." Kyle's voice took on the lilt of suppressed mirth. "Or maybe not so kindly."

"I'm in the director's suite?"

"It's not the director's anymore." Kyle smiled at Billy's surprise. "If you're going to pass out on us, you're bound to miss some drama."

He helped Billy to the bathroom, and when he came out, the living-room table was set for one. "Meds first, then soup."

Billy managed a few bites before a wave of fatigue threatened to overwhelm him. "I better go lie down."

When he next woke, sunshine and wind and tree limbs wrote a lovely script across his windows. Kyle was bedded down on the parlor sofa. Billy made it to the bathroom on his own steam, and felt the better for it. He stripped off his bedclothes, took a moment to inspect his bruises, and reveled in a long, hot shower. When he emerged, Kyle was there to help him dress. Kyle saw his winces and said, "Meds with coffee."

"Maybe I should give them a miss this morning."

"Don't you dare try to play hero. Plus, you need to be ready."

"For what?"

"They didn't tell me anything, except they're on their way up."

"Who is 'they'?"

As if responding, there was a knock on the door.

Vince Edwards entered first. He stopped midway across the parlor and scattered an angry gaze around the room that was no longer his. Once again, he refused to meet Billy's eye. Not even for an instant.

Peter Veer was dressed in pressed gabardine slacks and a navy polo shirt. The studio executive was an inch or so taller than the director and a good fifty pounds lighter. The differences between the two men went much deeper. Ada, Billy's grandmother, would have said that Peter Veer was all of one piece, as in, trim and fit and focused.

Vince was mostly just angry.

"Tell him," Peter said. When Vince remained silent, Peter's voice hardened. "You know the alternative. Tell him or go pack your bags."

"I am very sorry," Vince said. "I overreached. I was simply trying to do what was best—"

"Stop with the justifications and give him the rest."

Vince reddened. His gaze did a moth's dance around the

room. "From now on, we will make do with one regular take and one close-up per day. And use your body double—"

"Three takes," Billy said.

Peter switched his aim from the back of Vince's head to Billy. Vince remained intent on looking anywhere but at his leading man.

"One take won't work with Connie, and we both know it. The pressure will only make it worse on her. I can handle three, if Vince runs them together like yesterday."

Peter nodded. "Three takes plus one close-up. That sound good to you, Vince?" When the director remained silent, Peter said, "Don't you need to be somewhere?"

Vince wheeled about and left the room. The pneumatic hinge made it difficult for him to slam the door. But he gave it his best.

Billy asked, "What just happened?"

Peter turned to Kyle, who stood openmouthed in the bedroom doorway. "Why don't you order us some breakfast."

Billy was tempted to dismiss Peter Veer as just another front-office exec. Climbing the corporate ladder, teeth sunk firmly in the guy up ahead, concerned with nobody but themselves. Ambitious and vain and important only because they gave the up-or-down decision on every new project. Their expertise limited to handling budgets.

All actors met more than their share of such people. They were so easy to despise.

But there was something about Peter. Maybe it was how he wore his authority with such ease. Or how he had remained one step off the front line, observing the team in action, until the moment he showed Vince the iron fist. Something.

Peter was aged in his midforties, give or take five years in either direction. Dark brown hair frosted by coming winter. Expensively dressed even when casual—alligator belt, polo

shirt of some silk and cotton mix, loafers so soft they probably could be rolled up like socks. Trim and precise. A slight
edge to his voice, Billy could not tell if it was an accent or
part of his mannerism. As Kyle helped him settle at the parlor table, Billy asked, "Where are you from?"

"I was born in Antwerp. My family moved to LA when I
was five." Peter brought over two cups from the Nespresso
machine. "My father was a diamond merchant, sent over
here to set up a California outlet. Milk?"

"Please."

"I don't spend much time looking back. But while I was in
the hospital waiting to hear whether our project still had a
leading man, I remembered something." Peter settled into
his chair and shifted around so he could stare out the sunlit
window. "My father basically worked all the time. Once we
moved to the States, he was just this stranger who showed
up now and then for a quick meal. The only chance my older
brother and I had to really be with Pop was Sunday afternoons. He had season tickets to the Hollywood Bowl and
the LA Philharmonic. My mother had health problems. She
joined us when she felt up to it. But usually it was just my
brother and I."

A knock on the door caused them both to turn. Kyle let in
the room service waiter, signed the form, then insisted on
serving them himself. Peter watched Kyle fill his plate and
went on, "I'd watch my brother and father lose themselves
in the music. Two minutes into the performance, they were
just gone. I envied them. But music never spoke to me, not at
that level. Not like them. I was always the outsider."

"For you, it was film," Billy said.

"The size of the screen didn't matter. Not then, not now. I
never held with the idea that features were where the real
artwork existed. The show was either good or it wasn't."

Billy was with him now. Not just listening. Caught in

the act of reliving his own start. "When it was good, it captured you."

"If my father was home and watching TV with us, which was almost never, he and my brother used to talk their way through shows. Which I hated. They used to make fun of how involved I was. Like I was some aberration. Like my tastes were too juvenile. Like . . ."

"Like you didn't belong," Billy said softly. "Like your passions were less important than theirs."

"I sat there in the hospital waiting room, trying to remember if my father ever took me to the cinema. I came up blank." Peter blinked slowly, drawing the room back into focus. "Let's eat."

But as Peter tucked into his breakfast, Billy asked, "Mind if I ask a question first?"

"You're not hungry?"

"Too overwhelmed," Billy replied. "Why are we having this conversation?"

Peter seemed to find nothing odd with eating alone. "You noticed how Connie didn't say anything to you when you got back from the hospital?"

"Of course I did."

"Vince ordered her to stay away from you. He said if she so much as offered you a 'good morning,' she'd be off the project. Of course he doesn't have the right to make such a threat, not this far along. But it scared her, just the same. I'm sure she would want you to know."

Billy watched as Kyle set down a glass of orange juice and a saucer with his morning meds. "Why would he do such a thing?" When Peter simply continued to eat, Billy supplied the answer himself. "Vince didn't want me on the project in the first place."

"Fought against it tooth and nail." Peter seemed to enjoy

the memory. "Said you'd be terrible in the role. He had a perfect actor in mind, someone who could turn this into a major hit. Want to know who that was?"

"Not really, no."

"Probably just as well." Peter rose and walked to the Nespresso machine. "Another coffee?"

"I'm good, thanks."

He watched the little machine whirr and the liquid fill his cup. "I've had my eye on you for quite a while now."

Billy had no idea how to respond to that. So he remained silent.

"Two projects back. The family drama." Peter returned to the table. "The one that was panned at Sundance."

"*Half a Chance.* It deserved better than a made-for-television release."

"Wrong again." Peter seated himself. "It *received* better."

"You've lost me."

"I bought worldwide rights."

"Your studio did. For a song. I remember that much."

"I was responsible for that acquisition. Me. Personally. And the producers did all right in the end. I made sure of that." There was a spark to Peter's dark gray gaze now. A hint of humor that lifted the edges of every other word. "I offered them a portion of the back end. The studio covered its expenses on the US television release. We cleaned up on international. Most of those markets did a limited theatrical release, and in a number of cases, they saw this extended to several months. Your producer and director both came out gold in the end."

The news pushed him back in his seat. "Why am I only hearing about this now?"

"Two reasons. First, you need to change your agent. Gerry Axelrod is a fat has-been who spends his time eating M and M's and dreaming of better days."

"He gave me my shot."

"He's history. Axelrod didn't know because he didn't ask. All he saw was, you got paid guild minimum for the shoot. His interest ended there. I doubt he's even read your last two contracts. Second, my offer of the back end was conditional on your being taken for their next project."

Billy stared across the table.

"You must have wondered why they took you on again, after the first film's terrible reviews."

"Of course I did."

"I am the sole investor in that second project, the one that just wrapped before you came to Texas. I own all rights. You're great, by the way."

Billy breathed in and out.

"A terrific portrayal of a guy on the edge who manages to hold himself and his family together. That's your strength, in my opinion. Playing a hero against the odds. The romance angle is important for the female portion of your audience, but this determination to remain a good guy when all the world is going dark . . ."

Billy managed, "Tell me."

"I think your time has come, Billy Rose. The world is recovering from a terrible juncture. There's a lot of fear around. The dismal dystopian outlook doesn't wash anymore, not for the audience in Kansas City. They're *living* the dystopia. They're too scared and too worried and too stressed to find any entertainment value in that. They want reassurance. They want hope."

Peter set down his fork, folded his napkin into a precise little tent, and set it by his empty plate. "Last time the world went through a crisis like this, our industry could hide the stars and their bad habits behind a well-oiled publicity machine. That's all gone now. The audience we're after, the people our highbrow members like to think don't matter, they want a real person, a *good* person. Someone who backs up the roles they play by living this life in reality. They want you. I'm banking on this."

Billy felt like he should stand. Speak. Something. But just then, the strength wasn't there for anything except to sit and gape.

"I'm headed back to LA. My work here is done. I've been holding on to the release of your last project until I decided whether to invest in you. I came out here to see who Billy Rose actually is. The man when the character is set aside. I like what I see." Peter rose from his chair. "My brother and I inherited a cottage up north of LA, a place called Miramar. It's quiet there. Restful. Once your work here is completed, I want you to go up and recuperate. Will you do that?"

Billy cleared his throat. "All right. Sure."

"I'll have Trevor confirm your wrap date. Then I'll set up everything." He smiled across the table. "Get in touch with me when you're ready. We'll talk about your future."

Chapter 16

Three days later, Mimi left school half an hour after the final bell rang. She had always enjoyed these breathless moments, while the corridors were still charged with the students' energy and yet the place was almost hers. When she walked past the administrative offices, Yolinda raised her gaze from the computer screen, but she did not speak. Which was just as well, for there was nothing Mimi could say that would make things any better.

She had never cared for such times as this, when people came to her with health problems. There was always the chance that she would be the one to announce their final year, or week, or hour. She dreaded being forced to relay such news to Yolinda and her family. For a time afterward, she dwelled within a mourning shade. So she did her best to follow what she considered a healthy pattern before such an event. Just like now, walking the main street past Miramar's finest restaurant, enjoying the happy late-afternoon chatter of families and couples, breathing in the fine coastal air. It did not completely lessen her burdens. But it did anchor her in life.

When she passed the coffee shop across from the diner, her eye was caught by five couples occupying all the outdoor tables. It was like an advertisement for coastal romance, all of them utterly blind to the people walking past and smiling at the tableau. Ten people holding hands and listening to the heart music that was meant for them alone.

Mimi walked on, accompanied now by memories of her two catastrophic relationships. She was attractive; she liked men; she enjoyed male company; she went on dates. However, she had given her full heart and soul only twice. Once, her junior year in university. Then, again, her first year in Miramar. Total disasters, the pair of them. Which, upon reflection, was hardly a surprise. What man wants to give himself to a woman who could catch him lying, merely by taking his hand?

Of course they had fled.

Mimi had made her peace with solitude, more or less. Every now and then, though, she caught faint whiffs of the three crones from her childhood, clutching one another in the Orthodox church, isolated from life and people. As she passed the city administration building, she did what she always did when such fears arose to damage her night. She tucked the thoughts back into her mental strongbox and told herself that she might be fated to walk through life without a mate. Even so, she had friends. She had her jobs, both at the school and the dance studio. She studied and she worked and she *lived*.

Of course she was different.

Mimi had loved Miramar's Catholic church since the first time she set eyes on it. All the town's oldest structures dated from the mid-1800s and were built with broad-plank redwood and coastal pine. They faced the roads with wide shaded verandas where locals still gathered.

The church itself had a uniquely storied past. Italian fishermen had made very good money braving the coastal waters. Some of these clans had also gone after abalone. Nowadays it was illegal to take abalone from the ocean. The mollusk had been reduced to critically low levels because of over-exploitation. Mimi had tasted farm-raised abalone on several occasions. The flavor was unique, more like a spicy deep-sea shrimp than clams. But equally important to these early fishermen were the shells, whose mother-of-pearl interiors held an iridescence that made them both highly prized and immensely profitable.

These same fishermen and their clans had built Saint Peter the Fisher of Men, as the church had been known for almost two centuries. Mimi had heard the tales often enough to accept them as at least partly true. How the stained-glass windows had been brought all the way from Italy. How each family had either carved a pew themselves, or paid a local carpenter to do it for them. How the long struts supporting the roof were masts from vessels lost to violent Pacific storms. Each mast was carved with all the names of those who went down with their ships. They remained permanently stationed between the penitents and heaven.

Mimi treasured these moments in the empty church. In many respects they carried far more importance than Mass. She would have prayed, if she had been certain that anyone was actually listening. She knew some would have considered it odd, perhaps even sacrilegious, that she had no idea what she truly believed. But whenever she tried to ask for answers of her own, they did not come. Perhaps if just one small response had been directed her way, she might feel there was a genuine connection between the divine and herself. But she had stopped asking questions. The silence was too depressing.

She had also stopped looking for answers in books written by other so-called seers. The gall of these authors repelled her. They treated their abilities as something special, as if it set them apart from mere mortals. For Mimi, it was like taking pride in her eyesight, or her ability to walk upright.

Mimi sat and savored the empty church and how the silence seemed comfortable here. Even welcoming. Times like this, she could sit for just a few minutes, and yet, when she left, it felt like she had been here for hours. As if time's hold ended at the doors.

The faintest hint of old incense hung in the air—just enough to link her to the memory of those three crones. Mimi started to push the thought away, then decided, why bother? Thoughts of them often arose prior to her meeting new people and facing their questions. Like it or not, she was linked to the trio. But this did not mean she didn't have choices all her very own. How she walked through her days. How she *lived*.

Her thoughts drifted for a moment, as if she could look out beyond the church walls and see the town she cherished. Drifting along, down the main street, back to where the couples sat at their tables, rimming the café with the sweet aroma of new love.

It seemed natural to ask the question of herself.

Actually, it was more like the thought rose of its own accord. As if she was not the one asking. Merely the vessel. Or something. She asked, *Will I ever know a lasting love of my own?*

After a time she rose and left the church. Of course there had been no response. There never was.

But as she walked the sunlit Miramar streets, Mimi reflected that sometimes there was a unique satisfaction in just asking.

CHAPTER 17

◆

Yolinda's home was two blocks east of the Catholic church. Back in the day, the entire neighborhood had been erected by the Italian clans, using the same first flush of money that had seen them build the church. The lots were narrow, the homes tiny by modern standards. Less than half of the original structures had survived. Yolinda and her ex had bought a near ruin and spent years redoing it from the ground up. Around the time they finished, they had realized they were no longer in love. Yolinda had gained the house in the divorce settlement. Her ex now lived in Chicago. He was married with two children by his second wife. Yolinda talked about him in the same unemotional manner she might describe a politician from a different state.

Nowadays the surviving Italian homes were hugely prized. They almost never went on the open market. Word of mouth was enough to find a dozen buyers. The rare sales were always cash transactions. Tourists and locals alike flocked down the narrow lanes. Artists had painted Yolinda's house any number of times, and postcards of her front porch were on sale as far away as Santa Barbara.

Her home was scarcely broader than a double-wide trailer, and fronted by a shaded porch larger than her living room. When Mimi arrived, she found Yolinda standing by her screen door, arms wrapped around her middle. She turned and put a finger to her lips.

Mimi quietly climbed the front steps, crossed the porch, and heard a man's voice from inside the house. "This is idiotic. What can she do? Nothing. That's what."

"So don't stay." The unseen woman who responded sounded beyond tired. "I'm not sure I even want you here anyway. Go for a walk. Go buy us dinner. Something. Just go."

The man harrumphed. "Now you're not wanting me around for my own séance."

"You're acting like a child. Of course I want you here. I begged you to come. And don't call it a séance."

"What do I call it, then?"

"I've told you a dozen times, Delon. I have no idea what it is. Yolinda didn't say because she doesn't know. Your sister wasn't even sure it has a name."

"This is nuts." When his wife did not respond, he went on, "I got a bad feeling."

"Nowhere near as bad as how you've *been* feeling. Think about the tread we've been wearing out, running from one doctor to another." Cloethe gave her husband time to complain. When he remained silent, she said, "I don't know a thing, except what Yolinda has said about this young lady."

"Mimi. That's her name."

"Maybe it'll amount to nothing. One thing I do know— it's a lot more pleasant than sitting in another doctor's reception room, both of us scared out of our wits of what we'll soon be hearing." Her voice broke then. "Or walking into the doctor's office, me feeling already alone, waiting to hear somebody say I'm about to lose the only man I've ever loved."

That silenced him long enough for Yolinda to raise her hand and start to knock on her own front door. Then her brother asked, "How much is this costing us?"

"I told you. She won't take a dime. Yolinda says it's a . . . service. Something."

Another quiet moment passed; then Delon spoke for the first time without his anger. "That'll sure make a difference from all those docs and their tests and those bills. I'll give you that much."

"So you'll stay? Don't give me that face. Yes or no, Delon." Her husband must have given her some affirmation, because Cloethe said, "I swear, you give me more attitude than our daughter. Go get yourself another chair from the living room. I'll see what's keeping your sister."

Yolinda's brother was an odd-shaped man. Mimi had the impression that two different people were uncomfortably residing together in the same body. One of these aspects could have been an Olympic athlete. Or an aging former model. His physique held this potential.

Then there was the shadow. Overlaid upon his entire form was a blanket of misery and struggle that twisted him slightly. As if he had grown so used to battling with himself, he no longer realized how the internal conflict had bent him out of shape.

Delon fidgeted nervously as his sister escorted Mimi to the card table set up by the parlor window. A velvet cover had been positioned so the corners dangled over each side. The table held a narrow crystal vase holding a single yellow rose. The flower glowed in the sunlight, as if somehow illuminated by its own internal flame.

As Mimi seated herself, she became fairly certain it was going to happen. That whatever they asked her would result in an answer.

Sometimes in these moments before she heard a request, Mimi detected a gentle shift in the atmosphere. Almost always this meant she would respond. These subtle changes only happened now and then. She was always grateful when it did occur, because the pressure or baffle or whatever it was also served as an invisible shield. No matter how difficult the information she was about to deliver, Mimi always remained separated from whatever came next. Weeping, distress, rage, scorn, angry denial . . . none of it touched her. She remained safe inside her isolation bubble. Sometimes for hours.

Delon brought the room back into focus by asking, "Should I light some candles?"

"Honey, come on. Really?"

"Hey, I just thought . . ."

"Get a chair and join us. Or don't."

Delon looked ready to argue further, but the sight of the three ladies settling around the table silenced him. He left the room, returned with another chair, set it down in the vacant space, and seated himself with a loud sigh. His wife gave him a hard look. But something in his posture, or his silence, kept her from speaking.

Mimi examined Cloethe from that safe distance. She was a remarkably attractive woman in her late forties. Not beautiful in any standard sense. Her features were too powerfully carved. Mimi thought perhaps Yolinda's sister-in-law had the blood of some Plains Indian. Cloethe possessed the fierce look of a bird of prey, with high cheekbones and almond-shaped eyes, and a voice of honeyed force. "What do we do now?"

Mimi heard herself reply, "Tell me whatever you want. Ask whatever you feel needs to be addressed."

Mimi waited while husband and wife exchanged a long

look. As the silence continued, Mimi studied the three and perceived an intense harmony, something neither Delon's hostile attitude nor his ailment could alter. She witnessed the patience these two women showed Delon. Mimi could see how much they loved him, how worried they were about his health.

For an instant Mimi felt the protective shield vanish. Swift as a needle popping a balloon, she lost her safe distance. She was flooded by a sudden terror over being the bearer of terrible news. Of fracturing Yolinda's heart, which she knew would happen if Mimi spoke of a future without Delon. And this couple, how they would view this stranger who invaded their world with the one thing they feared most of all: destroying their life together, bringing grief and empty nights.

Then the bubble was restored.

Her protective distance fitted itself back into place. Mimi found herself able to breathe again.

And just in time, because Delon spoke to her for the very first time. "Do we hold hands or something?"

"Delon."

"I'm just asking, is all."

Behind the tension that grated his every word, Mimi detected a frank curiosity. She knew he hated having his privacy invaded. This happened so often with first-time requests. Even those who came to her in desperation, they loathed the prospect of her actually being able to peer inside and see the hidden. And with Delon, this came in the guise of a strange young white woman who taught at his sister's school. Mimi replied, "There are no rules. Say or do whatever makes you comfortable enough to speak openly. It can sometimes help if I touch your hand. But it is not necessary."

Mimi saw how her calm demeanor helped to disarm him. The rancor eased from his dark gaze, and with that, the women relaxed a notch. Delon asked, "I say anything I want?"

"Say, ask, it's up to you."

When he did not speak, Cloethe said, "Maybe I should—"

"No!" Delon was definite now. "I want to do this."

"Hon, are you sure?"

"Yes."

"All right." She reached for his hand. "All right, fine."

He looked down at her fingers laced with his. Yolinda took this as permission to reach for Mimi's hand. They sat there a long moment, the two pairs linked. Together. Then Delon said, "I've had spells."

"Some time now," Cloethe said.

"Eight months and nine days," Delon said. "The first time it happened . . . I've been healthy all my life."

"And strong," Cloethe said, kneading his hand with her own. "My big, strong, handsome man."

"I wasn't ready," Delon said.

"Who is?" Yolinda spoke for the first time. "Can anyone ever be ready for what you been going through?"

"These spells, they come without warning," Delon said. "Sometimes it happens at work, or I get woken up at night."

"A week goes by without a thing," Cloethe said. "Longer."

"We all hope and pray it's over," Yolinda said. "Then . . ."

"Sometimes he can't see. Other times he freezes up."

"My thoughts don't come together like they should," Delon said. "Like my hold on the world just vanishes."

"Last week it was at breakfast," Delon said. "That was the worst time yet."

Cloethe said, "He dropped his fork. Just sat there. Like he was frozen up solid. Scared me to death, seeing him like that. Telling me his vision was all fractured, he was close to going blind."

"But there's no pain," Delon said. "Not a whisper. Not a moan."

"We're the ones moaning," Yolinda said.

"He didn't want to go see the doctor," Cloethe said.

"Never been to a hospital in my life. Until then."

"He had a bad spell . . . When was it?"

"Five months ago," Yolinda said. "When they started coming more often."

"He didn't want, but I made him go."

"How could you not? The man was waking you up, scared to death with what was happening to him."

"But the breakfast thing, that was the worst one yet." Cloethe released one hand long enough to wipe her eyes. "He just sat there like a stone. For almost half an hour."

"The doctors, they don't have one idea," Yolinda said.

"Doctors," Delon said. "Don't get me started."

"Every time we go, they scare us worse," Cloethe said. "All their tests. And the diseases. So many awful, terrible names."

"They poke and they prod and they take so much blood." Delon shook his head. "The only pain I've had is from them and their tests."

"All the things they talk about," Yolinda said. "Like our worst nightmares been brought out and given names."

"Amyotrophic lateral sclerosis. Aneurysm. Stroke. Bell's palsy." Delon's voice took on a staccato tension. "Epilepsy. Brain tumor. Guillain-Barré syndrome. Parkinson's. Multiple—"

"Stop, hon. Just stop. You're going to make me sick."

"You getting sick? Hmm. That's a funny one."

Even in their pain the three of them joined together in that momentary shared smile. Then Cloethe found the strength to look at Mimi directly and ask, "Can you tell us what this is?"

"I can, yes."

The fear her words caused. The tension. She felt it vibrate up through Yolinda's grip on her hand. Etching its way into the sunlight.

Mimi said, "It's none of these things."

They all held their breath as she went on, "You're having migraines."

"But . . . there's no pain."

She nodded. "I don't know the proper name. But I know this is true."

"You *know* this."

"Yes." She kept her gaze on Delon. "You have a very rare ailment where you are having all the symptoms of migraines without the pain."

"But . . . how do I stop it?"

"You don't *stop*. They will never stop. You will keep this for the rest of your life. And sooner or later, the pain will start. But you can control it. And it will not kill you."

Perhaps it was the calmness of her words. Or the complete sense of detachment. Mimi could hear it herself, as if it were someone else who spoke. Whatever the reason, the room took a long and steadying breath. Cloethe asked, "What do we do?"

"There are migraine medicines. You need to use one that is fast acting. Take it as soon as you have the first sign of an attack. Carry a dose with you everywhere."

Yolinda was already on her phone, checking sites, her thumbs a blur. "Would you just look at this now!"

"What have you found?"

"It's right here. 'Silent migraines,' they're called. Extremely rare, but a condition recognized by the American Medical . . ." Yolinda's chin began trembling.

"Let me see that." Cloethe took the phone, scrolled down, and came as close to breaking as her sister-in-law. "All your symptoms, Delon. They're right here."

Delon's own hand trembled as he reached over.

"All this time," Cloethe said. "All those *doctors*."

And then it was over.

More often than not, Mimi was drawn away long before the others were ready to release her. Even so, she knew she needed to go. Her time inside this close-knit family was finished. Her work was done. They needed to move forward now. Without her.

She released Yolinda's hand and rose to her feet. "It was nice meeting you both."

CHAPTER 18

❧

Billy's physical condition improved, but only a little. He continued to use the walker and the wheelchair because he had no choice.

Four afternoons following his reduced number of takes, Billy returned to the hospital. Kyle had called ahead, and the doctor was ready for him. She found nothing out of the ordinary about either his level of pain or his lack of progress. The only test that frightened Billy was the one she had not performed early on, because symptoms did not appear until a few days after the incident—a search of his eyes for development of cataracts. But both eyes came back clear. This was followed by another body scan and heart EKG and the thorough examination of his joints, a cleaning of his wound, and check of the bruising. She saw him off with, If he noticed any change to his vision, anything at all, he was to immediately seek medical care. Otherwise be patient with his body's natural ability to recover—even from a blast of man-made lightning.

Billy had no idea how he would have managed without Kyle. The physician's assistant fitted himself to Billy's side like he had been born for the job. He was there when Billy woke. He readied Billy for every take and then helped him recover afterward. He became besties with any number of the crew, including JoJo, which astonished Billy.

Whenever possible, he and Trevor took their meals together. What Vince thought of this, Billy had no idea. The director did not speak to Billy again, save for the occasional barked order.

Connie's response made up one of the most interesting components of those next few days. She basically came into her own. Her lines were near perfect, her emotions clear and beautifully portrayed. For the first time since they had started working together, Billy was able to involve his character in what she was generating and doing and saying, rather than playing off an imaginary lady who only existed inside his head.

Before and after each take, she granted looks of liquid heat and caring concern, a straight shot of spicy passion, right from the heart level. Billy felt those looks right down in his toes. Whatever rules and restrictions their director might have put in place could not stifle her. Not without making Vince seem more of a dodo than he already was.

Billy might have been on meds, but he could still see clearly that Vince Edwards was not making any friends on set. The director barked at everyone. Except Connie. But even here Billy thought there was a book of new rules in play. From Connie's side. Not Vince's. Connie's attitude toward the director became very formal. Very cool. Very distant.

On the fourth day after his incident, when Billy traveled to the set from the hospital, Vince ended the take by rolling his hand and saying, "Again."

The entire team seemed to catch its breath. Billy thought the previous take was first-rate. Connie's responses had been right on the money. But when she looked the question at him, Billy responded with a single tight nod.

Vince saw it. He must have. Because he came close to shouting, "Again."

The scene was a long one, and three ongoing takes later had them both sweaty and tired. Added to this was the fact that Billy's meds were wearing off, and his body was shouting for a pause. Vince had shifted one of the cameras each take, and the Steadicam had continued to move around them, going for different angles. Which also allowed Vince to do numerous close-ups where both of them were in the frame.

Vince said, "Again."

Billy did not think it out. He did not speak, he did not protest. Not a word. He simply pushed himself away from Connie's arms and rose to his feet in slow, careful stages.

"Did you hear what I just said?"

Billy did his best to hide the pain from his features. Clamping down on his discomfort meant Vince's anger could not touch him.

"*Come back here!*"

Thankfully, Kyle stepped up and handed him the walker. Billy gripped the handles a lot tighter than he needed to for balance. Together the two of them walked out of the lights. Kyle whispered, "Where to?"

"Hotel," Billy said. "Bed."

"Gladly," Kyle said. "Now you just stand right there and let me grab your chair."

"*You're finished. You hear me! Your career is over.*"

"No chair, no stopping," Billy said. He felt Kyle hesitate, then fall back into step. "Go bring the car around. Fast as you can."

* * *

The next morning Billy was awake and staring at the ceiling when the first call came through at a quarter to seven.

He had been woken by the same dream as in the hospital, the same one that had pushed him from much-needed rest every day since the incident. Billy heard a brief snatch of his mother's voice. Each day it was a different tune. Today's had been a Perry Como hit, "For the Good Times." She had a fine voice, his mother, full and liquid and smooth. Made for the soft melodic tunes that had predated rock and roll.

Billy lay there remembering how she used to sing before another of their road trips. She had always seemed so happy. Excited and youthful and . . .

So ready to leave her child behind.

The adult Billy had managed to suppress the emotions that had dominated his childhood. The loneliness, the hollow ache, and the rage caused by a mother who preferred the road to her son.

Many of his fellow actors, Billy knew, fed on such internal cauldrons. They confessed their inner demons in acting class. They used the emotions to fuel their characters. They *embraced* the pain. Billy had viewed the inevitable aftereffects all too often. Such people never let go of their early pains. They could not afford to. They built their professional lives and their success on *fostering* the pain, *reopening* the wounds whenever required. They only felt real when they were reliving old pains.

Billy kept his past and the resulting emotions inside a container as tightly controlled as a distiller's vat. Not one ounce of the molten fury, not one drop, was released until or unless he required. He had no idea if he could ever truly heal, or if his boundaries made any difference. All he could hope for was, if the opportunity ever came to leave his past behind, he would take that step.

The repetitive nature of this dream remained a mystery. Billy could not recall the last time he had suffered the agony of hearing his mother's voice. How old had he been? Nine? Ten? Long enough to almost forget how hard it had been to find breath when he woke up. How hard it was to reknit his world. Find a way to pretend he didn't need the two people who had abandoned him. Build his life on his own terms. Not based on the loss of the pair who never lived up to the word "parents."

This was why he was awake when the first phone call came through.

An hour later, Billy had dressed and breakfasted. Kyle accompanied him through the lobby; then at a sign from Billy, he halted just inside the front doors.

It had been easy enough to determine Vince's schedule. A single phone call was all it took. Any star could and often did make such checks, timing their arrival to the director's clock. Not trusting the official schedule was a matter of course. Especially for someone like Billy, a journeyman actor who was apparently in the director's bad book and did not want to give him any further reason for rage. Small-time actors hoping for their big breaks had every right to be terrified of their directors' ire.

Only that was no longer the case.

Five minutes before Vince was scheduled to depart for the set, Billy exited the hotel on his own and took his time approaching the director's limo.

The morning's second bus was loading up, which meant most of the senior behind-camera crew watched his slow progress. Including Trevor, who started over, then reversed course when Billy shook his head.

The limo driver opened his door and rose uncertainly. "Help you?"

"I'm having a word with Vince." When the driver opened

the near-side rear door, Billy slipped in, then said, "Leave the walker. I won't be staying."

Billy left his door open so Vince would see him. The motor was running and the heat pushed against the January morning chill. Billy watched the bus shut its doors and sit there, idling. He figured Trevor had probably had a word with the bus driver, asking him to hang on a second. Let them all watch the show.

Three minutes later, Vince stepped through the hotel exit talking on his phone. He spotted the walker, saw Billy seated in his limo, and stuffed his phone back in his pocket. He stood there in the strong morning shadows, uncertain how to respond. When he finally started forward, Billy figured the director had been pushed forward by all the eyes aimed his way.

He stopped five feet from the open rear door and said, "Get out."

Billy could hear the director's hard breathing. Like crossing the asphalt had cost him. Which it probably did. Billy said, "Tell the driver to give us a minute. You and I need to have a word."

"You're making me late."

Billy leaned forward so as to face the director square on. "You want to hear what I have to say. You really do."

Vince was clearly tempted to refuse, but he finally gestured to the driver, who did a jackrabbit jump away. Billy slipped across the seat and waited until Vince was seated. Then, "This morning I got a call from LA. Two, actually."

"We're shooting a crucial scene and I've got a hundred more important issues—"

"Listen to what I'm telling you, Vince. The *studio* called *me*." Billy gave that a beat, then went on, "The calls came from one of Peter Veer's assistants. I forget her name. She said for me to tell you that you're barred from the editing room."

Vince's face went chalk white. "They can't do that."

"Actually, she can. That's why she called me a second time. Because I insisted on her reading me the exact language of your contract. Your participation in the editing process is dependent upon the studio's wishes."

"I'll sue them . . ."

Billy held up his hand. "Save your tantrum for later, Vince. I'm not interested. And, like you said, you're due on set. And there's more."

Billy was tired of observing the director and his rage. He turned to the opposite-side window and watched the light strengthen. "I've had time to think this through. So let me save you the effort. Two things. First, there's a spy on set, because Peter's taken a personal interest in how things go. Second, they called me so the message would get through loud and clear. Whether they actually do what they've threatened depends on how you treat me going forward."

Billy opened the other door and took his time climbing out. The process took long enough for the bus to pull from the lot. He offered his audience a silent apology for the lack of visible fireworks. He leaned over and said, "You don't have to be nice to me, Vince, but you do have to be civil. Starting with two takes and one close-up. If you need more, you're going to have to discuss it with me. Politely. And we do another only if I agree." Billy tapped the roof, then added, "One more thing. Connie and I are on speaking terms. Starting now. She is going to come over and we are going to talk. Today. Before the first take. Otherwise I'll make sure you and LA have words."

Billy retrieved his walker and entered the hotel to find Kyle standing just inside the sliding-glass doors. "I am positively breathless with anticipation."

"It's a beautiful day. It should warm up nicely, soon as the sun crests the ridge." Billy continued past him, aiming for the elevators. "I could use another coffee."

"That's it? After I've been poised here for hours, terrified I'll need to vacuum up your remains?" When Billy did not respond, Kyle huffed and joined him in the elevator. The PA did not speak again until Billy was prone on his worktable. Five minutes into their morning session, Kyle declared, "You're doing much better today."

"It hurts as much as yesterday." Billy stifled a groan as Kyle switched to his neck. "Maybe more."

"That's to be expected. No, don't stiffen up, you dolt. Relax and let me work my magic." He waved one hand in front of Billy's face. "These fingers don't lie. Your muscles are actually talking to one another again."

Billy dozed on and off, then fell into a deeper sleep. When he woke, it felt like he'd been out for hours. "What time is it?"

"Just gone ten."

"We better be heading out." Billy eased himself up. "What say we do without the wheelchair today."

Kyle brought the rental SUV around, helped Billy settle, put the walker in the back, and they set off. Ten minutes into the drive, Kyle said, "His wife is a dentist."

Billy glanced over. "Who?"

"Vince. My partner used to be her hygienist. They have the loveliest children. Three girls. He's watched Vince play with them any number of times. Apparently, he loves being the at-home dad when he's not filming. My partner describes Vince as the sweetest man alive. Can you imagine?" When Billy remained silent, Kyle went on, "Why he insists on playing the ogre when he's on set is beyond me."

Billy watched the yellow and ochre hills parade past for a time; then, "You've worked with your share of stars."

"Six years on the studio payroll, I should say so."

"Some you like. Others . . ."

"Best not say what I think of the others."

"What would you say is the difference?"

Kyle was silent until they pulled onto the interstate that served as El Paso's ring road. Then, "A person in my position, I suppose it's inevitable that I see what they prefer to keep hidden."

"You've seen them up close and personal," Billy said. "It's a part of your job description."

"Anybody involved in the film world learns to live with the pain of rejection." Kyle glanced over. "You know what I'm talking about, don't you?"

"The auditions. The acting classes. The readings. Of course I know."

"It hurts, doesn't it?"

"Agony."

"And yet you keep at it."

"Day in, day out."

"You don't have any choice. It's part of your life."

Billy watched the hills glide past the front windshield. "Until it isn't."

"There you go," Kyle said. "That is the point where stars fall into two categories. Most of them carry the pain and the rage of rejection with them. For them, it's a permanent stain on their psyche. I don't know if they can't help it, or if it's, well . . ."

"Tell me."

"Sometimes I wonder if perhaps the pain has been so constant for so long, and bitten so deep, they identify with the pain. It is a core component of their character. Or at least who they see themselves to be."

Billy returned to his morning reflections. After a time he said, "Hard not to let that happen."

"And yet some people become stars, and they walk away from all that."

"Or they hide it better."

"No." Kyle was firm now. Definite. "That might work with outsiders, but not with someone in my position."

"The makeup is off. The lights turned down low. You see them as they really are."

"And some artists are able to free themselves." He shot Billy another glance. "I don't know if they become someone new, or if they revert back to who they always were. You know. Before."

Billy heard the words. But what he thought was, he wondered if that was why his mother had begun singing to him again. Which was silly. Totally illogical. But there had to be some reason why the dreams would return after so long. As if she reappeared to remind him of who he was. Who he was bound to always remain. No matter how high he climbed up the LA ladder. The lost and lonely kid, the man destined to remain an orphan all his life long.

CHAPTER 19

There was an electric quality to the set. Billy noticed it as soon as he rose from the car. He could not put his finger on precisely what if anything had changed. Most of the technicians remained intent and busy as they prepared for the next scene. About half-a-dozen others, including the cosmeticians and costume lady, were seated at the trestle tables by the cooking van, enjoying an early lunch. Several of them waved to Billy as he passed. The hair lady called to say she'd be right with him.

Vince stood by the chief cameraman, viewing the set and two stand-ins through the viewfinder. He spoke too softly for Billy to hear, and the cinematographer motioned to one of the lighting gaffers to shift one of the kliegs. All part of a normal day.

Billy made his way to the makeup chair under the canvas awning on his own steam. The cosmetician and hairstylist entered the makeup trailer, grabbed their gear, and beat him by a mile. Trevor approached before Billy had settled. "You know what's happening." As usual with Trevor, it was not a question.

"The love scene," Billy confirmed. "I can't wait."

"Me either," the cosmetician said. "My heart's already going pitter-patter."

"I didn't sleep a wink," the hairstylist agreed.

Billy asked, "You ladies get off on bruises and moans?"

"Personally, I always enjoyed a little of the rough trade," the stylist said.

Kyle was seated on the nearest weight bench. He hummed a line from a song Billy did not recognize.

Trevor said, "We've spent the past three hours shooting the movements with your stand-in."

"He asked me to thank you for getting electrocuted," the cosmetician said. "You've made his day."

"Not Connie," the stylist said. "The lady wasn't a bit pleased over losing out."

Kyle laughed out loud.

Trevor said, "Speaking of the lady."

Connie walked up, holding a script. She greeted Billy with a smile. A first. "How's my lover boy?"

"Creaking and groaning," he replied.

"Billy is doing just fine, thank you very much," Kyle said.

Connie waited until the two stylists finished their prepping, then asked, "May I have a word?" When everyone moved away, Connie stepped forward and pretended to show Billy a page from the screenplay. "What did you say to Vince?"

"I forget."

"Liar." She pointed to a line neither of them bothered to see. The page was heavily annotated with her handwriting. "It's good to be able to talk with you, even like this."

"Likewise."

"Any advice on today's scene?"

"Yes," he replied. "Don't roll on top of me."

Connie bit her lip and managed to keep her laugh down, where it merely made her middle shake. "See you in bed."

The technicians had taken one of the empty Old Town storefronts and turned it into Connie's bedroom. The raw plank flooring and beamed ceiling and brass bed formed a romantic atmosphere with a rough-hewn flavor. Perfectly in keeping with Connie's role and supposed past. The tall bay windows with their ancient handblown glass were carefully veiled, the room lit to portray late-afternoon sunlight, soft and brooding.

Trevor and the chief cameraman spent what to Billy felt like hours, getting the folds of the wrinkled sheets just so. Connie pretended to snore through it. He would probably have become enormously uncomfortable, not to mention sore, had it not been for how his face was posed inches from one of the most beautiful women on earth.

Finally they all stepped away. Vince called, "Sound check."

Billy said, "Remind me what I'm supposed to be doing now. I forget."

Connie lay with her eyes closed. She murmured, "Liar."

"Sound's good," the technician called.

Vince said, "Quiet on set. This is a take."

The aide struck the clapper. "Scene forty-seven. Take one."

"And . . . action."

Then Connie opened her eyes.

Moments like this were rare indeed. When the outer world was no longer just something Billy had to push away on his own. When the scene's other character became *real*. When the scene bonded everyone involved. When they did not speak their lines, but *lived* them. When the so-called real world simply vanished, as insubstantial as mist in the Texas dawn. And all they had, all they knew, was the magic of what they were making. Together.

Connie breathed her lines. Soft as Mexican moonlight. Spiced by the languor of a woman in love. Her eyes were dusky emeralds, her every breath was an invitation for Billy to dive in and lose himself.

When it was over, they remained as they were. Held by what they had just created. The set was completely silent. As if everyone down to the most distant technician knew they had just made something incredibly, well, *real*.

Vince cleared his throat and said, "Billy, all right if we—"

"Let's do it," Billy said, without taking his eyes off this woman he almost loved. "Connie?"

"Yes," she whispered. "Yes."

"Take two," Vince said. "And . . . action."

CHAPTER 20

❧

That evening Mimi returned from teaching a Pilates class and made herself a solitary meal. As she prepared for bed, she found herself thinking back on Yolinda and Delon and Cloethe. Whenever she reflected on such events, which was seldom, the actual conversation was little more than a soft hum in her brain. Instead, Mimi was drawn to how those three had acted toward one another. The love they held, the heartfelt concern, the sheer closeness of their lives. The mental images grew so vivid, Mimi wanted to weep for all she did not possess.

She was halted by her reflection in the living-room window. She tried to remind herself of everything she had here in Miramar: Friends who cared for her. Work that meant a great deal, both to herself and to at least some of her students. She danced in the town's best studio, and helped others to extend their bodies' reach. People asked her for counsel, and valued what she could offer. She lived a full and good life.

But the reflection remained as it was. Silent. Solitary. Surrounded by the endless night.

Until it was not.

What came next was similar in feeling to her contacts with people seeking answers. Mimi found herself unable to be frightened. Even though she became swept up in an event unlike anything she had ever known before.

This time the bubble of isolation was not intended to protect her. Instead, as the sense of energetic presence surrounded her, Mimi knew without question that the purpose was to *draw her away*.

Reality became as indistinct as a dream. Mimi became captured by . . .

Mimi remained frozen in front of her own reflection. But what she viewed was herself leaning over a narrow wooden railing. As she did so, she . . .

Hummed or cooed or sang.

The effort required to draw that sound into focus created an intimate clarity with the event itself. She did not see herself do this. She *lived* the experience.

In a smooth, practiced, gentle motion, Mimi lifted her baby girl.

The child seemed almost weightless, a tiny bundle of life. Mimi settled the infant to her upper chest so that the baby's face nestled by her neck and chin. She could not see the child's face. But the sound her baby made, and the feel of her breath on Mimi's bare skin, was so very . . .

Precious.

She became filled to overflowing with love, and more. A life-changing tenderness pulsed with every heartbeat. She was utterly, completely fulfilled.

And then it was over.

CHAPTER 21

⸺❧⸺

The next day Mimi drifted.

Thankfully, it was Friday. Which meant many of her students and fellow teachers were already focused on the coming weekend. No one seemed to notice how detached Mimi remained. She watched and moved and listened and spoke from some great distance. And in the solitary moments, Mimi returned time and again to the moment she leaned over the crib and picked up her baby.

My baby.

It was an instant when her entire world changed. Before, she was one person. But when she held her child, she became another.

Again and again, Mimi felt the emotions well up inside. She marveled at how the simple act of holding her child left her . . .

Complete.

That evening she canceled her Pilates class, the first time since forever. Mimi simply did not want to risk such intense physical exertion pulling her away from the event. She went home, ate a solitary meal, then spent the evening sitting in silence. Reliving.

By Saturday the emotional bond to her experience had faded. In its place came the questions. The most pressing issues centered upon her absent partner. Because Mimi was certain of one thing above all else.

There had been no man in her image.

All day the questions rose unbidden: Was she destined to love and lose her lover? Was he untrue? Did he simply not want to be a father?

There was also the question of timing. She had no idea if this was a promise to be fulfilled years in the future. The prospect of being forced to wait left her restless inside her own skin.

As she prepared for bed, Mimi found herself wondering if this was what happened after she left a meeting. Did those with whom she spoke relive the event, and in the process come up with a dozen more questions? A hundred? Did they desperately wish they had asked for more information? Did they feel as she did, looking back, as if the power of asking anything more had been stripped away? Did they wonder, as she did now, if the message regarding whatever came next was intentionally limited, a mere glimpse beyond the bend of time? Was this how life always would be, one answer delivering a thousand more mysteries?

Sunday morning dawned with a rare touch of frost. Mimi dressed in layers, for the cloudless sky promised a day that would warm swiftly. She drove to church for early Mass, then went straight to the dance studio. She taught her class, stopped at her favorite deli for a take-out sandwich, then drove to Lighthouse Point.

The headlands lay three miles beyond Miramar's southern border. Mimi considered it an almost-ideal distance for her monthly gatherings. Many of the younger people who joined her for these acts of departure were too young to drive. Three miles made for a significant cycle trip, long enough for them to feel a distinct separation from their everyday world.

Families and dog walkers tended to avoid Lighthouse Point. The headlands ended in jagged cliffs that fell almost four hundred feet to the Pacific. Only a rusted-out metal fence prevented children and pets from falling off the edge. Far below, waves crashed upon glistening black rocks. In languid summer evenings, when sunsets lingered for hours, Lighthouse Point was a favorite spot for young lovers. The mix of frigid air rising from the Pacific and the heat radiating off the earth filled the salt-tangy air with a promise of good tomorrows. But on a Sunday afternoon in late January, with the temperature hovering in the low fifties, Mimi arrived to find an empty parking lot.

The lighthouse dated from the late 1800s, when over a dozen such warning beacons had been erected along California's northern and central coasts. The lighthouse was built of close-fitting stone quarried from neighboring hills. In the century and a half since its construction, the structure had been weathered to where it looked like it had grown naturally.

Over to Mimi's right stood the keeper's cottage. She had always loved the place. It looked to her like the lighthouse's little sister. It was built from the same gray stone and was surrounded by a weathered picket fence. The current owners had extended the house on the rear side, almost doubling its internal space. But they had used the same quarried stone, and dressed the windows with cedar shutters of palest blue. Mimi had never seen anyone use the place. She had heard it was owned by some rich film executive. Miramar locals tended to look upon all such vacation homes as if they represented a tribe of invaders. But Mimi liked these owners, whoever they were. She had walked around the cottage any number of times. It seemed to her that the owners had built the extension with an eye toward the next century, marrying the future to the point and its heritage.

Mimi rarely made this drive alone. Usually, some of the young people needed a lift. In bad weather she crammed as many as eight passengers into her Honda CR-V. Such solitary moments as today were rare indeed. She watched an offshore wind flatten the tall grass to either side of the lighthouse, and wondered what it would be like to lead adults. There was a distinct comfort to sharing these moments with young teens. Their sense of helpless tumult, the raw wounds of youth, the confusion over a future that often made no sense, she identified with them. She had no idea if her little ritual would hold any meaning for the people coming today.

Her thoughts drifted back to the images of four nights ago. The emotions were a mere whisper now. The experience itself had gradually become just another memory. It still held her, but in the sense of any other past event. Mimi stared at the silent cottage and thought about the home she might have with this man who did not stay. What it would be like to live without him, how it would be to experience the loss, if the baby would be enough to fill the void . . .

My daughter.

Then the gravel crunched behind her, and two vehicles pulled up to either side. Mimi waved and opened her door.

Everything seemed familiar yet slightly different, joining the adults at the parking lot's edge. There were eleven, plus Mimi. Which was fairly normal for such gatherings. The youngest she had ever brought here had been nine years old. Most were in their early teens. A few were university age, accompanied by younger siblings. Today's eleven adults were anywhere from Mimi's age to a couple and a lone woman in their late seventies. Mimi let the elderly trio set the pace as they started down the graveled path.

Linh's mother was not among them.

The walk to the pasture beyond the lighthouse seemed shorter. The emotions these adults carried with them were just as potent, and yet they seemed to handle it better. On several occasions, usually with preteens on their first visit, Mimi had been very worried that they might throw themselves off the cliff. Those young ones had seemed so bereft, their lives so utterly shattered. By contrast these adults appeared much more self-contained. Even the ones who were already shedding tears did so with a stoic calm.

Back in the late 1970s, the lighthouse had been turned into a museum for seamen. But this had been closed for years. There had been talk in Miramar of buying it back from the state and turning it into a public space for city functions. Now it stood in stolid patience, a weathered beacon to bygone days.

Mimi stopped the others as soon as the ocean came into full view. The pasture continued on for a further hundred paces, far enough for Mimi to feel safe even when she shepherded the most desolate of teens. She always took her place to one side and slightly ahead of the others, and stationed another trustworthy regular to the other side. Doing all she could to keep her charges safe, no matter what wild temptations they might carry with them.

The wind blew strong off the land, carrying the pungent flavors of sorrel and sage. A bracing chill rose from the Pacific waters, creating a sharp-edged clarity to the moment. Mimi studied the faces gathered around her. She saw a few sad smiles, something utterly absent from the younger gatherings. Some of these people actually looked eager to be here. It was not happiness, of course, but rather a tense anticipation.

Mimi found herself wanting to be a part of this.

On occasion she had brought a half-finished letter addressed to her father. They were always incomplete attempts to say how much she missed him, the result of being woken far too early by the prospect of another such gathering. Sitting at her lonely kitchen table, hands around a steaming mug, missing him as if he had disappeared a few months ago, rather than nineteen years. The letter was rarely more than a few words.

This was different. For one thing, Mimi had brought nothing. But mainly she just wanted to join with these others. Not stand out as a teacher or counselor or whatever. Simply be one of the group. Allow her wounded spirit to stand here with people who included dear friends and seek both solace and the chance to say a final farewell.

Which was why, instead of her usual introductory remarks, Mimi said, "I'll go first."

As she stepped forward, Mimi reached down and plucked a trio of daffodils. Their blooms were still tight, not yet fully open. She straightened and held them in both hands. Her face was directed at the ocean. The wind pressed on her back, like it was pushing her forward, urging her to speak.

"When I was eight years old, my father disappeared. We lived in Donetsk, in eastern Ukraine. I am Polish. The Poles formed a minority population there before the conflict forced most families to flee. Even in my early years, the Russian separatists were making trouble. This was almost fifteen years before the real civil war began."

Mimi felt the words rise up from deep inside, as if drawn by the desert wind, and flung far out into the cloudless sky. She had never spoken freely of these events. A few words uttered here and there, the subject swiftly steered onto safer grounds. She could feel the group's eyes on her now. Mimi had no idea why she spoke as she did. Only that it felt right. No, more than that. It was *vital* that she talk to the wind and the sky and the day.

"My father was chief surgeon at the Donetsk central hospital. He also ran surgical clinics in some of the neighboring cities. My mother desperately wanted us to emigrate to the West. My father refused. He knew that if he left, the Polish minority would receive little or no medical treatment. So he stayed, and he treated everyone who came to him. No matter what their background. As the years went on, and the conflict worsened, this included wounded paramilitary forces and, in at least two cases, Russian soldiers. I know because those were the nights when my parents fought. My father's reply never changed, no matter how loud my mother screamed at him. One person can make a difference, my father always said. If they do the right thing, one person can help bring peace."

The wind was strong enough to blow her hair into a tangled veil. Mimi knew she was crying. But she could not be bothered to clear her hair away and dry her face. Such an act of confession was simply not part of who she was. She did not take the sacraments because she refused to sit in a wooden box, scarcely larger than a coffin, and tell her secrets to a man she could not see. Yet here she stood, releasing the words with the same ease as her next breath.

"Then one day when I was eight, my father held a clinic in Pervomaisk. He never returned. Over half of Pervomaisk has been bombed, burned, turned to rubble. The hospital where my father worked to save lives is gone. Virtually the entire population fled west."

Mimi tossed her flowers to the sky. She watched them tumble through the air, across the meadow, out over the blue waters. "I miss my papa. His goodness and his smile. His big hands and the way he held me. His strength. His intelligence. His good heart. Every day I miss him."

She took a step back. It was partly to conclude her action, tell the others that it was now their turn. In reality, she did it to escape a sudden and most unwelcome thought.

She had never released flowers for her mother. Or written a note. Or said any form of farewell. Or offered her up in quiet moments, at church or here or anywhere else.

She heard the murmur of other voices, and drew the day partly back into focus. Mimi would not stain this beautiful day with thoughts about that woman.

CHAPTER 22

❧

The day they wrapped, Billy flew back from El Paso with the rest of the crew. To his utter astonishment, a dark-suited limo driver stood by the baggage claim with Billy's name on his electronic board. A first. The other returning cast and crew treated it as merely confirmation of what they already suspected: Billy Rose was a man on the rise.

Billy did his best to thank his team, especially when it came to Trevor and Kyle and Connie. The people most responsible for him feeling so satisfied with the project. Vince Edwards stepped around them, head down, tight and angry as usual, and slipped into a second limo. Not even glancing their way as he departed. Kyle handed him a slip of paper with two names and Miramar addresses and appointment times: massage every morning and Pilates each afternoon.

Billy insisted on riding up front, then lowered the seat back and dozed his way north. He opened his eyes a few times, but did not raise his seat until the limo pulled up in front of the cottage. Peter Veer's vacation home was nothing more than a silhouette carved from the starlit night. Farther down the point, a lighthouse rose high enough to block the moon. Billy had stiffened up during the drive and needed the walker to make it inside the cottage. He stood gripping the rails as the driver deposited his case and departed. Billy scarcely managed to strip off his clothes before giving in to his first real rest in what felt like months.

He woke to sunlight rimming his bedroom drapes and the whisper of an unseen ocean. He rose in stages, testing each joint, glad the walker was stationed there beside his bed. He used the bathroom, then slowly dressed in the same clothes he had worn the previous day. He padded across the stone-tiled floor, entered the kitchen, and found a Nespresso machine with a crystal bowl of coffees waiting for him on the counter. He kept his back to the room as he waited for the first cup to brew. When he had arrived, he had seen enough of the cottage to know it was a work of art. He wanted to make his first inspection when he could fully appreciate his temporary home. First he had to erase the night's final shadows.

Billy sipped his first cup and stared at the cabinet eighteen inches in front of his face. He had been woken by yet another dream of his mother, just as he had every night since the accident. As always, an invisible woman had sung the lyrics. He finished the cup and brewed another. Billy watched the dark liquid drip into his mug, wishing he could distill the series of dreams down to their meaning. Fearing with uncommon strength the mystery behind the nightmare's return.

The shower was almost as big as Billy's LA bathroom and only slightly less complicated than a shuttle launch. There was a sauna setting and a soap spray and massage jets and an overhead outlet big as a dinner plate. He turned the jets on hot. They pulsed from three walls, strong as the hands of a professional masseuse. Billy turned in slow circles, letting the water probe and loosen.

It didn't take a psychiatrist to know why his mother always remained invisible. It was the song, the music, that had drawn her away. She had made a choice between Billy and the road. Billy had lost. Every time.

He dried off and wrapped a blanket-sized towel around his middle. Entering the bedroom, he was hooked yet again by the whisper of his mother singing. This morning it had been a Righteous Brothers' hit, "Unchained Melody." Billy stood in the dim light and rubbed the space over his heart. Waiting for the song to fade.

When the room went quiet enough for Billy to hear the ocean again, he knelt on the floor and opened his case and pulled out clean clothes. Then he raised the bedroom blinds and gave his temporary home the sort of appreciative inspection it deserved.

The only remaining portions of the original cottage were the stone exterior walls and ceiling rafters. Everything possible had been done to overcome the limited space. Brass-rimmed lights shone from the high-peaked roof. The floors alternated between ancient flagstones and cedar planks. The master bedroom and bath took up most of the original structure, with just enough space left over for a narrow guest bedroom. The kitchen-dining-parlor area occupied a glass-fronted extension. The drapes covering the sliding-glass doors were a mystery he only solved by accident, when he pressed what he thought was just another light switch, and all the curtains rose together, revealing a magical vista.

The cottage and lighthouse occupied a tabletop of emerald meadow. Billy estimated the area of shimmering grass covered a dozen acres. Surrounding this, in every direction save one, from all the windows, was . . .

Blue.

Billy had never spent much time around the ocean. A couple of stolen weekends while in university, traveling seven hours each way in an overcrowded van. Since moving to LA, he occasionally made the trek to Zuma Beach and Malibu, fighting traffic for hours from his minuscule apartment in the Hollywood Hills.

Billy unlatched the glass doors and stepped out onto the narrow stone veranda. There was just enough space for a cast-iron table and chairs, a rectangular fire pit, and a grill. Beyond this rose a weather-beaten picket fence. A second fence, this one of rusting barbed wire, ran along the rest of the cliff's boundary. Rusting DANGER, DO NOT CROSS signs rattled nervously in the wind. Beyond the fencing the land just dropped away, out to where the Pacific swelled and crashed and sang. Billy stood there for what seemed like days, breathing the air and willing himself to accept that this was really happening.

The cottage had been stocked and prepped for his arrival. The fridge was full to overflowing. Billy could have easily camped out there for a month. He made a late breakfast and ate it on the rear veranda. The frigid air rising off the Pacific made for a pleasant contrast to the brilliant sunlight and off-shore breeze. It felt exquisite.

The only interruption to his solitary hour came as Billy carried his plate and mug back inside. Voices drifted his way, carried from somewhere he could not see. Billy made his way around the side of the house and found a group of people walking from a parking lot he had not noticed before. There were maybe a dozen of them, all ages; about two thirds of them were women. Some carried bunches of flowers. A few held framed photographs. As they continued down the path and passed the lighthouse, he shifted around to the cottage's other side so he could watch them.

The grass surrounding the lighthouse had been cut back. Farther on, it grew almost to waist height. The group halted where the wild pasture began. A lone woman stepped forward. Billy could not see her clearly, the sunlight was too strong. But from her silhouette he would guess she was young, perhaps his own age. When she bent over and plucked flowers, the woman's long hair flowed out like a veil captured by the wind. She used her hand not holding the flowers to tuck it back behind her ears. She held herself impossibly erect, poised almost on her toes, like a ballerina might stand just before leaping onto the stage.

Billy could see the woman's mouth move, but her words were lost to the wind. He found himself mesmerized by the scene. He saw several people wipe their faces, and could feel the moment's power resonate in his chest. He remained standing there until the woman tossed her flowers into the air, then stepped back and joined the others. When another person stepped forward, Billy retreated to the cottage.

An hour later, Billy left the cottage. He thought he would probably be okay using just the cane. But he took the walker as well, in case weariness reduced him to needing that level of support. He walked to a second structure built of the same quarried stone. He thought it probably had once been a stable, large enough to hold two horses and perhaps a small wagon. Nothing so grand as a carriage, of course. But a workingman's cart and all the equipment would have fit snugly.

The stable doors were electric. Billy pressed into the keypad the code supplied on the same plasticized sheet that held all the cottage's other instructions. The doors slid back on silent pneumatic hinges, revealing a Land Rover. Billy had no idea of its age, but he could see it was not new. Maybe ten years old, possibly older, but so lovingly kept it was impossible to tell. He had actually driven several, back when he earned his summer bucks parking cars at Asheville's ritziest hotel. As he stowed his cane and walker, he wondered what kind of person kept an eighty-thousand-dollar ride on hand for the occasional visit to the central coast.

Driving the magnificent vehicle into town, Billy felt as

though he was taking sips of some dangerous elixir. He had never had money. Up to now, he had escaped the burning urge to own what he could not afford. But all this—the cottage and the ride and the easy days ahead—fashioned an utterly new experience. One thing he could say for certain: All this was bound to come with a price.

Billy drove with his windows open to the sweet-scented air. He found the town of Miramar so charming he actually became lost. This was very hard to do, given how well the business district was laid out. But he wasn't paying attention, and became trapped inside a one-way system. He drove down narrow streets in a district that included city buildings and rustic houses and a truly beautiful Catholic church. Finally he admitted defeat and stopped a statuesque African-American woman carrying two shopping bags along the sidewalk. He called over, "Excuse me, I'm lost."

She recognized him. This happened occasionally, but not that often. So many people in LA lived for their next sighting of a star that even somebody as minor as Billy Rose would get recognition.

But instead of telling Billy where she'd seen him, and how much she had liked the show or movie, she asked, "Doesn't this car have something to tell you where to go?"

"Probably. But I can't hardly figure out how to turn it on."

She liked that enough to walk over. "So you're visiting."

"Just came in last night," Billy replied. "I'm already in love."

Her eyes sparked with humor. "I bet you say that to about a million ladies a week."

"Sorry. You must have me mistaken for somebody who gets his way with women."

"Where you headed?"

"The Miramar dance studio."

"Say what?"

He could see an instant's shock, but did not know the reason why. "I've had an injury. My physical therapist wants me to start doing Pilates. He says it will help the healing."

She squinted into the sunlight. "You don't want to try and get there from here."

Billy laughed out loud. "You sound like folks from my hometown."

"Where's that, hon?"

"Asheville, North Carolina."

"Then you are lost. I guess I'm going to have to show you." She carried her shopping bags around the front of the Land Rover. "Are you going to let me in or not?"

CHAPTER 23

The dance studio was seven blocks from where Billy picked up the lady. Her name was Yolinda, and she used the journey to pry out his entire life's story. She revealed very little about herself, other than how she worked in the school where Mimi, the Pilates instructor, taught. When he pulled into an open space in front of the studio's plate-glass window, he said, "I'd hate to be a student on your bad side."

"They don't stay that way for long, not if they're smart." She opened her door. "You need help coming inside?"

"No thanks." But the drive had been long enough for his muscles to stiffen. Rising from the car took long enough for Yolinda to hurry around and take his arm. "I'm all right, thank you."

"Sure you are." Even so, she opened the rear and pulled out his walker.

"I'd rather use the cane."

"Hon, you don't need to prove yourself to anybody around here. Now take hold and let's get you settled." Billy allowed himself to be guided inside, where Yolinda called, "Mimi honey? I brought you a new customer."

Billy recognized her the instant she appeared in the studio's hallway. Even before the light illuminated her face, Billy knew her silhouette and the way her hair fell around her shoulders.

He watched as Yolinda walked over and spoke with her. Mimi's only response to whatever the older woman said was to raise both arms, sweep back her hair, and bind it into a ponytail. She then walked up and said, "Mr. Walker? Mimi Janic. Would you like to get started?"

Mimi started him on very simple exercises, mostly working his core. When these proved too much, she stopped and asked, "May I see your injury?"

Billy unbuttoned his shirt, dropped it to a nearby chair, then kicked off his trousers. She stared at him in wide-eyed amazement. "What *happened* to you?"

"A lighting cable broke loose." He touched the small bandage on his shoulder. "I was electrocuted."

"I've never seen anything like this." She leaned in close to the bruises lining his left side. The discoloration had not changed much. But at least the angry swelling had started to go down. Mimi murmured something in a language Billy did not recognize.

"The doctor said it resembles a lightning strike." He shrugged his good shoulder. "My heart stopped."

She straightened and looked at him, her gaze round and solemn.

"The medic was almost close enough to catch me. He saved my life."

She nodded once and took a step farther away. Studying him intently. "You can put your clothes back on now."

"If it's just the same, I'd rather stay like this. The clothes rub on my bruises."

"Let's start again. Slow and easy."

Mimi Janic proved to be a highly professional instructor. She remained very intent upon his movements, and skilled at gently testing his limits. Gradually he relaxed into a state of trust, knowing she would not press him to the point of genuine pain. Each time she started him on a new exercise, she first demonstrated what she wanted him to do, then moved in close enough to hold her hands inches away from his form. Not touching. But showing that she was there for him.

Mimi was marvelous to observe close up. There was a pale freshness to her skin, like a redhead's complexion, but with a vivacity and strength that was all her own.

They took a break after another fifteen minutes. Mimi could see he was tiring. Billy sat in the folding metal chair next to the one holding his clothes and leaned his head against the wall. She said, "My friend told me you're an actor."

"Guilty as charged."

"I'm sorry. I'm certain I've seen you in something. But I can't remember what it was."

"I've mostly played small roles. And doing TV ads to pay the rent."

"But Yolinda says you're one of her favorite actors."

"I've starred in some TV films and low-budget movies." He hesitated, then added, "I've heard things might be changing for the better. Finally. But I don't know anything for certain."

She studied him a moment longer. "Are you being modest?"

He shook his head. "I've made it this long being realistic. Or trying to."

"That sounds, I don't know, odd for an actor."

"You know the LA scene?"

"I lived there for nine years."

"Where?"

"Santa Monica. A couple of blocks off Montana."

He was about to say that she didn't strike him as being anything like the LA ladies he had come to know. But something about her statement, just saying where she had lived, had brought out shadows. So Billy swallowed his comment and made a process of rising from his chair. "I think I'm ready to start again."

She helped him settle on his back, then knelt beside him and resumed working him through a routine to release and strengthen his core. "You have kept yourself in excellent shape. I imagine that helped you survive as much as anything the medic did to you. Perhaps even more."

Billy could feel perspiration being pressed from his body by the strain. When they finished the next exercise, he asked, "Could I have a towel?"

"Of course. Sorry, I . . ." She rose in a fluid motion and left the room. She returned carrying several. She handed him one, then helped him rise far enough to settle a second around his shoulders. "We have another fifteen minutes on the clock. But perhaps we should stop now."

"One more."

"As you like."

Mimi had a good deal of red in her hair, but more brown, and these mixed with a golden strain. If Billy had been pressed to name the color, he would have called it early autumn. She wore a sleeveless shirt over leotards that did nothing to hide her form. Even when kneeling, she held herself with a dancer's beautiful poise.

Billy waited until they finished the session, and he was dressed, to ask her out. It was a simple enough request. Meet him for a coffee. Or a drink. Her choice.

Mimi unfolded the walker and picked up the cane. "Let me see you out."

As they slowly progressed along the side corridor, the outer door opened and a trio of ladies in their twenties bounced in. They tossed Billy flirtatious glances, watching Mimi shadow him, and then they were gone. A pair of slender young men with dancers' lithe grace followed. More of the knowing looks, the smirks, flashing Billy's way and then gone. Clearly, Yolinda did not limit her news to the lady helping him down the hallway. Mimi ignored them and kept her gaze fixed firmly on Billy's progress. He had to assume this was her polite way of saying no. Which was perfectly understandable. She wore no ring, but a woman this attractive had to be surrounded by wannabe suitors.

Mimi held the door, ushered him into the sunlight, then waited while he beeped open the car. All the while keeping her gaze fixed on his hands, the walker, his next step.

But as he opened his door, Mimi reached out and touched the hand still holding the walker.

Her three fingers rested on the back of his hand, a featherlight touch that lingered.

Then she said, "I think . . . dinner would be nice."

Billy heard his voice rise a full octave. "Dinner would be great."

"Can we do this tonight? I've been given a meal . . . It's a long story."

"Tonight is fantastic."

"Seven o'clock, then." She still did not meet his gaze. "Castaways restaurant on Ocean Avenue. I'll meet you there."

Chapter 24

❧

"Let me get this straight." Yolinda could scarcely keep the laughter from her voice. "You're calling to ask me, do I mind you finally going out on a date?"

Mimi stared out her front window, watching a trio of young children and their mothers play an elaborate game among the trees and shadows in the park. "That's not why, and you know it."

"With a *movie star*."

"You were the one who made the reservation for tonight. And it was for us to have dinner together."

"Girl, what is wrong with you?"

Yolinda's pretend anger made Mimi smile. "Why do I feel like you're having one conversation and I'm having another?"

"What I know is, you haven't been on a date in years."

"That is absolutely not true."

"Seems like. It's been too long, I know that much. You don't go out enough. You're young, you're lovely as a sunrise . . . Girl, you deserve to have some *fun*."

"Are you done?"

"Huh. Are *we* done? We're finished when you tell me what I need to be hearing."

"Which is what, exactly?"

"Thank you so very much, Yolinda. You be sure to tell Cloethe and Delon how grateful I am. And you might want to mention how I'm treating a *movie star* to dinner. Because of them."

"I still feel uncomfortable about them paying."

"Don't you even start. They wanted to do this. They need a chance to do more than just say thank you."

Mimi did not know how to respond. She stood by the open window and listened to the mothers calling and the children's shrieks of laughter.

"Oh, I know you don't want payment. But, girl, you *helped* them. You have to accept this. Let them do it. For their sake."

She heard Yolinda slip into her schooltime voice, which commanded and scolded all at once. Because she expected Mimi to argue, come time to pay for their meal. Yolinda was prepared to push just as hard and as long as it took.

"It's so nice of them," Mimi said. "I hear Castaways is very expensive."

"You've never been?"

"No. But I've wanted to."

"Why on earth not?"

"The owners . . ."

"Sylvie and Connor." When Mimi remained silent, Yolinda breathed sharply. "You don't mean . . . they were clients?"

"Don't call them that."

"So they were."

"I don't ever talk about such things. Not to anyone."

"This just keeps getting better. Delon and Cloethe will be thrilled to hear they're giving you something you've wanted. And to answer your question, the place is definitely not cheap. But they can afford it. Not to mention all the time and stress you've saved them."

"The meal, but not the wine," Mimi decided. "He'll probably want to decide on that himself." Then she started to amend herself, because he had told her he was still on meds, which probably meant no alcohol. But in the end she decided there was no need to get into his current medical situation with her friend.

"Listen to you." Yolinda's good humor resurfaced. "'What Billy wants, Billy gets.' Is that what you're telling me?"

"I'm hanging up now." But she spoke around a smile. "Please thank Cloethe and Delon for me."

"Come on, girl. Put some spice into that gratitude. 'Whatever Billy wants . . .'"

Yolinda was still singing as Mimi cut the connection.

CHAPTER 25

The Pilates session left Billy utterly drained. He made it home and fixed himself a sandwich, which he ate standing on the rear veranda, then lay down for a nap. He woke an hour later and groaned his way from the bed. He had been woken as usual by the sound of his mother singing. It had only been a whisper this time, the melody so soft he could not even name it.

Billy gradually straightened as he teetered into the kitchen for a cup of coffee and a half dose of his meds. He knew he needed the drugs, and knew also that he didn't want his brain to go all foggy in the middle of dinner.

By the time he showered and dressed, he was moving well enough to know he could leave the walker behind. His back and all the joints along his left side felt immensely tender. But he knew this was not why he had slept so deeply, or so long. The strain of the shoot was leaving him now. The pressure of performing for a director who did not want him on set was part of his past. He was no longer dancing to the tune of a man who loathed the very sight of him. The studio had taken a personal interest in the film's edit. And all because . . .

He pulled away from the cottage at the wheel of the Land Rover in the dusky golden light of a fading day. Billy tucked away all the thoughts of what his future might hold. He wasn't ready to deal with that yet. Not by a long shot.

Billy arrived at the restaurant twenty minutes early. He found a parking space almost across the street from the restaurant's entrance. He settled into one of the decorative iron chairs outside the establishment. A lovely Latina came out as he settled. Billy explained he was waiting for his date, and accepted her offer of an espresso. He watched the evening people crowd the sidewalk and saw a number of couples enter the restaurant. When the lady returned with his coffee, he asked, "Is there a party tonight?"

She had a face that was made for flirtatious moments, and eyes to match. "Party?"

"The people I've watched enter your place all look so excited."

She paused long enough to greet a party of four, hugging two of them, shaking the others' hands. Then, "You don't know what's happening?"

Billy shook his head. "I'm the new kid on the block."

"Well, new kid, I'm not going to spoil the surprise." She flashed what for her was probably just her customary smile. "Enjoy your coffee, new kid."

He spotted Mimi soon after. She climbed the gently sloping hill, pausing twice to greet people. Even from this distance Billy enjoyed seeing her smile. He had the impression it was not a natural act, and probably did not happen very often. She did not strike him as a sad woman. Rather . . .

Billy watched her start back toward him, only to be halted by yet another family. He tried on several words to describe his date. Solemn, certainly. But not somber, or tragic, or . . .

Mimi Janic looked timeless.

It was a silly affectation, he knew, standing there by his table and empty cup, looking for a word to describe a woman he had only met that afternoon. But he had not so looked forward to the company of a woman in a long while.

Watching her approach held a singular pleasure, like tasting a spice for the first time. Mimi carried herself with a calm so strong it defied whatever temporary storm might strike her world. She was certainly a lovely woman with a caring nature, but he suspected a lot of people would find this timeless calm of hers a hard trait to handle. Especially men. One look from those golden brown eyes and they would know she had seen right through them.

Ada Rose had been exactly that sort of woman. She had silenced the young Billy's attempts to lie his way out of trouble with the same sort of look Billy thought Mimi might use on any male weasel who tried out his best lines.

Mimi wore mint-green trousers of some material that shimmered as she walked, probably silk. A beige sleeveless top, gold-link chain necklace, pale open-toed shoes. She carried a small purse in one hand, a pastel jacket in the other. Her hair was caught in a gold clasp so that it fell over one shoulder. Her autumn eyes offered him a smile that did not quite touch her lips. "Good evening, Billy."

"I haven't looked forward to anything this much in a long time."

She studied him a long moment. Billy could only hope whatever she saw was enough to separate his words from whatever had kept her alone until now. All she said was, "Let's go inside."

Their table was situated near the bar, a copper sheathed semicircle that divided the restaurant's two chambers. From where he was seated, Billy could look over the tables and patrons, back to where the sunset's final glow illuminated a huge bay window. The place was cheerfully packed.

Over a splendid first course, Billy described the film he had just finished shooting. Mimi did not pry so much as invite. Her questions were so gently spoken, it was easy to ignore how probing they became. Billy responded with an ease that surprised him. Normally, he did not talk so much about himself or his work. Inside the LA scene such conversations often became exercises in self-adoration. But Mimi seemed genuinely interested, so he tried to talk about it as if he was describing any other job. Only with more lights. And egos.

Their second course came, sea bass on beds of saffron rice. Grilled asparagus. Mimi had a second glass of wine. Billy stuck with sparkling water. They ate in the comfortable silence of old friends. Billy suspected such quiet moments were a natural part of Mimi's nature, and did not press. Though he wanted to. He had a dozen questions. A hundred. But he was uncertain how to begin.

Finally he set his fork down and said, "The truth is, I don't know all that much about people. Small-town upbringing in the Carolina hills. Theater scholarship to the only university in reach. My time in New York and Los Angeles has all been aimed at finding a way into the world of acting and film. It's pretty much dominated my existence."

Mimi waited through a final bite, touched her lips with the napkin, sipped her wine. Then, "Why are you telling me this?"

"I want to know you, is all. But I don't know enough to even ask the right questions."

She tilted her head, letting the hair spill down over one shoulder. Inspecting him from a different angle. "You are being honest with me."

"As much as I know how." Their waitress came by, picked up their plates, asked about dessert and coffee. Billy let Mimi reply for them both. That they'd like to wait a bit. When she was gone, Billy said, "If I'm wrong to try and ask about you, just forget it."

"No, no. It's just . . ."

"You're a private person. I get that. I'm having a really nice time. Don't let my curiosity wreck things."

She sipped her wine. "A man being so honest, it's . . . different."

"Different good or different bad?"

She set down her glass. Smoothed the tablecloth in front of her. "What do you want to know?"

"Will you tell me where you're from?"

She continued to stroke the tablecloth, avoiding his gaze. "I was born in a war zone. My family lived in the outskirts of a city called Donetsk in eastern Ukraine. The war had not officially started then. That came about eight years ago. But the conflict was all around us. All the time. My family was part of a hated minority. I am Polish. Most citizens of eastern Ukraine are of Russian heritage. My family emigrated there between the First and Second World Wars. One grandfather was a professor at the university where his father was chancellor. My own father was a surgeon. He . . . died."

"I'm so sorry, Mimi."

"Thank you."

"No, I mean . . . Well, sure. I'm sorry about your father. But I'm more sorry for asking. I've made you sad. I didn't—"

"You didn't *make* me anything. I carry this sadness. You merely brought it out. So the question is, were you wrong to ask?"

She still had not looked at him. Nor was there any hint of anger, or even irritation, in how she spoke. The word he had thought of outside the restaurant came back to him. Timeless.

"I don't know," he answered.

"Neither do I know. So if you find an answer to this mystery, you will tell me, yes?"

He nodded. "Your accent has gotten stronger."

"I never talk about my early years. Never. Never. Never. And now I have done it twice in one day."

Billy was still searching for a response when the lights dimmed. Instantly a rush of excited murmurs filled the restaurant.

Mimi had wondered how the meal might turn out, ever since accepting Yolinda's invitation. She rarely had contact with people, once they came to her with a question. There was no hard and fast standard, like how she felt about being paid. She simply did not want to endure their attention, especially when the news she delivered was unwelcome. It wasn't like she had come up with the answer herself. She had simply delivered the message. Life was just easier to handle when such moments were avoided.

But she had a Pole's delight in good food, and Yolinda was a dear friend, and she had literally begged Mimi to accept this gift from her brother and sister-in-law. Plus, Mimi had wanted to dine in Castaways ever since moving to Miramar. But after that session with Connor and Sylvie . . .

Now here she was, watching Billy struggle to find something proper to say. Knowing he felt bad over bringing up her past. Knowing she should probably say something to help him out. But just then, she heard the thump of someone making a heavy go of the stairs that opened between the hostess station and the kitchen.

Marcela, the attractive hostess, swiftly came around to help a heavily pregnant woman step into view. A number of patrons at other tables smiled and cheered and applauded. She waved to them, then took aim straight at Mimi's table.

"I couldn't believe it when Marcela told me you were here," Sylvie said. "Your name isn't on the reservation. I know because I checked."

Mimi stood in order to accept the woman's embrace. Feeling the massive bump press against her own middle caused Mimi's eyes to mist over. The recollection of her own nighttime image came back, sharp as a knife. She managed, "It's good to see you."

"Why now, after refusing our invitation for almost a year?"

"It's complicated."

"It better be."

By this point Billy had risen slowly to his feet. "I'd like to introduce Billy Walker."

"Hi. Welcome to Castaways." Sylvie gave Billy half a second. Less. She asked Mimi, "Does this mean we can meet for a chat? Finally?"

"I suppose . . . Of course we can."

"Good." She hugged Mimi a second time. "Now the whale has to make her way up front."

Mimi remained standing because she heard the male voices and soft laughter and multiple footfalls on the stairs. Billy looked a question at her, but she merely shook her head. There was no way she was going to get into that.

Then Connor Larkin came into view, and the applause grew louder still. He cast the room a generic smile. Then he pretended to be shocked by the sight of Mimi. "So it is true. You haven't moved to Alaska. Or Tahiti. Somewhere so far away you can't return Sylvie's calls."

She felt her face flame as he embraced her. "I'm so sorry."

"You should be." Connor then glanced across the table. This time his double take was genuine. "What do you know? Billy Rose in the flesh."

Billy offered his hand. "I can't believe you remember me."

"Hard man to forget." Connor told Mimi, "Three years back I was in this crazy techno-thriller."

"*Virtual Control*," Billy said. "Over four years now."

"Whatever. I'm playing just another bad guy, my job is to go down in flames." He pointed at Billy. "Mr. Rose here had a grand total of, what, ten lines?"

"Seventeen," Billy said, smiling now.

"Seventeen lines. He steals the show. The star who walks off with the girl and the prize, what's his name?"

"I forget," Billy said.

"So did the critics. All they talked about was Billy Rose here. Even the female lead said she wished she could have been rescued by this guy."

"No, she didn't."

"Well, she should have." Connor told Mimi, "You should check out that movie, see for yourself."

"I've seen it," Mimi replied, her face flaming for a different reason now.

Billy said, "You're kidding."

"Connor is correct. You were great."

Connor asked, "How long are you in town?"

Billy seemed to struggle over his response. "Hard to say. Maybe forever."

"Miramar will do that. Sure has to me." He surveyed Billy. "How are your injuries?"

"You heard?"

Connor Larkin found that humorous. "Miramar isn't on the back side of the moon. It only seems that way. Of course I heard."

Mimi said, "Billy is doing fine, all things considered."

"Get my number from Marcela," Connor told Billy. "Come up and we'll have a chat about the Wild West."

"I'd like that," Billy replied. "So much."

He turned back to Mimi. Serious now. "What you did for us, I can't begin to say."

Mimi patted the air between them. Not saying it, but hoping he would understand, just the same.

Connor nodded and stepped back. "Any requests?"

Mimi breathed easy. "Something from Michael Franks would be nice."

Connor slipped away, stopping briefly by several other tables as he made his way toward the front. Mimi watched Billy settle into his chair, wondering which of the many uncomfortable questions he would ask. Bracing herself.

Instead, he leaned across the table and asked, "You like Michael Franks?"

CHAPTER 26

⤝⤞

Connor seated himself behind the piano to considerable applause. He adjusted the mike and said, "This is dedicated to the lady who's about to bring twins into our home."

While the audience still applauded, he slipped into a highly stylized rendition of "Fly Me to the Moon."

Billy was so overwhelmed by the conversation with Connor Larkin that he felt immune to how he listened to a tune straight from his mother's playbook. This was followed by the Etta James hit "A Sunday Kind of Love," and then "The Way You Look Tonight." Connor segued easily from one to the next, granting the audience no time to applaud. Billy remained mildly astonished by his lack of any internal reaction.

Connor's arrangements and tempo were far more modern and upbeat. Even so, Billy would have expected it to be a wrenching experience. Instead, he found himself able to listen and absorb and then let the song go. As if tonight's experiences were completely separate from the melodies that so plagued his dawns.

Another two songs, then Connor stopped, and during the applause three others rose from a table near the stage and took up their instruments. A woman played stand-up bass, with two men on drums and sax. Connor introduced them and said, "I'm sorry to report that my crew is doing their best to haul me into the twenty-first century."

The bassist leaned toward her mike and said, "Only mildly kicking and screaming."

The drummer said, "Apparently, Connor thought they stopped making new tunes around 1970."

"At least all the tunes that mattered," Connor said. "So I was wrong. So sue me."

They played six melodies from the modern era, songs by Sade Adu, Michael Bublé, Natalie Cole, Diana Krall, and then ended with two by Michael Franks. A short break, then the entire group played a Sammy Davis Jr., a Como, a Sinatra. Five more by contemporary artists, and it was over.

As the restaurant emptied, Billy watched as several patrons stopped by their table. Some had children in Mimi's classes. Others seemed to share the same heartfelt gratitude as Sylvie Cassick and Connor Larkin. Billy stepped slightly back from the table, content to wait and observe. Mimi's response was very curious. With the parents of her students, she was warm and welcoming. With the others, Billy had the impression that Mimi Janic stopped breathing. She held herself with a sense of patient resignation.

Finally they were alone with Sylvie, who hugged Mimi a final time and made her promise to return. To Billy, Sylvie offered a professional's farewell, then allowed Marcela to help her back up the stairs. From the stage Connor waved his towel in a weary farewell, then made the hand sign of a phone and pointed to Billy.

As they stepped into the night, Billy said, "That was amazing."

Mimi nodded. "I wish I could have danced."

"Why didn't you?"

"They don't allow it when he plays. There simply isn't room."

Billy took each step carefully. He had learned to let his joints unlimber gradually after he'd been stationary. "Do you mind if we walk just a bit?"

"Not at all. My first class isn't for another..." She glanced at her watch. "Nine hours."

"Was that a joke?"

"A small one, perhaps."

Mimi directed them down the gentle slope leading toward the sea. Billy started to ask where she lived. Then they passed beneath a streetlight, and he caught sight of her face. Mimi's features had taken on the same calm resignation she had shown the people who had come and thanked her in that sincere and mysterious fashion. As if she knew he was about to shatter the night's aura. As if there was nothing she could do about it.

So he remained silent. They walked together another block, and Billy stopped. "I think that's enough for me."

She seemed taken aback. "Thank you for a lovely evening."

"I was the guest tonight, remember?"

"I stand corrected." She tasted a smile. "Until tomorrow afternoon, then."

"Mimi . . . would you teach me to dance?"

She stared at him. "You do not know how?"

"Oh, sure. I know how to dance *badly*. I'm probably the best *bad* dancer you'll ever meet."

"How is it, you love music and yet you've never learned to love it with your body, with motion?"

Billy relished the sound of that, loving music with motion. "I have a list of all the things I want to study. Someday. Dancing is definitely on the list."

"But not at the top?"

"Not even close. My bad."

"So, what is first on your list of lessons?"

"The British accent. Don't laugh."

"I am not even close to laughing."

"Some of my favorite British and Australian actors do great American dialects. I want . . ."

Then and there, standing together in the middle of a midnight-empty sidewalk, Mimi reached out. She cradled his face in hands as strong as they were gentle. She pulled him down a trace and kissed him soundly.

"Good night, Billy."

And she was gone.

CHAPTER 27

Mimi's week settled into a most unnatural routine. Unnatural, as in feeling comfortable in a man's company. She found a distinctly new happiness whenever she was with Billy. Along with fear, of course. She woke up scared and carried it through every waking hour. But happy, just the same.

By Tuesday afternoon the entire school knew Mimi was dating a movie star. Which was mildly untrue, since they had not actually dated but that one time. Instead, each afternoon she left school and went to the studio and had her hour-long session with Billy. If she had another class or private lesson, Billy waited. When she was free, they went for coffee. She refused his offer of another date night, saying she needed to maintain a regular schedule during the week. Billy did not press, which was interesting. She wondered if he felt as she did. That their time together was so multilayered and so unsettling, they both needed space.

Billy Rose Walker constantly challenged Mimi to step beyond her comfort zone. Each night when she recalled their latest conversation, she knew another moment's terror. Now she was the one seated at the sidewalk table, talking easily with a man who drew looks from most of the women and some of the men who passed. A man who only had eyes for her.

On Wednesday he entered the studio without his cane. Mimi worked him a bit harder that day, then had to go fetch the cane from his ride when they were over. He insisted on walking the three blocks to the café, which gave her a chance to hold his elbow, as if wanting to be there and support him. He said, "I called Connor Larkin. He said he might stop by. I hope that's okay."

"Of course it is." Though, in truth, she felt a moment's jealousy over someone else entering their private moment. Which was silly. But still.

"I've got a problem. It hit me yesterday out of the blue."

"A problem with your work?"

He nodded. "It was there waiting for me when I got back from seeing you yesterday."

She could see how it troubled him, so she did not ask for details, much as she found herself wanting to know. "You think Connor can help?"

"Maybe. I hope. Otherwise . . ." He shook his head. "The whole thing is just crazy."

When they entered the café, they found Connor Larkin seated at the window table, his chair placed where he could see the Castaways' entrance a block down the street. His phone was set on the table by his cup. He greeted them by saying, "I don't know how long I have."

Billy stood nervously by the table. "Why don't we leave it for another time?"

"There's no telling when that will be." Connor used his foot to push out the chair. "Right now, I'm on permanent standby. Tell you the truth, it's good to have a reason to step away."

Mimi asked Billy, "Regular black coffee, yes?"

"Thank you." To Connor, "I feel kind of silly, taking your time when your whole world is about to change."

As she started away, Mimi heard Connor say, "Tell you what. Why don't we get past all the superficial how-do-you-do's and get straight to the nitty-gritty. Like we're already pals."

Mimi approached the counter and watched Billy ease himself into the seat. She heard him say, "You almost sound down-home."

"Richmond born and raised. You?"

"A little nowhere valley-town west of Asheville."

She placed her order and paid and walked down to the delivery station. The noise level was such that she could no longer hear what was being said. Just the same, it was nice to have this opportunity to observe the two men. Even in his weary and semiwounded state, Billy exuded a visceral energy. So too, she saw now, did Connor. Not even the man's harried and stress-filled state could extinguish the natural magnetism. It was not how two incredibly handsome men shared the same table that drew so many stares. Their innate power, a subtle magnetism, set them apart.

It made for a unique moment, watching the two actors seated together. The room's energy and the afternoon light seemed to coalesce around them. They almost seemed to pose, as if they maintained a subtle readiness for the camera to catch them. Even here.

As Mimi accepted her two coffees and started back, she thought she could actually feel Billy's charged presence. Strong as heat.

When she set the cups on the table and took her seat, Connor asked, "So, what's on your mind?"

Mimi realized the two men had waited for her return to

start talking. It was silly to find that so big a deal. Just the same . . .

Billy said, "I got a delivery yesterday afternoon. Seven scripts."

Up to that point Connor's attention had swiveled from Billy to the phone to the window and back. Paying attention to the other man seated at his table, but also aware of his wife's needs. Now the shifts halted. Connor's attention became tightly focused. All he said was, "Well, now."

Billy sipped his coffee. The tension radiated from him. Mimi had no idea why he appeared so stressed. And worried. But Connor did. She could see that. Connor asked, "Have you read them?"

"One. Started the second. Then . . ."

"You stopped because you have no idea what you're supposed to be doing."

Billy nodded. Sipped his coffee. When he set down the cup, it rattled softly against the saucer. Giving away the man's tight tremors.

"How did they arrive?"

"By studio limo."

Connor smiled. "You don't say."

"Along with a pair of wicker baskets," Billy said. "One had fruit and cheese and stuff. The other was a sort of wine sampler. Bottles from places I've never heard of."

Connor's grin widened. "You need help with that, let me know."

"Detailing what they are, or drinking them?"

"Both. Your call. Was there a note?"

Billy nodded. "Handwritten. From the newest member of the studio's executive board."

"So. Their new green-light guy wrote you a note. What did he say?"

"He hoped I was improving. Asked me to give these a

look. When I was ready, I should call." Billy stared across the table. "What is going on?"

"You know what's happening. You just want to know, is it real?"

He started to lift his cup, then set it back down.

"All your dreams, all your hopes and wishes," Connor said, "they're about to come true."

Billy asked, "Why does that make me sick to my stomach?"

"Because you're human," Connor said. "Because you're worried what it might mean, and afraid you might not be able to make it last."

Billy pushed his cup away. He turned and stared out the window.

Connor's voice grew gentle. "Tell me what you know about the film that just wrapped. Not the story. The commercial elements."

Billy described the problems he had experienced on set with his director. The news delivered by Trevor, the AD. The conversations with this studio executive. Mimi thought Billy's delivery came in broken snatches. But Connor merely nodded, as if it all made perfect sense.

Billy did not finish so much as run out of breath, or so it seemed to Mimi.

"The word they'll be using around the studio is counter-programming," Connor said. "That means they'll be setting your project up to be released the same weekend as their failing tentpole feature. Counterprogramming means they'll be switching as much attention your way as they can, without actually saying they expect the bigger film to be a bust. In reality, all the publicity and marketing dollars are going to be dropped in your lap."

Billy directed his question to the window. "What does that mean, exactly?"

Connor replied with a question of his own. "What's the release date?"

"For which film?"

He leaned back in his seat. "Say that again."

"They were holding back on the release of my last film."

"Who told you that?"

"The studio exec. While he was up. Sorry. I forgot to mention."

"You sure did. What's the date for that one?"

"Middle of next month. Television and streaming. He said something about an overseas cinematic release around the same time."

"And the one that just wrapped?"

"July fourteenth weekend."

"Right at the height of the summer blockbusters. Come the last week in June, your new personal publicist will hand you a schedule. Basically for the ten days to either side of that weekend, your life will be lived in fifteen-minute segments. Except for when they fly you to New York for the late-night shows. Be sure and ask for a voice coach to fly with you, help you prep. There won't be time once you land." Connor paused. "You all right there? You've gone all green."

"Give me a minute."

"Come late June, you won't *have* a minute."

"But what does it all *mean*?"

"That's simple enough. The studio is setting you up. They want to develop you as the next star who's able to open a movie."

Billy's swallow was audible. "And the scripts?"

Which was the moment Connor's phone buzzed. The tension broke with an almost-audible snap. Connor glanced down, and instantly rose to his feet. "Sorry. Got to run. Why don't you give them all a read, then we'll chat." He offered Mimi a quick hug, patted Billy's shoulder, and was gone.

Billy sat there a long moment, then finally managed a soft "Oh, man."

CHAPTER 28

❧

On Thursday afternoon Mimi finally realized what lay behind her rising surges of sheer terror.

Billy Rose Walker was not the man from her image.

She sat at the dance studio's small desk, watching the wall clock count off the minutes until his arrival. The desk was situated in an alcove between the studio's entrance and the corridor running down one sidewall. The hall ended in a second alcove, which was fronted by five doors: the staff's dayroom, an office, a storeroom, and restrooms. The studio itself was reached by two glass-fronted doors, one up by Mimi's desk and the other down by the restrooms.

The hallway was broad enough for a line of wooden benches to run down one side, facing the dance studio itself. The interior wall was glass from the waist up, which allowed parents to sit and watch their children perform. It also ensured that all off-duty staff could keep an eye on whatever private lesson was happening. That meant everyone had seen Mimi working with Billy. The star who was *visiting* from Los Angeles.

Emphasis on the word "visiting."

By then, everyone also knew he was staying in the cottage on Lighthouse Lane, the place owned by some Hollywood bigwig. This meant Billy was not just an actor. He was *important*. He was a man on the rise. In *Hollywood*.

Mimi neither liked nor disliked all the attention being cast her way. Whenever their questions became too personal, she steered the conversation around to a safer topic. People accepted it because that was how Mimi handled everything to do with her life. "Reserved" was the word she heard friends use most often to describe her. It was a lot better than other descriptions applied over the years. Secretive. A blank wall. Too guarded for her own good.

Then Billy pushed through the doors, and gave her a smile that brightened the afternoon, and said what he always did when they met: "You look especially lovely today."

And she responded as she always did. Ignoring the multitude of other people who had found some shred of an excuse to linger down by the kitchen or the dayroom or the office. She rose from her chair and asked, "Shall we begin?"

Their conversation followed the same pattern it had every session. How was he feeling? Fine. Did he do any exercises on his own? One set after Abril, the masseuse, was finished with him. Abril was as strong as she was massive, and as gentle as a Mexican teddy bear. Mimi knew all this because Billy told her. All their conversations inside the studio were about his health, his progress, his range of motions. The only difference today was, Billy had not taken his meds.

She asked, "Are you sure that is wise?"

"The pain is less, my movements are better, and my cane stays in the car." Billy breathed out as she guided him through a second stretch. "I want to see if I can make do with Advil."

That was the last they spoke until Billy finished his workout and lay on the mat, waiting for his strength to return.

She had pushed him hard that day, hard as she would the students in her advanced class. But he hadn't complained. Billy never did. Which was another thing she liked about him.

So many things. And so very much.

Too much, really. Which was the problem.

Mimi remained where she had been during the final routine, kneeling by his side, there to support him if required. His eyes remained closed, which meant she could examine him openly without worrying about the staff making their way up and down the side corridor.

There was no question in her mind. There hadn't been since leaving him outside the restaurant.

She was head over heels in love.

Which, of course, made Billy the wrong man for her image.

The reason was simple enough. Billy was going back to Los Angeles. All their afternoon coffees had pretty much followed the same pattern as that meeting with Connor Larkin. Billy talked about his work with evident reluctance. He had repeatedly said he never wanted to become one of those actors who only had one topic that interested them: themselves. But Mimi did not respond to questions about herself. She never did. And she asked questions about him and LA and such. And he answered. Honestly and directly. She loved his answers, his clarity of thought, the way he held himself with a modesty she had to assume was genuine.

It was all too much, really.

The reason was simple, direct, and beyond argument or debate. Billy was going back. And she would never leave Miramar. Never, never, never.

And there was far more besides.

Billy was going to become a star. She had not seen this in any sort of image or vision or whatever. She didn't need to. His conversation with Connor Larkin was all the confirmation she needed. Besides, everything he related about his most recent film added to her certainty, even while he apparently refused to accept it.

But that was not the real reason.

In her image *the man was not there.*

What was more, *she was happy.*

And one thing she knew for certain: Without the slightest doubt, if she gave in to her feelings about Billy Rose Walker, she would never recover from losing him. Not in a billion years. A week in the man's company was all she needed for that to frame the reality. If he left, she would be completely and utterly shattered.

Which made him the wrong man.

Mimi came to her feet and watched as Billy stood in stages. He smiled around his discomfort and said what he always did, "Do you have time for a coffee?"

She knew now was the time to break it off. Say he had improved to where they didn't need any more sessions together. Walk away. Forget him. While she still could. *Maybe.*

But there just wasn't enough air in the room.

"Not today," she managed. "I need to take care of things that can't wait."

The excuse sounded feeble, even before she spoke. But Billy seemed to accept them as real enough. His disappointment was clearly evident. As if this actor up from the LA dream machine was actually . . .

Falling for her.

During Friday's lunchtime Yolinda's patience finally ran out. She waited outside the faculty break room, then silently tracked Mimi inside and pointed her to the lone table set in the window alcove. It was as close to a private space as the faculty lounge permitted, with chest-high bookshelves serving as dividers. Yolinda removed the RESERVED sign from the table, thunked down her lunch bag, and pointed to the chair next to her own. "Sit."

Mimi wanted to argue, give yet another of her many excuses, and just walk away. But the truth was, she needed to talk this through, she needed to clear things up, she needed . . .

She sat.

Yolinda walked to the fridge under the coffeemaker, pulled out two juices, dropped money into the basket, and walked back over. "Cranapple, right?"

"Thank you, Yolinda."

"Oh, so the lady has a voice. What do you know." She opened her bag and pulled out a sandwich, a yogurt, and a spoon. "Talk."

"I don't even know what to say."

"You've been having a good time with the actor fellow."

"Billy. Yes. We do. Did."

"And you're still seeing him for treatments."

"Every afternoon. I think that's about to end."

"What, the treatments or the two of you?" When Mimi did not respond, Yolinda set down her sandwich, wiped her hands, then reached over and took hold of Mimi's wrist. "Girl, look at me. What do you see?"

"A friend."

"You got that right. Now tell me what's got you so wound up."

"He's an *actor*."

"And?"

Mimi told her about the meeting with Connor Larkin. She released the words in a rush, so fast they kept colliding with one another. About Connor's response and Billy's fear and the incredible tension. And . . .

"I got it now," Yolinda said.

"I'm so excited for him. Thrilled. Because . . ."

"It's the man's big chance, and you like him, so you're happy for him."

Then everything just became so clogged up inside, Mimi had to cough before she could repeat, "They're making him a *star*."

"They might be, sure enough."

"And what, he's going to be happy with *me*? In *Miramar*?"

"You like it here."

"It's the only real home I've ever known."

"Does your Billy know that?"

"He should. I've told him often enough."

"So here he is. Billy Rose Walker. A man on the brink of seeing his name in lights."

"Connor said the way they put it is, Billy will have the power to open a movie."

"The man just might be the next big star. And so you're not looking at him as just, you know, this good-looking man who treats you fine and you're having a great time stepping out with him. Not anymore."

"It's a lot more than that."

"You sure about that?"

Mimi nodded. Just having it out in the open like that made her sick to her stomach.

Adela Perez, the school principal, chose that moment to step up to the divider and ask, "Everything all right over here?"

"Give us a minute," Yolinda replied, not taking her eyes off Mimi. "You ought to eat."

"I can't."

"Girl, you got three more classes. Take out that rabbit food you brought and eat something." She waited until Mimi unpacked her apple and banana and the ziplock bag of veggies. Yolinda said again, "It's a lot more than just spending time in the man's company."

"Yes."

"You in love with the man?"

"I don't . . ." Mimi pushed the food to one side, planted her elbows in the table, mashed her face into her hands, and mumbled, "I'm so scared."

Yolinda gave that a long moment. "Tell you what. Cloethe and Delon are coming over tonight. She's making her shepherd's pie. Why don't you bring Billy."

Mimi lifted her face.

"Cloethe does the best shepherd's pie you ever tasted. You think Billy might like casserole?"

"I have no idea. He keeps claiming he's a country boy at heart."

"We'll give him a good inspection, try and help you see what's really going on here. Because I tell you the truth. If my brother and his wife catch one whiff of the man playing with you, they won't leave nothing but a greasy spot on the pavement."

CHAPTER 29

❧

Billy's Friday started bad and grew steadily worse.

As usual, his mother's singing woke him. Only this time the dream held a new edge.

Billy dreamed he was inside a square building, not big, a few rooms wide and long, completely empty. Her singing was there as soon as he became aware. The song was alluring as always, only now it was edged with menace. Instantly he realized the singing meant someone or something was hunting him. The dream did not need to make sense to fill him with a sense of almost-overwhelming panic. Billy raced to the back, but the singing was faster. As always, he did not see anyone. He did not recognize the song, could not hear the actual words. And every now and then, a wrong note was sung. Which never happened. But it did now, and the mistakes filled Billy with a certainty that it actually was no longer his mother who was singing. He raced back and forth, from window to door, certain that someone had stolen the voice and was now using it to draw him in and consume him . . .

He woke gasping. Billy wrestled off the covers and rose from the bed, too fast, bringing back the pain for the first time in three days. He hobbled to the bathroom and stood looking at his reflection in the mirror over the sink. Doing his best to anchor in a real world. Only then did he recognize the melody still drifting through the dawn light, Ella Fitzgerald's "That Old Black Magic."

He showered off the dream sweats and dressed and pressed the buttons to raise all of the cottage's blinds. But it did no good, because a marine layer had settled in with the dawn. He had seen a few of these since moving to LA. They rarely got so far inland as the Hollywood Hills. When it happened, the mist was a thin silver veil that only lasted until the sun was fully up.

This was something else entirely. The fog was as solid as a translucent wall. Just enough light made it through to turn the mist a sullen gray. As Billy made his first cup of Nespresso, it seemed to him that the world had erected the barrier with one intent. To force him to get started on the work he had spent all week avoiding.

The previous afternoon he had returned from his session with Mimi to discover a second carton bearing the studio logo placed on his front step. The box contained another seven scripts. On it was a terse note from Peter Veer, very similar to the first, hoping he was improving and enjoying his time in Miramar. Asking Billy to give these a look when he felt up to it.

He ate a bowl of berries and granola, staring at the pile growing in the center of his dining table. He had managed to work his way through a grand total of three screenplays. In a week. Out of fourteen scripts now stacked on the table, all bearing covers with the studio's blue-gray logo. Just like it flashed on the screen before the films started.

He didn't need to be a genius to understand why the nightmare had struck with such viciousness this particular morning.

Billy simply had no idea what to do with this pile of opportunities.

He picked up his phone and dialed Connor's number from memory. Again. The call went straight to voice mail. Again.

All his classes. All the instructors. All the roles he had played. All the books he read. None of it had prepared him for the challenge he now faced.

Of course he had played lead roles before, in theater, school, small films, TV specials. But in every case the power of the play or film, the direction of his role, had been *dictated*.

Billy opened the next script. He took his time. During his time with Abril, the masseuse, Billy mentally reviewed the pages he had read thus far. He worked through a late lunch. Sketched out the role, and how his character played against the other roles. Everything he thought the powers that be might expect of a . . .

He fought down the tension. Spoke the word out loud. "Star."

As with the other three scripts, almost every page became covered with notes. Yet as he stared at the final page, Billy mostly saw all the unanswered questions.

Thankfully, Mimi chose that moment to phone. A first. Billy felt an unaccustomed rush of pleasure. "How are you?"

She took her time responding, as if the question required a great deal of thought. "I am . . . on my afternoon break. How are you?"

"Working too. I'm glad you called." The rush of pleasure was gone now, erased by her flat unemotional tone. It was her normal way of speaking, at least to him. Even before she closed the distance and kissed him on the night-clad street. Their one and only taste of intimacy. But hearing her now, without the woman's intensity and sheer physical presence, left him feeling . . .

Hollow.

Billy knew he was falling for her. He knew his feelings were coming on too strong and too fast. Which was why he discounted them whenever he woke in the night and thought about their last session, or their most recent coffee, or walking the Miramar street, or standing by his car, him hoping desperately that she might offer him one of her very rare smiles.

"I think . . . we shouldn't meet every day anymore. You are improving. It is no longer required."

Billy started to ask if that was what she wanted. But he stopped with the words almost out, his mouth open, and just exhaled. Because it sounded like what a teenager would be saying. After he got dumped. Which he was fairly certain Mimi was doing.

"Billy?"

"You're the boss," he said. Truer words, and all that. When it came to them, Mimi was the one in control.

"I am thinking, one day each week. And, of course, you must continue to do your exercises every day. How long are you staying?"

"That really depends on you." He winced at how that sounded. If he could have taken the words back, he'd have done so. But it was true, just the same.

She hesitated a long moment. Then she said, "My friend, you met her. Yolinda. She is wondering . . . would you like to have dinner with us tonight?"

"Of course. That would be nice."

As Mimi gave him the address, a school bell sounded in the background. "I must go now. Seven o'clock. Until tonight."

The fog never lifted.

When it finally came time to leave for dinner with Mimi and her friends, Billy had only made it through half of the fifth script. He showered and dressed and carried the cane out to the car. Moving slowly, but on his own unaided steam.

As he pulled the Land Rover from the garage and drove through the gloom, Billy decided he had no choice but phone Peter Veer and admit defeat.

The dashboard clock said he had just over an hour before he was due at Yolinda's. On a whim he drove down the length of Ocean Avenue and found himself at the entrance to a beachfront parking lot. He pulled in, rose from the car, and stood so the hood took most of his weight. The fog had thinned to where he could just make out the white water. The sun was so dimmed by the lingering veil, Billy could watch it approach the horizon. He was filled with a sense that his problems with the screenplays were reflected in every other part of his life. His body's refusal to nearly heal. The weather.

Mimi.

Falling in love with a woman who pushed him away was futile in the extreme. The dimming dusk illuminated the truth well enough. That was exactly what she was doing, of course. She might be making her farewells with an infinitely gentle pressure. She might ease the moment by inviting him to dinner that night. But any idiot could see she was not going to drop her reserve and let him in.

He had never seen himself as a guy who pushed and pushed with growing desperation. Who refused to accept that his feelings were not shared by the lady in question. And they never would be.

Finally Billy rounded the driver's side and slipped behind the wheel. The time for being foolish about a love that would never happen was over. He had to stop this before he dug himself any deeper into emotions that were not shared.

He would break things off tonight.

CHAPTER 30

The four of them met at Yolinda's an hour before Billy was scheduled to arrive. Within minutes they were moving smoothly around one another, like they had been together on any number of occasions. Like they were the closest of friends. A simple word from one drew comments from the others, little snippets that did not need to be fully formed into sentences and paragraphs and complete thoughts. They were that close.

Which meant Mimi was fully aware of the anxiety Delon and Cloethe carried with them. She helped Yolinda set the table, then started cutting vegetables for a salad, while Delon opened a bottle of wine and Cloethe put the casserole dish in the oven. Four people in Yolinda's small kitchen, all of them comfortable in their own space, even with the couple's tension. When she thought it was time, she said, "Something's the matter, isn't it?"

"I told them about you and Billy Rose." Yolinda kept her hands focused on the salad bowl. "I didn't want you to have to go through all those questions another time. Which Delon would insist on making you do."

"Like a dog with a bone." Cloethe checked the oven's setting. "That's Delon when he's picking at somebody else's life."

"Oh, thank goodness." Mimi breathed easier. "I worried you had news about his health."

"My brother is doing just fine, thanks to you," Yolinda said.

"He's got a new migraine medicine. One dose and all those symptoms just fade away." Cloethe pulled over a stool and seated herself. "Now Delon's doctor is making it sound like this silent-migraine thing was part of his thinking all along."

"Doctors." Delon handed out glasses and poured the wine. "Don't get me started."

Yolinda watched Mimi sweep the vegetables from her chopping board into the salad. "What I didn't know was Delon's attitude toward Hollywood."

"I got nothing against the town," Delon said. "It's actors I don't like."

Cloethe demanded, "And when exactly did you ever meet one to know?"

"I never met a plague carrier, but I know I don't like them, either."

Cloethe shook her head. "The things that come out of that man's mouth."

"What . . ." Mimi's phone chimed. She glanced at the readout and started for the door. "Excuse me. I need to take this."

In the days following Anastasia's death, a San Luis Obispo attorney contacted Mimi and announced that she represented Anastasia. Why the woman whom Mimi had come to view as both aunt and her closest friend needed a lawyer three hours north of Los Angeles, the attorney would not say. The lawyer's name was Megan Pierce, and in the four years that followed, Megan had continued to play a vital role. "How are you, Mimi?"

"Well, thank you. And yourself?"

"Busy. I've just had a request to set up a conference with you."

Despite the added distance, the number of LA contacts seeking Mimi's help had remained fairly constant. All such meetings took place in Megan's conference room. "When?"

"Tomorrow, if at all possible. I told them no, of course. But I have been assured it is extremely urgent." Megan sounded the same as always, crisp and direct and counting the minutes as having genuine value. "He is a long-standing contact of yours. Do you want to know who it is?"

"No." She had always made it a practice not to know anything in advance. She started to put it off, then realized she was delighted with the prospect of leaving town. "Tell them I'll see them at eleven."

Billy left the cottage early enough to stop by Miramar's largest market for flowers. He set them on the seat next to a bottle of wine from the studio's gift basket. The Land Rover's GPS led him back into the same old-timey area where he had gotten lost that first day. He passed what appeared to be city or county buildings, all dressed up with wooden-shingle roofs and wide shaded verandas. Then the Catholic church, a wooden structure so lovingly built it belonged in some vintage magazine. When the GPS told him he had arrived, Billy found himself exactly where he had stopped Yolinda walking down the narrow lane and had asked her for directions. He remembered precisely where she had been because of the four jacaranda trees lining the space between her house and the neighbor to the north. Billy realized the woman had been about to climb her front steps when he showed up. Instead of dropping off her shopping, she had carried it with her and then carried it back a second time.

Billy found a space big enough for his vehicle four houses down. The evening air was caught in a distinctly California space between the day's heat and a wintry night chill. There was neither traffic nor wind. The street was so quiet he heard kids playing a video game through an open window. In the next house a couple sang snatches of a tune he didn't recognize as they clattered around their kitchen.

The exterior of Yolinda's house struck Billy as a teacup palace. The town's heritage was there on lovely display. The four planters lining her porch railing were fashioned from reed oyster baskets. The porch lights were brass whaling lanterns. The front windows held handblown glass that shone like burnished copper in the day's final light.

Billy found himself unaccountably nervous as he approached Yolinda's front steps. That, and his absence of any meds, slowed him to where it was almost natural to pause on the first step. Which was when he heard the voices through the open front door.

Billy heard a man say, "So the fellow scares you."

"That's not nearly strong enough," Mimi replied. "What is a thousand times worse than saying he's scary?"

The man huffed softly. "Sounds like the right attitude to me."

A woman demanded, "What on earth are you saying? You never even met him."

"That *actor* is paid to make people believe his lies. He's a professional at it. What else do I need to know?"

"Glad to know you're going into this with an open mind."

Yolinda said, "How do you feel about him? That's what I want to know."

"That's not the point," Mimi replied.

"There you go," the man said.

"Will you just hush with your nonsense and let the lady speak?"

"The question is," Mimi said, "can I let myself feel anything at all?"

"No," the man said. "Absolutely not."

"I love it here," Mimi went on. "Miramar is the first place I've ever called home. Sooner or later, Billy is going to wake up from his dream time here and go back to LA."

A woman said, "You hated Los Angeles?"

"That's not it," Yolinda replied. "You heard what she said. Billy is part of the scene down there. It's not just the place. It's the *life*. It's the *scene*."

"Yes," Mimi said. "Yes."

Billy knew he had heard enough.

He could not say what hurt worse just then, his wounded side or his heart. He coughed and climbed the stairs and shuffled across the front porch, moving slowly enough for Mimi to step into the open doorway, there to greet him with that lovely, solemn gaze.

Of all the roles he had hated, none came close to this. Billy said, "I'm so sorry. But everything just locked up."

She stepped forward. "Oh, Billy."

"I've got to go back and take it easy tonight." He knew his smile was mostly grimace, which fit his words precisely. He held out the flowers and the wine. "Tell Yolinda I'm sorry, would you? Maybe we can do it another time."

Reluctantly she accepted his gifts. "Can you make it home?"

Billy waited until he was down the steps and ten paces along the sidewalk to turn back. He gave Mimi a last and final look, then waved farewell.

Mimi took a slow, deliberate path from the front porch back to the dining table. The candlelight flickered and danced over the starched linen tablecloth. The three of them,

Yolinda and Delon and Cloethe, watched her set the bottle down in the middle of the table, between the salad bowl and the copper plate for the casserole. Mimi lowered herself into one of the two empty chairs. The four of them were seated as when Delon and Cloethe had come looking for answers. Only now, it was Mimi who had no idea how to move forward. After all, she had just been handed exactly what she had claimed to want. What she had convinced herself she desperately needed. And yet . . .

Delon said, "The man heard us talking."

"Of course he heard," Cloethe replied. "You shooting off your big mouth like that, they heard you in Marina del Rey."

"Well," Delon said, glancing at Mimi, then away. "That's probably not a bad thing."

"That's not for you to say, now, is it?"

He reached out and lifted the bottle, checked the label. "Man's got taste, I give you that."

When he rose from the table, Cloethe said, "You are *not* opening the man's wine."

"Why not? The first bottle's gone, our glasses are empty." But when his wife did not reply, Delon resumed his place at the table.

"I'll do it." Mimi took the bottle from him and entered the kitchen. She picked up a kitchen towel and mashed it hard to her face. There was no reason for tears. None whatsoever.

When her eyes cleared and her hands steadied, she used the corkscrew and opened the bottle. She returned to the silent table and filled her glasses. No one looked her way as she set down the bottle and lifted her glass. Mimi focused on the fractured candlelight and said, "To better days."

CHAPTER 31

～

Billy stopped for Mexican takeout and ate it on the cottage's rear veranda. He opened the current script and read a few more lines, then gave it up as wasted motion. He spent the rest of the evening trying to convince himself that what he felt was mostly wounded pride. He had come up here to heal from being electrocuted and basically dying on set. In this vulnerable state he had been blindsided by a woman with a healer's touch and eyes of deepest mystery—eyes he saw every time he closed his own.

Billy finally gave the evening up as a lost cause and went to bed, only to spend an hour or so wrestling with his sheets. Finally he rose and padded back into the main room. Billy opened the glass doors and stood there, breathing in the night. The breeze off the Pacific carried a wintry edge. Clouds like silver moonlit islands drifted overhead. The longer he stood there, the more certain he became that it was time to head back. Los Angeles held no real appeal to him. Maybe he would return here one day, but on his own terms. When the place was not tainted by a woman who did not want Billy in her life.

The whisper of another half-heard melody woke Billy a little before nine. He had just enough time to shower and drink his morning coffee before the masseuse arrived.

Abril Martinez was almost as tall as Billy, a big-boned woman with a sensitive touch and whose eyes constantly sparked with good humor. As usual, Billy dozed on and off through the session. Whenever he rose to a near-awake state, he found himself returning to the midnight decision. It was time to pack up the unread scripts and put this place in his rearview mirror. There was no reason his departure should leave him so bereft.

He was about to tell Abril that he wouldn't be needing her services any longer when a rush of noise lifted Billy's head from the cushion. Abril walked to the window, pulled back one edge of the drape, and said, "You've got company."

Billy levered himself off the table, wrapped the towel around his middle, and padded over. He watched Connie Adler rise from a gleaming red Porsche convertible.

Abril took a sharp intake of breath. "Is that Consuela Adler?"

"We acted together in my last film."

"Oh, my mother thinks she is an angel." Abril let the drape go. "No, well, not a *good* angel. One coming from down there." She giggled like a schoolgirl and pointed at the floor. "You should hear what my mother says when *la bruja malvada* steals away the good girl's man."

"I need to shower and dress. Would you mind telling her I'll be right there?"

"It would be my greatest pleasure." Abril pried the drape open again. "So many tears, this one causes."

He started for the bathroom. "I'll join you fast as I can."

"No, no, do not rush." The doorbell rang, prodding Abril

into motion. She almost skipped across the tiles. "My mother, she is just going to die."

Billy showered and he took his time dressing. Connie's sudden appearance unsettled him in ways he could not explain. Another uncertainty added to an already overburdened day.

Billy opened the bedroom door and followed the voices out to the rear patio. Soon as he passed through the open glass doors, Connie broke off her animated conversation with Abril and rushed over. Then she stopped an arm's length away. Connie tucked her hands under her chin, like a wary little girl. "Was I wrong to come?"

"You look fantastic." And she most certainly did. She wore a black-on-black ensemble that clung to her splendid form like shadows. Her only piece of jewelry was a jade bracelet, which matched her emerald gaze.

Connie pouted. "Is that your idea of a polite no, Billy?"

"Anybody as beautiful as you would be welcome anywhere." Then he added, "I'm glad you came."

She seemed as surprised as he felt. "Really?"

"Yes." And to his astonishment, he really was.

Connie insisted on posing with Abril. Billy shot the pictures with Abril's phone. The lady folded up her table, sang her thanks, and left. Billy watched the big lady skip down the graveled lane leading to the main parking lot and said, "You make friends everywhere."

Connie followed him back into the kitchen. "Speaking of which. Kari Simmons. Remember her?"

"The *Variety* reporter. Sure."

"We drove up together. We met yesterday for a drink. She wanted to come, but was afraid you'd say no. So I said . . ." Connie's attention was caught by the screenplays piled on the kitchen table. "*Qué demonios?* Billy, what are these?"

"Homework." He walked back over and took the cup from Connie's hand. She did not seem to notice. "Peter sent them."

"Peter Veer? He sent you scripts?"

"By limo."

She sank slowly into Billy's chair. "When?"

"The first batch arrived Thursday. More the day before yesterday."

She took one of the screenplays with a bent cover and flipped through the pages, running her finger down his sidebar notations. "Billy, Billy, Billy, what are you doing?"

"I have no idea."

She used her foot to push out the chair to her right. "How many have you read?"

"Four and a half." He seated himself. "In a week. Out of fourteen. Don't laugh."

"Do I look even the teeniest bit close to humor?" She took another of the wrinkled scripts and slowly turned the pages. Her fingernails were the same color as her eyes. He only noticed this when she began tracing one along his notes, reading slowly. "You're blocking out your part."

"Well, sure."

Connie turned a few more pages, then rose to her feet. "You need to speak with Kari."

"Connie, now really isn't a great time—"

"I wasn't asking." She was already heading for the door. "You just come with me."

When they rounded the cottage, Billy surveyed the red Porsche convertible and said, "I bet you're a terrible driver."

Connie sniffed. "I've never had an accident that counts."

He turned toward the stables. "How many have you caused?"

"I don't stay around long enough to see." She followed

him over and watched as the electric doors opened, revealing the vintage Land Rover. "It suits you."

"Boring and ancient?"

"Dignified and discreet. Shall I drive?"

"Not on your life."

She used her phone to text Kari, and received instructions where to meet. She guided them via her GPS down Ocean Avenue. Billy pulled into a parking space opposite the Castaways restaurant. Connie noticed the grim look he gave the place and said, "It looks very nice. You don't like?"

Billy shook his head. "That place and I have a history."

"How long have you been in Miramar?"

"You know exactly. A week."

"You have been here before, perhaps?"

"First time."

He expected either some sort of snide remark or a series of probing questions. Instead, she waited until he finished parking, then said, "Terrible thing, histories."

Connie remained stationary, which Billy took as the signal to come around and open her door. She slipped one arm around his waist and gripped his nearside elbow. "You're moving very well, Billy."

"Three days and counting without meds. Nights are a trial."

"Because of your injury, or the history?"

He caught a whiff of her perfume. Some exotic spice. It suited her. "You smell great. And you look better."

The moment felt uniquely charged. Walking up Ocean Avenue, taking their time only partly because of his fragile state. Every eye they passed was drawn to her, or perhaps them both. Connie Adler was quite possibly the most beautiful woman he had ever been around. And certainly the sexiest. She held an almost animal allure, a draw that made it almost impossible for Billy to feel sad or wounded or . . . He found himself smiling as they passed a café whose outdoor tables treated them as passing theater. For the moment it was enough to simply relish the closeness of a lovely woman.

Connie nudged him. "*En qué piensas?* Talk to me, Billy Rose."

"I'm glad you came."

She lifted up on her tiptoes, agile as a dancer. High enough to briefly nuzzle his neck. "That is the right answer."

They met Kari Simmons in a diner three blocks up Ocean Avenue from the Castaways restaurant. Their window booth looked out over the sunlit road and an old-fashioned motel whose hand-painted sign advertised newly renovated studio apartments. The *Variety* reporter wore another monochrome outfit, this one of pale lavender. Kari did not even let Connie finish describing Billy's work on the script. "Darling, that's not your job anymore."

"The director will do that for you," Connie said. "*With* you, if he or she is any good. But this work you are doing, Billy, it's what a quality small-time actor does."

"A *supporting* actor," Kari agreed.

Connie extended one arm around his shoulders and drew him closer still. "I may be new to Hollywood, but I'm big in Mexico. Do you understand, Billy?"

"A supporting actor is all I've ever been," he replied.

"That's all behind you now," Connie replied. "What do you want to be now?"

"I'm afraid to say it."

Connie stroked the line where his hair met his neck. "Because it's not just a word anymore, is it?" She felt him shiver, and smiled. And kept stroking. "It's not somebody else they're talking about. Not anymore. Now it is Billy Rose. The man who opens a movie."

Billy found himself needing space to breathe. "Can we please order? I'm starved."

Connie pulled back her arm, but only so she could poke him in the ribs. "Your job is to *listen*."

"Not eat?"

"All right. Yes. You can eat. But only if it doesn't get in the way of job one."

Kari watched the exchange and smiled. But the reporter did not speak again until they had ordered. And then it was to say, "What exactly did Peter's note say? The one with the first batch of scripts."

"Give these a look, let me know your thoughts. Signed with his initials, PV."

"And the second note?"

"Pretty much the same as the first."

"Then it's a test," Kari said.

Connie nodded. "No question."

"But a test of what?"

"That's simple enough." Kari's voice went flat—the sound of a woman who had seen all too many people come and go. People eaten by the Hollywood machine. "Peter is looking for the answer to two questions. First, are you sensitive to what the audience wants? Second, are you happy playing those sort of roles?"

"The roles the audience expects you to play," Connie said. "The roles that they'll pay to see you in."

"Most actors who rise to where you are now see success as an opportunity to thumb their collective noses at the studio executives." Kari's gaze was intent enough to peel away skin. "They go looking for roles that will satisfy the critics. They want to be *challenged*. They want to be *stretched*."

"They want something new and unique," Connie said.

"They sneer at investors," Kari said. "They think going for roles in films that make money is suddenly beneath them."

Billy nodded. "Peter wants to know if I can help him do his job."

"Exactly." Kari leaned back, clearly satisfied with his response. "Here's what you need to do. You read all the scripts. Choose two, maximum three. Call the studio. Ask for an appointment to speak with Peter. Tell his assistant you want to set up a conference call to discuss possible projects."

"I should be taking notes," Billy said.

"I'll help you remember," Connie said.

Kari went on: "When it's time, you talk about the scripts from the standpoint of audience potential. Remember those words, Billy."

"'Audience potential.' Got it."

"Ask who he thinks might be a good director for each project. That's why you need to limit your scripts to two, if possible. Because this isn't going to be a discussion about your role."

"It's the project," Connie said. "Your next hit."

"Say you want to watch other films the director has done. Don't feel pressure to decide on anything. That's not what this conversation is about. Ask who he sees as your co-star . . ."

Billy felt a tightness streak through Connie's body, there and gone in an instant. Fast and potent as a lightning rush.

At that very same moment, a woman walking along the sidewalk froze outside Billy's window. He recognized Yolinda, Mimi's friend. The woman who had fixed the dinner he had not stayed around for. Yolinda was tall enough to stare him straight in the face. She gave him three seconds of frigid disdain. Then she walked on.

The event was strong enough to push him away from the table, the conversation, everything. The meal arrived then, and Billy used it as an excuse to disengage. He ate without tasting. Kari continued talking, but he had trouble focusing. The world became split into two very different segments. The table and their conversation belonged to Hollywood. But there was a distance now. When Connie next spoke, he slipped further away mentally and studied her fully. Her beauty was certainly not an act, nor, he suspected, the sexual magnetism. She *wanted* him, it was as real as the daylight. Even so . . .

Finally Kari stopped talking. He had no idea what she had just said. But he knew she was waiting. Billy wiped his mouth, balled up his napkin, set it on the plate, and said, "I owe you."

Kari nodded. "That's what I wanted to hear."

"Connie said you wanted to interview me."

"Not now, Billy Rose. But soon. You understand?"

"The interview I will never turn down," Billy said. "The exclusive I would never give anyone else. Of course I understand."

She lifted her hand to the passing waitress. "Check, please." As she slid from the booth, she said, "I think it's time I made myself scarce. Where can a girl go for a walk?"

CHAPTER 32

Mimi left her condo early, walked to the studio, and danced until her limbs trembled with exhaustion. She returned to her home, showered, and ate a meal standing by her front window, watching mothers play with their children in the park across the street. As she left Miramar and accelerated down the southern highway, a red Porsche convertible passed her, heading into town. The top was open and Mimi could see two women chattering gaily. The driver was a spectacular beauty, perhaps Latin or some Mediterranean blend. Through her open window Mimi caught a brief conversational snatch of two vivacious ladies talking loudly over the radio and the car's growl. She wondered what it would be like to experience such a moment, when she could feel so open and engaged and excited about life.

Mimi had rarely looked forward to getting away as much as she did that morning. She had slept poorly and woke up angry with herself. She had no reason to feel so sad. It was ridiculous. She had made the right move, for all the right reasons. Billy Rose Walker was a man on the rise, and his trajectory was up, up, and away from Miramar. Her home. Of course they had no future. Of course she needed to break things off.

She was entering San Luis Obispo when her phone rang. Yolinda greeted her by asking, "You want another reason to walk away from that man?"

Mimi waited until she had stopped for a light to say, "Tell me."

"I just spotted that man in the Ocean Avenue Diner. There was this Hollywood glamour queen doing her best to attach herself to his side. You know the type."

Mimi had no idea how long she sat there. Finally a horn beeped from behind. Another. She drove through the intersection and pulled into a parking space. She sat there and listened while Yolinda finished describing the two women eating lunch with Billy.

Mimi found herself certain that the events inside the diner were not as Yolinda assumed—that there was a completely logical reason for Billy to be with those women. And yet . . .

Why on earth did it matter? She and Billy were not an item and never would be. Why should she care?

"You there?"

"You were right to call," Mimi said. It was the proper thing to say.

"You sure?"

"Yes, Yolinda. Thank you. I have to go."

She cut off the motor and just sat there, staring at the sunlight splashed across her windshield. It was supposed to rain later, but the day was fine now. A couple walked the sidewalk past her car, wearing shorts and hiking boots and carrying backpacks. They held hands and chattered happily. Just another couple with time to enjoy a sweet day. Mimi was not the least bit concerned about this woman with Billy.

What upset her was how she couldn't control her feelings. Even now, after getting exactly what she wanted . . .

She missed him. So much.

Mimi drove into San Lu's old town and parked on Monterey. She walked up the street and entered the city's original mission church. The Mission San Luis Obispo de Tolosa dated from 1772, founded by Father Junípero Serra. The interior smelled of incense and wax polish and age. Normally, Mimi found a pew and seated herself and lost all track of time, herself, the coming appointment, it all just drifted away. Today she struggled not to let Billy crowd into the church with her.

Try as she might, however, the day remained fractured. Just like her heart.

Finally she gave in to the fact that her peace was not coming. That she could not clear away such elements and prepare. Instead, Mimi found herself thinking back to the last time she had been seated in a church. The fishermen's chapel in Miramar was much smaller and far more intimate. Even so, the two structures held to a similar heritage, as if the eons of incense and prayer bound them together, sanctuaries which ignored the rush of time and events.

Without warning, Mimi found herself returning to the image she had discovered that night, standing before her front window, leaning over the crib. She did not just recall the moment. She experienced it a second time. Picking up her daughter. Feeling . . .

The sense of being complete and so utterly in love and so totally at peace filled her again.

Finally Mimi blinked, returned to the church, and looked down at her empty hands. She wondered at the mystery that awaited her. The utter certainty that someday she would be holding her baby girl.

It was in this moment when the question came naturally. There was neither room for fear nor anything else. All the barriers to asking about something for herself simply drifted away. As inconsequential as the old incense.

She asked, *Can I have a lifelong love with a man?*

There were so many better ways to ask the question. So much yearning tied up in this tight little bundle of words. She sat in the silent church and felt the moment slip away. Greeted by a silence that was almost welcome after the morning's tumult.

When it was time, she rose and left the church.

CHAPTER 33

❧

Mimi walked the six blocks to the law offices of Sol Feinnes and Associates. Their building was relatively new, but built to resemble the neighboring Spanish-mission structures. Mimi gave her name to the receptionist and settled in an unoccupied corner of their lounge.

The first time she had met Megan Pierce was at Anastasia's funeral. An intense and highly intelligent woman had approached Mimi, introduced herself, and explained that she had represented Anastasia on several legal matters.

The funeral had been as dire an experience as Mimi had feared. As if losing her oldest friend was not enough, Mimi had been forced to endure the cold resentment of Gregor's wife. Long before the church service was over, Mimi decided this would be her final visit to Los Angeles.

Megan had approached her as they were leaving the church. Mimi had found it immensely difficult to connect the woman's words into something coherent. "I don't understand. Anastasia had legal dealings in San Luis Obispo?"

"Some. A few. Of a highly confidential nature."

"She never mentioned anything like that to me. And I live there."

"I'm not at liberty to discuss a client's legal affairs." Megan pointed to the line of cars parked outside the church. "Can I offer you a ride to the cemetery? Unless you'd rather ride with the family . . ."

Megan stopped midsentence when one of Mimi's contacts came up, embraced her, and started talking about how much Anastasia had meant to them, and how sorry she was for Mimi's loss, and how she hoped Mimi would still be available. This had happened a number of times before the service began. And each time Gregor's wife had shot Mimi another of those icy looks.

Mimi waited until her contact walked away, then told the attorney, "I won't be attending the graveside service."

Megan nodded, as if she had expected nothing less. "I need to speak with you at your earliest convenience."

"What about?"

"Anastasia asked me to serve as go-between with regard to your LA clients—"

"Don't call them that. They're not clients."

"How should I refer to them?"

"Anastasia suggested I simply refer to them as contacts. That has always worked well enough for me."

"As you wish." Megan offered her a card. "As per her instructions, I have been in touch with everyone on the list she supplied. I have already received several requests from LA residents who seek your . . . services."

Mimi studied the woman's heavily embossed card. "All right. Yes."

"You agree to my taking on this role?"

"If that's what Anastasia wanted. But I can't pay you. I don't take money from them."

"Anastasia has taken care of all that." Megan offered her a typed sheet. "These are the people who have requested appointments. I would ask that you let me know whenever you are ready to . . . resume your work. You are most welcome to use my firm's small conference room. Unless, of course, you'd rather meet your . . . contacts in your home?"

"No." Mimi found herself drawn to this woman, despite Megan's very formal air and her severe dark suit and the reason why they were speaking at all. "Go ahead and set them up. Tuesdays and Thursdays I have no classes and work on my thesis. Any of those afternoons."

"Very well." Megan started to turn away, then said, "Anastasia was one of the most remarkable women I have ever met. I liked and admired her very much. I will miss our conversations."

Mimi stood and watched the attorney's departure. Several other people stopped to offer condolences and lingering embraces. Mimi scarcely saw them. She thought it was just like Anastasia to arrange such a connection. Especially now, when Mimi's need was greatest.

Two weeks later, after a day filled with multiple appointments, Mimi had returned home to find a letter from her student loan officer, informing her that all debts and accrued interest had been fully repaid.

Mimi had to assume Anastasia had secretly charged these wealthy Angelinos, then sworn them to secrecy. And used this intelligent young lawyer to offer Mimi this helping hand. Just when the lonely void was most intense. And when Mimi had no choice but accept that Anastasia had spent years secretly charging for Mimi's services.

Mimi could almost hear Anastasia laughing.

Megan Pierce came out personally to greet Mimi. That was one of the many things Mimi liked about the attorney, how she treated Mimi like a respected client. A few eyes tracked them as they walked the side aisle past the central bull pen, back to the corner conference room. Mimi had no idea what the other people in Megan's firm thought of these meetings. What mattered was that Megan seemed more than happy with the arrangement.

Normally, Mimi used the smallest of the firm's three conference rooms, a snug little space that held a maximum of eight people. But the internal window showed a collection of young associates in sweat-stained shirts working frantically over open files. Megan said, "We're using the main room today."

"All right." Mimi followed Megan past the senior partner's office. Megan knocked on the neighboring conference room, opened the door, and stepped back. "You know where to find me if you need anything."

"Thank you, Megan." Mimi stepped inside, and smiled with genuine pleasure. "Hello, Peter."

Peter Veer set down his phone, turned over the pad where he had been making notes, and rose to his feet. "Mimi. So good to see you again."

"Didn't Megan tell you I had requested this appointment?"

"Megan never informs me." As always, Peter held her chair and remained standing until she had settled. "It's best I don't know anything in advance."

He was aged somewhere in his late forties or early fifties, and had the buffed and polished look of a Hollywood executive on the rise. What made Peter Veer unique in Mimi's eyes was the manner of his questions. They met every six months or so, and had done for years. She knew he owned a vacation home in Miramar, one inherited from his parents, but not where it was located or how often he visited. The one time he had mentioned it, Mimi had politely insisted that their relationship remain strictly on a professional basis. Peter had never raised the subject again. Nor had he ever suggested they meet anywhere but here.

Peter's reason for visiting with her never changed. His questions were always the same. Could he trust this person? Could he rely on them?

The way Peter spoke took Mimi straight back to that very first experience with Gregor. Sharing her gift with an honest man, who simply sought clarity over a new and possibly risky contact. At least, Mimi amended, she hoped Peter was honest.

Peter wore a sports jacket of some elegant weave, Mimi suspected a blend of silk and linen. Silk T-shirt. Midnight-blue gabardine trousers. Alligator belt and matching loafers. "I'm entering into a make-or-break relationship," Peter said. "With someone I know almost nothing about. Yesterday I finally admitted defeat. I'm so scared, Mimi."

" 'Make-or-break' sounds very serious."

"The stakes could not be higher," he agreed. "For him and for me. I have just been promoted to a new position with the studio. He is my first major find."

The sudden awareness of where all this was headed shot through Mimi like lightning.

"We have a major production this summer that is going to be a complete and utter bomb." If Peter noticed her sudden alarm, he gave no sign. "I've had my eye on this man for over a year. And his new project could be just what we need. But my concerns go far deeper. Because I'm in a position to gain prominence with this move, other members of the executive board are gunning for me. You understand what I'm saying?"

Mimi was unable to respond.

"He is an actor. His latest project is the film I'm planning to use as a counterbalance to the studio's bomb."

Mimi planted both hands on the table. Wanting to shove herself away. If only she could find the strength.

"His name is Billy Rose Walker."

Mimi groaned.

Peter's gaze widened. "You *know* him?"

"Peter, your studio's physical therapist set me up as his trainer."

He studied her with a very worried gaze. "From your expression, I'd say you did more than that."

"Yes. It is . . . was. We're not . . ."

Peter gave her a very tense moment, then asked, "Can we still do this?"

"I don't . . . All right. Yes."

"Is there a risk of bias?"

"I have told a dear friend that their mother is dying. Bias is not the issue."

"With complete honesty," Peter said.

"There is no other way." Mimi reached out. "Give me your hand."

CHAPTER 34

Billy and Connie left the diner and walked along Ocean Avenue, heading down the gentle slope toward the sea. She seemed more than happy to match her stride to his. Her body moved with a liquid grace, lithe as a jungle cat. Every now and then, she rested her head on his shoulder, a brief gesture, just long enough for his senses to be filled by her fragrance.

The message was clear enough. She wanted him. And he . . .

What did he want? Billy had no idea. He could not even tell if the desire he felt was actually his at all.

She asked him the same question as before they entered the diner. "*En qué piensas,* Billy?"

He could not bring himself to discuss her potent allure. "Thank you for bringing Kari. I owe you."

"*Hablas español,* Billy?"

He replied in English, "I get by. Four years in university, then night classes when I first arrived in Los Angeles. I've done some commercials for Telemundo."

The news seemed to cause her to shiver. They walked on a bit before she said, "Ask me to stay."

He stopped, which granted her the chance to move around in front and press herself to him. "Connie . . ."

"Just a few little words, Billy." She held him closer still. "Whisper it. I will hear you."

CHAPTER 35

When Mimi remained silent, Peter repeated his questions. "Can I trust Billy Rose Walker? Can I rely on him?"

This time there was none of her preferred distance. Instead, Mimi was viscerally connected. She was *bound* to this experience.

"Mimi?"

"He is a very good man." The words were drawn out almost against her will. "He is afraid of this change in his professional life. Terrified."

"He should be." Peter's words became clipped. Carved with precise speed by his tension. "Billy is being given a chance to rise from the minor leagues. He *needs* to be afraid. And that does not answer my question."

Mimi felt herself drawn away—from the questions, the Hollywood executive, the conference room. All of it faded into the mist-clad distance. "He is a very honest man."

"Again, that does not . . . Mimi, why are you crying?"

The answer was, Billy had shown her total honesty. He had offered her an open heart. And she . . .

She had run away.

"Mimi, honesty is only a start. Can I rely on him to deliver when it counts?"

She saw . . .

It was her choice. But to come to him, she had to face . . .

The image had only been this clear once before. Only then, when she vividly lived the moment of bending over the crib, she had known such a complete and utter connection to what had not actually happened.

Only this time there was no peace.

The experience threatened to tear her apart. Because to return to Billy, to restore their relationship, to *love* him, meant . . .

"Mimi, *please*."

Mimi opened her eyes. She made no effort to clear her face. "Billy is utterly trustworthy. Whether your project succeeds or not, I cannot say."

Peter leaned forward. "That is not enough."

Mimi closed her eyes. Resigned to what awaited her.

She saw herself walking forward. Billy turned to meet her, then lifted something in his arms. Mimi saw . . .

Billy held a mirror.

If she continued to move forward, she would be forced to see herself. All the elements she had so carefully hidden away. Her entire life of secrets and locked doors, all the tightly guarded elements to her past. Exposed.

When she remained frozen to the spot, Billy turned and walked away. Leaving Miramar. Never returning.

Never, never, never to be hers.

Her one chance. Lost.

"Mimi . . ."

Peter stopped when she shoved back her chair and rose to her feet. "I have to go."

"But you haven't answered me!"

She knew with utter certainty this relationship with Billy

would be her one and only chance to reveal herself. In safety. Otherwise . . .

She would find another man.

One who left because he grew tired of living with her secrets.

Billy offered something else, something she had never thought she might one day want. The chance to be open with another person, to reveal herself, to . . .

To heal.

Billy's love would serve as mirror and shield both. If she let him. The choice was hers.

Mimi said, "I have to go."

CHAPTER 36

When Mimi had covered less than half the distance back to Miramar, a storm swept in from the Pacific. California winter storms were legendary affairs, with wind gusts of hurricane strength and blinding rains.

Many locals had no idea how to drive in bad weather. They fought the storm, grimly determined to hold to their normal speed. Blasts of wind and rain waited in the valleys and punched down from the hills, veering the unwary into the oncoming lane. Mimi slowed to a crawl, and when a parking area came into view, she pulled off entirely.

She used the pause to phone Yolinda. Her friend answered, "What's that noise I hear?"

"The storm hitting my car. I'm on my way back from San Lu and got caught in the middle of it."

"You want the bad news now, or would you rather wait until you're back safe and sound?"

Mimi knew it had to be about Billy. "Tell me."

"The lady I spotted in the diner with that man. Turns out she's this telenovela star up from Mexico."

Mimi stared at the rain striking her windshield. The wind was so strong it shook her car even while stationary. The news only strengthened her certainty that she had to get to Billy before he left. Hearing he had spent the day in another woman's company changed nothing.

"You there?"

"Yes."

"They've been spotted walking Ocean Avenue. The lady had a dead-solid lock on that man's arm."

Still, the news did not touch her. She knew Yolinda was expecting sorrow, outrage, relief, something. But all she could think to say was "Didn't you tell me Billy was staying out on Lighthouse Lane?"

"Girl, did you not hear a word I just said?"

"Of course I did. But there's something . . ."

"I can't think of a single thing that would come from giving that man a piece of your mind. He's *Hollywood*. They make them bulletproof down there."

"Yolinda. Please."

"The answer is yes. He's in that house out on the point. But, Mimi, you listen to me. The best thing you can do just now is come straight here, we'll open a bottle of wine and talk over how good it is you're not—"

"The storm is clearing, I need to go."

It was almost dark by the time she reached Miramar. She drove straight to Lighthouse Point and pulled into the main lot. Hers was the only car, hardly a surprise with weather like this. She parked so that she faced the cottage directly. Then she sat there. Waiting for inspiration, hoping the right words would come to mind. It had seemed so simple during the drive. Arrive here, walk in, tell him not to leave. Tell him . . .

The sky overhead was a whirling mix of slate. The Pacific was a tumbling mess of waves and white froth. She watched a rainband sweep across Miramar, erasing the city from view.

She loved it here so very much. She had never thought she would find a place that suited her, that *welcomed* her. She wondered what it would feel like, to have the same sense of welcoming closeness with a man. The thought was so alien it hurt her heart to even consider such a thing. Mimi sat and stared at the cottage and its blank windows, as confused and uncertain as she had ever been in her entire life.

Then her phone buzzed.

She checked the screen, and the afternoon slipped away. The storm, the cottage, Billy, it all just vanished. There was simply no room for anything else.

CHAPTER 37

❦

Mimi was so captivated by the text message displayed on her phone, she did not notice Billy's approach. Only when his shadow fell upon her window did she look up and give a little gasp. As if the man she had come to see had levitated over.

Mimi rolled down her window. Billy said, "Are you here for me?"

She just looked at him. The tumult in the sky overhead, the storm wreaking havoc in the sea, it was nothing compared to what she felt inside.

"I wasn't sure." He looked out past the lighthouse. "My first day here, I saw you come with a group. I don't know what was happening. But it seemed . . . important."

"It was."

Billy looked at her. "I just . . . You were out here so long, and maybe watching the house. I wanted to come see if you wanted something. From me." He shook his head. "Does that sound as lame to you as it did coming out of my mouth?"

"I need to talk with you."

He seemed resigned to it. "Let me go ahead and get one thing out of the way. I saw your friend Yolinda, when I was with the actress from my last film. It wasn't anything, Mimi. Not for me anyway. She wanted—"

"That's not why I'm here." Even so, Mimi tasted a faint relief. It was good to have him confirm what she had already thought, or sensed, or hoped. Something. "But thank you for telling me."

"Do you want to come inside?"

She rolled up her window and rose slowly from the car. She fumbled with the door and dropped her phone. Billy picked it up and handed it back. "Are you all right?"

"No."

"Is it me?"

The look he gave her chipped another piece from her heart. *A good man brought low* was what she thought. Mimi heard herself say, "I have a problem."

"Can I help?"

"I don't know if anyone can."

The first drops of an incoming shower touched her face. When she remained planted to the spot, he took hold of her elbow and said, "Let's move this inside."

The cottage was as lovely as Mimi had imagined, all those times she passed and wondered how it might be inside. Billy pulled two parlor chairs over next to the rear windows. As if he knew there was nothing she would like more than to watch the storm from this safe haven. "Would you like tea?"

"That would be nice, thank you." She angled her chair so she could both see the rain pelt the glass and watch Billy move about the kitchen. "This is a lovely place."

"It belongs to the studio executive who's giving me my big chance."

Mimi nodded slowly. It all fit together now. Billy staying in Peter's cottage, the way they met, her meeting with the executive today, she could almost hear the crystal clear events chime together, fashioning this very moment. Seated here. With Billy.

His back was to her as he took a teapot from the cabinet. "Would you like milk? Lemon? Honey?"

"Lemon and sugar, if it's not too much trouble."

Billy proved capable of making a tea in the Eastern European style. Another surprise in a day filled with astonishments. He opened a metal tea canister and put a good pinch into the pot. Poured in the steaming water. Set the pot on a wooden tray, then sliced lemon while he let it steep. "Glass or ceramic mug?"

"You have tea glasses?"

"Not me. But this place is a full-service operation." He opened another cabinet and pulled out two glass cups with sides etched in some royal emblem.

"How is it you know the proper way of serving tea?"

"My grandmother. Ada Rose made hers with sassafras and licorice." He placed the cups on matching glass saucers. Container filled with brown and white sugar cubes. Tiny sugar forceps. Tea strainer. Matching silver spoons. He picked up a small coffee table and placed it between their chairs. He set the tray on the table, then poured two cups of tea through the strainer. Added lemon and sugar. Stirred. Settled back and turned to the windswept rain rushing over the glass. Waiting.

Mimi managed, "There is so much I need to say, I don't know . . . I can't."

"It gets all clogged up inside," Billy said to the glass door. "Until anything you try to speak feels wrong."

"How are you knowing this?"

Billy pointed to the scripts sprawled over the dining table behind them. Then said, "That's for later, okay? I'll tell you. But not now."

She nodded. Sipped.

"Why don't you just tell me the first thing that comes to mind. We'll start there and see where it takes us."

The image popped into her head the instant he spoke. "The dinner at Yolinda's. When you met me on the porch and then left. You heard us talking about you."

"I did. Yes. Two women and a man."

"Yolinda's brother and his wife."

"He doesn't like me."

"It's not . . . Yes. All right. He does not trust actors. But that's not what was really behind what you heard."

"They care for you. They want to protect you from people like me."

She heard the resignation in his voice, and knew this was the right place to start. "I need to tell you something about myself."

CHAPTER 38

❧

"I have been hearing things," Mimi began. "Or receiving messages. Impressions. None of the words fit. All of them do. A little."

Mimi took the phone from her purse and sat holding it against her thigh. The message she had received carried such portent she had no choice but to share her secrets. At least a few. So here she sat, across from this incredibly handsome man, and spoke about what had shattered her two previous attempts at love.

"It started when I was fourteen. I've been doing this ever since."

Billy asked, "Doing what, exactly?"

"There is no *exact*. If it was *exact*, I wouldn't have such trouble telling you."

His response surprised her in a day and evening and night that had been knit together by the unexpected. Billy sipped his tea. Watched her across the table. "This is very hard for you. Telling me."

She nodded. "Terrible."

"If it helps any, know this. I have already accepted what you're trying to tell me. I believe you. And I'm grateful that you'd even try."

The words came in a rush then. As if she had waited all her life for a man to say just exactly that. "People come to me with problems. I give them insights. Sometimes."

"Not always?"

She shook her head. "Sometimes I only hear . . . silence. And other times it's not what they want to hear. Whether I help them or not when the news is unwelcome, I have no idea. I try not to have contact with these people afterwards."

He nodded. As if it all made sense. "That was what Connor and his wife were talking about. You helped them?"

"Yes. Sylvie gave birth yesterday. Twin boys." She rubbed the phone up and down her leg. "The first day we met. At the studio. You asked me out."

He recalled, "You touched my hand."

"I wanted to know if you were . . . ."

"Safe," he finished. "Good for you."

"Afterward, I felt like I had lied to you. I didn't hear anything. But it still felt wrong."

Billy rose and walked to the fireplace. He hit a switch and gas flames began flickering. Only then did Mimi realize the room had taken on a wintry chill. He asked, "More tea?"

"Yes, please."

He took cups and teapot back to the kitchen alcove. He poured fresh water into the kettle, and said with his back to her, "So people ask you a question. You touch them."

"Sometimes I touch. Not always. Usually, they come with a question. Not always. Delon, that's Yolinda's brother, he's had a health issue."

"Delon is the man who doesn't like me."

"I can't believe I'm telling you all this."

"Are you hungry, Mimi?"

"I couldn't possibly eat anything."

"When was your last meal?"

"I don't . . . Breakfast."

"Maybe food would be a good idea." When she did not object further, Billy pulled out a loaf of sourdough bread and various items from the fridge.

Mimi rose from the table and walked over. The L-shaped kitchen was separated from the rest of the room by a granite-topped island. Mimi leaned against the polished stone, her hand clenching the phone. "I don't understand how you can be so calm about all this."

Billy glanced over, studied her face, then went back to making sandwiches.

"Aren't you going to tell me all this is impossible? How I have to be completely unhinged to even suggest such a thing?"

He continued slicing the loaf, then set four pieces in the toaster. "This bread is two days old. I'm going to heat it up a little."

"Isn't that what you're thinking? That I'm being delusional? That I've completely left reality behind?"

He watched the toaster, not her. "Those are other guys talking, Mimi. Not me."

"That's it?" She watched him pop out the bread, put in another four pieces. "You believe what I'm saying?"

He spread mayonnaise on two slices, coarse French mustard on the others. "Back where I come from, a lot of the families have attended the same church for generations. Some of the remote valleys still hold to the old ways. They're often called foot washers. Communion services start with all the parishioners washing the feet of the person next to them. Hard-shell Baptists, that's another name you hear. Hidebound. Outsiders dearly love to heap scorn on traditions they don't understand."

His accent had strengthened, the first time she had ever

heard a hint of his country upbringing. She found it endear-
ing, how it surfaced now. Him not meeting her gaze, his motions smooth and somehow comforting. Slicing more bread
and slipping them into the toaster. Making sandwiches she
could not possibly eat.

"Most of these hill clans and their churches, they have one
or two elders called diviners. The ones you hear about down
in the lowlands, they use divining rods to hunt out water. In
the churches, though, they serve a lot of other roles. Truth
tellers, they're the most common. A few are healers as well.
In valleys where the nearest doctor is two or three hours'
drive, these healers play a vital role. They spend a lifetime
learning about what roots and herbs can be used to help with
the healing process."

She watched him prepare sandwiches with bean sprouts,
crumbly goat cheese, and slices of vine tomatoes. He pulled
cloth napkins from a drawer, cut the sandwiches in half, set
them on the cutting board, and then slid it over between
them. "*Bon appétit.*"

Mimi shifted closer to him. Forced herself to release her
grip on the phone. Took a bite. "These are delicious."

They ate in companionable silence. Night fully blanketed
the windows now. The wind and lashing rain buffeted the
glass facing the Pacific. Crashing waves formed a muted rush
of sound. Mimi finished one half, picked up another, and
said, "The woman who raised you."

"Ada Rose. My grandmother."

"She was a diviner?"

"She never let anyone call her that." Billy selected another
portion. "She said it was too lofty a term for what she did."

"How did . . ."

"Ada was always partial to her teas. She and her guests
would share a pot. Then if they asked, she would read the
leaves at the bottom of their cup. Sometimes. Not always."

"She never charged?"

Billy shook his head. "The thought of taking money was obscene to my Ada."

Mimi found her throat suddenly constricting. She forced down a final bite. Set down the remnants of her sandwich. Drank her tea. "Thank you, Billy. This was delicious."

"No more?"

"No." She took a hard breath. "There's something I need to tell you."

"Can it wait? You look exhausted."

"Not this."

And then she told him about Peter. Because he needed to know. Not the details of what she had seen revealed. That would only come later. She knew at some point she would share that as well. Just now, however, he needed to hear what Peter had asked about him. Billy Rose Walker. The man Peter Veer desperately wanted to trust.

He remained motionless throughout that final chapter. Almost as though he had managed the feat of not breathing for such a long time. Or perhaps the unseen storm was capable of breathing for him as well. When she was done, he walked to the rear windows. He stood for a long moment, staring at his rain-splintered reflection, rocking back and forth, heel to toe.

Finally he said, "You need to call Peter."

She nodded. In the midst of her telling, she had come to the same decision.

"Tomorrow would be best. It's too late now."

"I'll do it."

"Thank you for trusting me with this." He faced her fully. "Do you want to talk more?"

"No. But I need to."

"Not for me, you don't."

"Billy, I need to explain . . ."

"We both have a lot that needs explaining. Soon. But right now, the most important thing has already happened. You coming in and sitting down and talking with me. From the heart. Everything else can wait." Billy walked to the central table and picked up his keys. "If you're half as tired as you look, you should let me drive you home."

CHAPTER 39

❧

The only time Mimi spoke during the drive was to offer directions. Billy was more than comfortable with the silence. The news she had just delivered required some quiet work on his part. Hearing that Peter Veer was one of her contacts, as she called them, had certainly been a shock. Just the same, he felt a definite sense of calm. Perhaps even stronger than that. A genuine feeling of rightness. Doing this. Driving her home. After the most intimate conversation Billy had known for quite some time.

She rode with the phone clenched between her two hands. The streetlights revealed features creased with strain and exhaustion both. He knew some mystery was about to come out. He could sense her desire to talk. But he was not going to ask. Something this big needed to come naturally. When she was ready. Or not at all.

She directed him down a narrow side street that fronted a large city park. The wind was strong enough to blow the swing sets in crazy patterns. Billy parked and cut the motor and turned to Mimi. Waiting.

She lifted her hands and stared at the phone. Rain spackled the front windshield, turning the streetlight into a liquid prism that creased her face. "This is going to sound crazy."

"No, it won't." When she did not say anything, he added, "Are you okay?"

"No, Billy, I'm not." She released one hand and rubbed her forehead. "I'm so scared."

"What can I do to help?"

She looked at him. Her gaze as liquid as the light. "I don't want to be alone tonight. But I'm not . . ."

He held up his hand. "You're asking me to be a friend."

She might have shed a tear. Or perhaps it was just a shadow from the rain. She whispered, "Yes."

"Say no more." He opened his door and started around the car, walking slowly. He felt the day's weight now. Still, it felt good to be moving without aid. And even better to be there for her.

As they started up the front walk, she asked, "Are you sure you're okay with this?"

"Absolutely." It was the last thing they said as she led him into the building's central corridor and unlocked her door. Her unit was trim and neat and precisely laid out, just as he would have expected. Artwork he did not recognize adorned the living-room walls. "You have a lovely home."

"Thank you." She pulled the drapes, shutting out the night. "The bathroom is off the hall to your right."

When he returned, she had made up the sofa with sheets and pillow and a lavender blanket. She picked up the phone from where she had set it on the parlor table, resumed her two-handed grip, and said, "Thank you, Billy. So much."

"Sleep well, Mimi." He waited as she went around, cutting off the lights. When the door to her bedroom closed, he stripped down to his boxers and stretched out. He found himself smiling at the ceiling, listening to her prepare for bed. Thinking about this incredible day, and how it had changed his state of mind.

Billy found himself comparing his present situation to his life in the big city. The best way to describe the ladies he had known in LA was, confusing. They had been sweet enough, at least starting out. Sweet and easy and, well, dangerous was the word that came to mind as he closed his eyes. They could shift from magnetic to man-eating in the space of a single breath. He had come to assume any LA relationship of his would follow the same big-city cycle, leaving him not so much heartsore as empty.

Billy sighed once and shut his eyes. There was a singular pleasure to be found in the word that carried him off to sleep:

Friends.

The next thing Billy knew, the front door opened and a voice he instantly recognized as belonging to Yolinda called, "You ready, hon?"

He heard footsteps rush across the front room. "You go on without me."

Sometime during the night, Billy had burrowed down where the cushions met the sofa's back. His head was partly covered and the blanket was up almost to eye level. Billy figured it was as good a place as any to play like a rock.

A long pause, then, "Girl, what on earth? Is that . . ."

"I can explain. But not now. I'm running late."

"Will you stop pushing me? I know where your front door is."

"You go ahead. Tell everyone I'll be there soon."

"Well, just give me one second so I can pick my chin up off the floor."

Billy waited until the door closed, then pried himself free of the sofa and sat up. "Well, that was awkward."

She was dressed in bright red tights and matching hair band, with a sweatshirt that read U OF SAN LU. Billy thought she looked utterly delectable.

Mimi said, "I overslept."

"That makes two of us." Then he realized, "Wow."

"What?"

"No nightmare." He rubbed his face. "What time is it?"

"Half past nine. I'm due to teach a class in fifteen minutes."

"Give me three minutes and I'll drive you."

"I can walk."

"I'd really like to do this, Mimi." He gathered up his clothes and headed as fast as his body allowed for the bathroom. When he returned, unshaven but moving better, he found a steaming go-cup planted on the front table. Billy picked it up and followed her from the apartment. Once in the ride, he took a long sip, again, then said, "You look rested."

"Someday I will tell you what it meant, knowing you were there with me." She waited until he had turned onto Ocean Avenue to ask, "You've been having nightmares?"

"Yes. And, yes, I want to talk about them. But not now. First things first."

She nodded, understanding. "My problem."

"Right." He didn't speak again until he pulled up in front of the studio. "How does your day look?"

"A half-hour break after this, then another class. Another half hour. Then . . . You remember when you saw me on the point?"

"Of course."

"They asked me to take them out again this afternoon. I used to do it every weekend with the students. Now it's down to once a month. But this is a new thing, taking adults. I said yes."

"Mimi."

"What?"

He hesitated, then shook his head. The words were not there. "Nothing. Go teach your class."

CHAPTER 40

※

Billy drove home and called Abril, catching the masseuse just as she was leaving for their appointment. The woman seemed genuinely thrilled to learn he needed to cancel the day's appointment. Only after he cut the connection did Billy realize she probably assumed it had to do with Connie. From where he stood, the previous morning's events seemed years ago.

He did a brief stretching routine, showered, dressed, and made a double portion of his morning smoothie. He drank half, the second half went into Mimi's go-cup. He started to leave the cottage, then picked up the top four unread scripts.

Billy arrived back at the studio and reached for the first screenplay. The news that Peter Veer had approached Mimi with questions about him had a surprising effect. He found himself calmed by how Peter was so deeply concerned. He and the executive responsible for lifting his career shared a mutual fear of the unknown, both of the future and what role the other might play. Billy opened the script's cover, read the first page, and stopped because . . .

He felt weightless.

This was the first time in his entire professional career that Billy had not viewed a script in desperation. Always before, there on the pages resided either his next role or his next rejection.

A few minutes of screen time, a larger role in a low-budget film, a one-episode gig in an ongoing series: His job was always the same. He was paid to play off the main character, strengthen the primary action or emotion or both. He was there to burnish someone else's star.

Not today.

Billy resumed reading. Turning the pages was like watching a flower unfold. Over and over, he lifted his gaze and struggled to absorb this new reality.

The lead role was his.

If he wanted it.

Forty minutes later, Mimi emerged from the studio carrying a towel and a shoulder bag. She did not sweat so much as glisten. She smiled and spoke to an older woman who followed her from the door. When Mimi slipped inside the Land Rover, Billy offered her the go-cup. "I thought maybe you could use a smoothie."

She wiped her face with the towel, sipped, and said, "Perfect."

"Would you like to go somewhere?"

"Just away from here." She took another sip. Yolinda chose that moment to emerge from the studio and shoot him a stink eye. Mimi gave no sign she noticed. "I need to talk with you about something."

"Sure thing."

They did not speak again until Billy found a space on the park's opposite side from Mimi's condo. The day had warmed up, so he rolled down all the windows before cutting the motor.

Mimi started in immediately, as if she had been waiting for this precise moment. "My father died when I was eight. My mother . . . died later. I had a sister. We were separated when I was nine and she was four. I came to America. I've never heard from her since."

Billy watched her lean over and pull the phone from her bag. Mimi went on, saying, "I come from near Donetsk, the capital of eastern Ukraine and the center of the current conflict with Russia. You have heard of this civil war, yes?"

Billy nodded, but did not speak. He found himself utterly fascinated by how Mimi did not release any emotion whatsoever with the words. Her voice remained so calm it sounded almost toneless. But the flat manner of speech was not so much a lie as her only means of maintaining control. He watched her and thought that Mimi had spent her entire life living this role. Hiding away a passion and a fire so deep it threatened to consume her if she ever let it out.

"When the real war started, people began disappearing on a regular basis. Soon after, several websites started up. Places where families could post pictures and ask for information. I used one called *Znykli Osoby*, Missing Persons." The act of speaking the name in her mother tongue brought out a sharper accent, a tragic tone. "But many such chat rooms have become places where people gather and wail. Then last year a new app began to gather momentum. It's called *Stina*, or Wall. Like after nine/eleven, when people taped photographs on fences and walls lining New York's downtown streets. Only this has a second meaning. Project Wall is a plan to build a fortified barrier along Ukraine's border with Russia, an attempt to halt the flow of fighters and arms coming in from the east. Here, you can see."

Her hands trembled as she scrolled. Billy leaned over, but made no move to take the phone. He doubted he could unclench Mimi's grip with a crowbar. He found himself looking at a child's face, one with the faintest resemblance to the woman seated next to him. "This is your sister?"

"Zofia. Yes. Is her. My only photo."

The child was smiling broadly enough to show a missing baby tooth. Her hair was much lighter than Mimi's, but held the same reddish tints. The photo was supposedly taped to a wire barrier, with something written in Cyrillic script above and below. An e-mail address followed. "Someone contacted you?"

"Not someone. My sister."

"When?"

"Yesterday. While I was waiting in the storm."

"Outside the cottage. When you didn't come in." Billy watched her stare at the phone's screen. He had a hundred different responses, but none of them fit the moment. Finally he said, "Mimi, it's time."

She lifted her gaze. "What?"

"Your class starts in five minutes." He gave that a beat. "I could go and cancel for you—"

"No, no. I should . . ."

He nodded. Started the motor. Drove her back to the studio. He let her off, then returned to the same spot there by the park. He pulled the next script off the pile in the backseat, but he did not open it. After a few minutes he rolled up the windows and rose from the car. He crossed the park, reveling in the simple pleasure of moving fairly easily. He selected a bench partially shaded by a pair of imperial palms. He watched parents and young children play at the park's far side, their cries and chatter creating a happy background music to his day.

The day was warming to where he slipped off his sweatshirt and tucked it under the script. Usually, a heavy rain in LA granted the city a day of relatively clean air, two at the outside. But it was never like this, when every leaf and blade of grass held a jewel-like beauty. The air was perfumed by a hundred different fragrances. The brown overcast haze that overshadowed so many LA afternoons was little more than a myth. It did not belong here.

He opened the script and read about a third. By the end of act one, he knew this was not a role he wanted to take on. It was the first time he had ever been able to set down a screenplay for this reason. He took a pen from his pocket and made notes on the cover, while the thoughts and emotions were still fresh. Just in case Peter asked.

Which brought him back to the matter at hand.

Billy had known his response to Mimi's crisis before she finished speaking. The question was not what to do, at least as far as he was concerned.

When it was time, he returned to the car and drove to the diner for take-out sandwiches and juice. He was back in front of the studio when the class broke up.

This time Yolinda was the first to emerge from the studio. She observed him standing by the front fender, and gave a tight little "hmm-umm" as she stepped to one side. She crossed her arms and waited. Billy saw no need to speak at all. When Mimi emerged, Billy opened her door. She walked straight over and settled into the leather seat. "Thank you, Billy."

"Well, I never," Yolinda said.

Billy had rolled all the windows back down. As he settled back behind the wheel, he heard Mimi ask Yolinda, "Are you coming this afternoon?"

"Is that all you've got to say for yourself?"

"I told you I can explain." Mimi's voice had resumed its steady ease. Her previous tension was gone. "But not until you're ready to listen."

"Wait until Delon hears about this." Yolinda hitched up her shoulder bag and turned away.

Billy drove them back to the park. He unwrapped Mimi's sandwich, then his own. "Apple or orange juice, I bought both."

"Apple, please." She let them eat for a time in silence. Then, "Do you have anything you want to say about . . . this morning?"

"That's not the question you should be asking." Billy bundled up the second half of his sandwich and set it aside. He couldn't eat and discuss this issue. "At least, not yet."

She took her cue from his actions and handed him the un-eaten portion of her meal. After he bagged that with his own, she said, "What comes first?"

"Are you sure you want my advice?" When she remained silent, he pressed, "Do you want me involved beyond just being here for you?"

"I don't . . ."

He nodded. "There's every reason for you to want to keep a distance between me and this issue. If you want me to be your friend, your support, and nothing further, that's okay."

She studied him with those amazing autumn eyes. "It really is, isn't it? Okay."

"Yes. I want to be involved. Very much. You are hurting, and it pains me to see you in this state . . ."

Billy stopped because Mimi reached over and touched his face. A soft caress, almost as gentle as the light in her gaze.

Once she dropped her hand, he said, "It has to be your choice, Mimi."

She nodded slowly. "I need to try and work this through myself."

He was genuinely disappointed, but all he said was "I under-stand."

"Do you, Billy? Do you really?"

"She's your sister. She's a part of your life before all this. It is a separate world from this and from me . . ." He stopped because she was shaking her head. "What?"

"This is *my* sister. *I* need to resolve this. *Me.* It's how I've always worked. It's how I survive. Handling things *alone.*"

This time he actually meant it. "I understand."

When she went silent and turned to face the front windshield, Billy decided to give her some space. He rose from the car and took another circuit of the park. The day was gentle, the light so strong he could feel it in his bones. The air that filled his chest carried a spark of something he could not identify. Perhaps it was nothing more than the simple pleasure of living a good day. But he hoped it was something more. Something permanent. Something . . .

Billy saw Mimi rise from the car and walk over. She graced him with the same gift as before, a gentle touch to his cheek. "Thank you, Billy."

He thought it was silly, how the words were not there. Him, an actor and all. But just then, it was all he could do to nod.

Mimi took his hand. "I need to be going out to the point. I like to be there before the others arrive."

They walked back to the car together. As Billy drove, she gave a fuller account of what was about to happen. How it had started with students, how adults were now involved, how good it made her feel to help. Billy entered the lighthouse parking lot and pulled into a space well removed from the cottage. He wanted a clear separation of this meeting on the meadow and his temporary home.

Then he spotted a trio of cars pulling into the lot. "Here they come." When she reached for the door handle, he said, "Mimi, wait."

"Yes?"

Asking such a simple question should not have raked his throat and chest like it did. "Can I come, too?"

CHAPTER 41

The onshore wind was strong enough for the ocean's chill to defy the afternoon heat. Mimi pulled a knit cap from her shoulder bag and slipped it over her head. She could still feel the drying sweat from her sessions, and welcomed the breeze. She watched Billy rise from the Land Rover, and knew his slowness was not just down to his injuries. She had no idea how she felt about his accompanying them. She knew he had lost his parents sometime during his childhood, but had no idea if that was why he felt a need to walk out now. Then she turned away and greeted Adela, the school principal, and another couple who had also come the previous weekend.

Then it was Yolinda's turn. "You sure are full of surprises."

"Anyone who feels the need is welcome to join us." Mimi lifted her voice. "Everyone, this is Billy."

Yolinda waited until they started walking across the meadow to say, "I guess you don't want to hear what Delon thinks."

Mimi stepped away from her friend.

They stopped at the mowed-grass boundary. Ahead of them, the waist-high meadow weaved and shimmered in the breeze. Here and there, uncut flowers winked in the crystal light. There were eighteen gathered with her today. Mimi stood on the right of the group, well separated from Billy. When they all were gathered, Mimi said, "The young people who join me here have renamed this place Cape Farewell. I hope it is because they have found an opportunity to say their good-byes and return to a future that is not controlled by loss. We do not seek to end our connection to those who are no longer with us. Our aim is to be free to shape a future where past wounds do not hold the power to hold us back . . ."

Mimi stopped speaking when Billy leaned over. At first, she feared the day had been too much, and his injuries had suddenly flared up again. He stood there, his forearms clenched together by his chest, bent so far his face was aimed at his ankles. Adela was standing next to Billy. The principal reached over and rested her hand on his shoulder. Waiting and watching as he took a long, shuddering breath and slowly straightened. The expression on his face, the pain that creased him from hairline to collar, touched Mimi deeply.

Then she noticed Yolinda.

Her closest friend stared at Billy, her lips pursed slightly, her forehead bunched in a concentrated effort to . . . what? See him anew? Accept that they had him wrong? Whatever the reason, Mimi found herself ready to continue, "Our aim here today is to offer a farewell, not to the lost ones, but to the chains that bind us to a past that is no more. To free us to move into the future on our own terms."

She had no idea where the words came from, only that they felt right. Mimi took a step back, signaling that it was time for others to have their say. One by one, they moved forward, some alone, a few as couples, and spoke words she did not bother to hear. Many of them spoke so softly they could not be heard at all.

Billy never spoke.

When it was time, she finished as she always did. "Thank you for coming. Go in peace."

Billy moved straight from the point to his vehicle. He slipped behind the wheel and sat watching as Mimi hugged any number of the people and said her farewells. Yolinda was the last to approach Mimi. She glanced at Billy, a look hard as agate. But Mimi halted whatever her friend wanted to say by punching the air between them with an open hand. The gesture was so sharp it backed Yolinda up a pace. She retreated, but said something in parting that Billy did not need to hear. He turned away and stared out to where the point met the sea and air. The wind was stronger now, mashing the meadow into tight nervous shivers. He could hear the rush and roar of waves striking the rocks down below. Now that it was over, he wished he could take it all back. Drop Mimi off, let her meet her pals and do whatever she felt was right out there on the point. He should have just taken the final two scripts back inside, settle down at the kitchen table, and keep doing what he was supposed to do here. Heal. Prepare for whatever came next. Not this. Not sitting here feeling like his actions had formed talons that tore at wounds he had carried his entire life.

Mimi settled into the passenger seat, ignoring how Yolinda shot Billy another hard look before turning away. Mimi asked, "Will you take me home, please?"

"No problem."

That was the last they spoke until Billy reached Ocean Avenue, when Mimi asked, "Are you all right?"

Billy had no idea how to respond, so he stayed silent.

"No, of course you're not." She turned slightly. "Do you want to talk about it?"

He was definitely not, but the lid had been pried off now.

And her question was all it took for him to release: "I've got this line about my folks. I've been using it so long, it's automatic."

"Your parents died when you were six," Mimi recalled.

"It's probably a lie. I have no idea. What I do know is, when I was six, they left on just another gig. I was old enough to make a lot of noise, which I did. It had been building for a while by then. Tell the truth, I don't recall it very clearly. What I do remember was how angry and hurt and terrified they made me, every time they went off like that."

Mimi's response was silent and very small, a tight little series of gestures. She sighed, shook her head slightly, and covered her eyes with one hand. But it was enough to fill his face with the flame of fresh memories, and almost choke off his air. He would have stopped if he could. Just let the silence build and the emotions boil. But there was more that had to be said. He had no choice.

"I knew they were leaving because of how *happy* my mother became." Speaking the word "happy" clenched his throat tighter still. "She sang little snatches, a line or two from whatever song was going inside her head. She sort of skipped around the house. For days. This time I started screaming at her that same instant. Up until that point I'd sort of saved up my rage for when they were leaving. Not this time. Screaming at them. Demanding they take me along. Throwing things. Yelling until my throat felt torn apart. It scared her. I could see that. But she didn't say yes. Which only made me angrier."

He could see her now. The way she had stared at him. Standing in the doorway to his bedroom the night before they left. The hallway light cut her into a silhouette. She had stopped singing earlier that day. Because every time she started in, even the slightest hum, he leapt on it. Tearing the air in their home with his screams. That night, while his mother stood in the doorway watching, Billy lay in his bed and sobbed. Because he knew it hadn't worked, and they were leaving, and he was powerless to do anything about it.

Billy could not see her clearly, but he knew Mimi was watching him. Waiting. He did his best to clear his throat. "They left the next morning. Just got in the car and drove away. My father was a gentle giant, silent in the way of a lot of hill-country men. He drove and did not look at me. I ran alongside my mother's window, screaming and begging. Then they were gone."

Mimi said, "They didn't die?"

"I have no idea. Whenever I asked, Ada always said they'd had an accident and they weren't coming home. And I needed to accept that and move on. But every now and then . . ."

"Yes? What?"

"She always met the postman, it was one of her unchanging daily habits. Whatever else Ada had going on, she was standing by the mailbox out where our drive met the rural road. Every now and then, I'd see her slip a letter into her apron pocket. If she opened those letters and read them, I never saw. Whenever I asked, she'd just say it was none of my concern. Ada was a great one for her secrets."

"Oh, Billy."

The rest was so easy to say then. He had already gone so far. Billy said, "I used to have these dreams of my mother singing. They were the worst nights of all when I was a kid. And now they're back."

"Since when?"

"They started again the night after the accident. I've had them every night since then. The hour before dawn. I never see her. But . . . they're getting worse. At least they did. Until last night."

"She didn't sing to you last night?"

He shook his head. "I've been wondering if it's her at all. I'm beginning to think it's a warning. Or pressure to resolve something. Or not make a mistake like they did . . . Tell the truth, I have no idea what it's about."

"You want me to help." Mimi did not frame it as a question.

"Can you? Will you?"

"The 'can' is impossible to say. Either it happens or it doesn't. I have no more control over this than I do if I make a call and someone answers or they don't." She turned in her seat so her knees were pointed at him. "If I can, of course I will. I want to help you."

He nodded, wishing he could tell her what it meant to hear that. To not have to face whatever this was alone any longer. Instead, he said, "I don't remember how they looked. My only clear images are shaped by album covers. They made four with Columbia. I remember the photographs. My mother's always out front, smiling and happy like she was before heading out on the road. My dad's always half-hidden behind the drum set."

"It is a wonder to me that you like music at all."

"What can I say? It's in my bones."

Still, Mimi did not make any move to depart. "I am thinking you do not want to be alone tonight any more than I do."

"You got that right."

"What would you like to do?" She hesitated, then said, "What I mean to say is . . ."

"The cottage has a small guest room."

"I'm sure it will be fine." She reached for the door. "I won't be long."

CHAPTER 42

⁓

When Mimi returned to the Land Rover, she wore pale blue cotton trousers that might have been designed to look like jeans, only these were formfitting and far too stylish to be denim. Over this, she wore an off-the-shoulder linen top one shade darker than her skin. Billy had an apology ready, and started the instant she closed her door. "I'm so sorry. I shouldn't . . ." He stopped because she gave him the same sort of sharp open-palmed motion she had used on Yolinda. "What?"

"You think only one friend at a time can have problems? You think you must wait until all of my situation is perfect, and then you talk? Is that it?"

"Mimi . . . well, sort of."

She crossed her arms. "Really, Billy? Really?"

"Okay, so maybe I didn't—"

"Did it ever occur to you that I might feel concerned over discussing my private life with you? Private things I have never shared with anyone? Like a contact who came to me for help? Or my sister reaching out to me after all these years?"

Billy said what he had been thinking since she first revealed the crisis. "I don't think it's your sister."

Mimi glared at him. Then, "Are we all done with this apology nonsense? Yes? Good?" She turned to the front windshield. "I'm ready to go now."

They stopped for takeout at a Chinese restaurant Mimi knew on the way back to the point. When Billy asked her what she wanted to eat, her only response was a sad, "Whatever." Billy figured she had resumed worrying over her sister and her next steps. He felt an increasing certainty over what needed doing, but she needed to ask him. She needed to be ready to listen.

He ordered a duck and a lamb and a beef and a veggie, probably double what they would eat. Then he stepped to one side and glanced through the restaurant's front window. Mimi sat motionless in the Land Rover. He could feel the pressure growing. He wanted to talk through her crisis issue. Give her his take on the situation. Get things moving. But he couldn't. The balance between what he wanted to say and do, and how he remained standing there beneath a poster of the Hong Kong harbor, it was like fitting himself into a new role. One that required him to step away from the person Billy Rose Walker had been since starting his professional career, doing whatever it took to climb the next rung. This particular role required him to stay silent. Be patient. Let Mimi remain in control. It might not have been the hardest role he had ever taken on. But it came close.

They returned to the cottage in silence. But once he began unpacking their meal, Mimi showed delight over his choices. "I always get the same thing. Cashew chicken. What is this?"

"Tibetan lamb."

"And this?"

"Mongolian beef strips. And this is duck, and the last one here is spicy tofu."

"How do you know about all these dishes?"

"Los Angeles is home to more great restaurants than any place on earth." Then he saw how naming the city brought back the faint pale wash of sorrow to her gaze, so he finished with the observation "I guess I was born curious."

She took birdlike portions of everything. And loved it all. The pleasure of good food drew her further into the evening. She asked him about growing up in the Carolina hill country, which led him to describe his early fascination with film. "A trip to the big city happened every few weeks."

"Big city?"

"Asheville. Little blip on your map. But coming out of the Blue Ridge valleys, it was just one step shy of New York. Ada would deposit me at the mall with enough money for two films and a food court meal. It was my idea of heaven. I'd spend the days before every trip deciding which movies I wanted to see."

"You had favorites, yes?"

"Dozens. More. Hundreds. If she was gone long enough, I'd sit through a new favorite twice, then sneak my food into the next one. Six hours camped in the cinema. Heaven." Billy rose from the table and began wrapping up the remaining food and storing it in the fridge. "*Back to the Future*. I saw the revival of it half-a-dozen times. *Chariots of Fire*—I never saw that in the cinema, but every time it came on the television I was right there, hooked. *ET, Raiders, Steel Magnolias, Breakfast Club*, those were my favorites from the eighties. From the nineties."

He stopped because Mimi had become withdrawn once more. "What's wrong?"

"They are all just names. I've seen a few. Not many. The family I lived with . . . they had no interest in Hollywood."

He resumed his place by the table. "That seems strange, living in LA."

"We were part of the Polish and Ukrainian communities. You'd have to sit through one of their gatherings to understand. Gregor, the father, ran a high-end home supply business. We're talking two hundred thousand dollars for a closet. Quarter of a million dollars for a bathroom. The adults would sit together and listen to Gregor describe the homes where he worked. Russian money, they called it. There was no greater insult, as far as they were concerned. These film people spend money like the Russians. They wanted nothing to do with that world."

When she went quiet, Billy decided to probe gently. "This family where you lived, did they have kids?"

"Two. A daughter three years older, a son two years younger. They took cues from their mother and treated me as competition for their father's attention. They . . ." Mimi blinked. "I don't want to talk about them anymore."

"Fine by me."

She shook herself, like coming out of a bad dream. Then, "Was there a film that had the biggest influence on you growing up?"

"Not one. Five or six. A few more."

"Like what? Tell me one."

The first name that came to mind: "*The Big Chill.* William Hurt, Kevin Kline, Glenn Close . . . what?"

"I never saw it."

"I don't remember how old I was the first time I watched it. But I remember . . ."

"Tell me."

"It was just another night in front of the television. Cable and satellite came late to our world. Ada paid for it because it meant so much to me. I don't remember her watching much of anything." He leaned back, captivated by the memory. "The description in the paper sounded so lame. A group of college friends gather after spending years apart for a funeral. I only watched it because there wasn't anything else I hadn't seen like a hundred and fifty times."

"It held you."

"It *changed* me. When it was over, I told Ada I knew what I wanted to do with the rest of my life." Billy pointed to the television set in the wall above the fireplace. "Would you like to watch it with me?"

CHAPTER 43

~∞~

Sunday morning Mimi woke to the gray wash of dawn. She had taken the lower bunk, which allowed her to look up and watch the sky gradually brighten. The window was a small square cut into the opposite wall. Mimi thought back over the previous night. How lovely it had been to sit there with Billy as the film unfolded. She had been deeply moved by the story. But now, in the growing dawn light, she found it hard to separate out her feelings about the film from . . .

How she was coming to feel about Billy.

She had watched him from time to time, seen how captivated he had remained from the opening credits to the soundtrack's final refrain. She had felt his passion for the story, the actors, and the world they created there on the screen. She tasted the yearning he had for his world, the desire that almost consumed him. To be that good. To do what they had done. Create art that defied time and space.

Be a star.

And then it was over. She thanked him and she said how glad she was to have seen it with him for the first time. Billy had offered her a shy smile and said watching it with her had made the experience almost as powerful as the first time. All those years ago.

They had stood up and cleared the last bits from the table, and he had started the dishwasher and turned off the fire. And then . . .

He had led her into the guest room, asked her to choose a bunk, brought sheets and pillowcases from the linen closet, then checked to make sure the bathroom had everything she needed. He had left and returned with a Lakers T-shirt. Then he had offered her a good night, and shut the door.

Friends.

Mimi had never before slept in a bunk bed. She found the room's confines very charming. With the ocean's constant rush and the tang of salt in the cottage air, she could easily imagine herself on a ship. Briefly anchored high atop this rocky atoll. Ready at any moment to break free and plow its way through the Pacific.

Mimi rose from the bed and padded barefoot into the kitchen. She had packed pajamas, but slept in Billy's T-shirt. She tasted the air and knew there was no reason to call his name. Billy was not there.

She filled the kettle and pulled a cup and tea bag from the cabinets. As she waited for the water to boil, she stepped to the side window and saw . . .

Billy stood far out on the point, almost but not quite at the cliff's edge. A dawn wind blew strong from the south, so Billy had taken shelter on the lighthouse's lee side. Even so, the high grass whipped nervously around his legs. He stared out to sea, motionless.

Billy had still not moved when the kettle's whistle drew Mimi back to the stove. She filled her mug, added sugar and a trace of milk, then returned to the window.

Billy was still there.

She could see a trace of her own reflection there in the glass, like the dawn was intent upon joining them whether she liked it or not. She saw . . .

She had been so wrong about him. The fears she had used to separate them had little to do with the man, and everything to do with her.

When Mimi finally turned away, she knew precisely what she needed to do.

Mimi refilled her mug and carried it back into the bedroom. The windowless guest bath was scarcely the size of a closet, but was fitted out with shipboard precision. Mimi showered and dressed and finished her tea, intent now on the coming task. She heard Billy moving about the front parlor, so she took her phone back into the bathroom, placing a second door between them.

She obtained the studio's main number from information. When a man answered, she said, "Could you please pass a message to Peter Veer? It's urgent."

"Ma'am, it's seven o'clock on a Sunday morning."

"He will want to receive this as soon as possible," she replied.

"Are you absolutely certain it can't wait?"

"Yes. Positive."

There was a long pause, then, "I guess I can send him a text."

"He will thank you."

"All right. Go ahead."

"This is Mimi Janic." She spelled her last name. "Tell him I have the answer to his question."

CHAPTER 44

There was no space in her room for a chair, just a padded bench built into the wall beside the bunk's headboard. She was seated there, watching daylight strengthen beyond her porthole-sized window, when Peter called back.

"Yes, Mimi."

"I have the answers you need regarding Billy Rose."

"The ones I *need*."

"Yes."

"Go on, then."

"I cannot say whether you or your films or Billy will be successful."

"You told me that before. I understand. There are too many variables."

"What I do know is this. Billy will remain honest and committed throughout your time together. He will give you . . ." Her throat caught up then, silencing her.

Peter was sharp. Impatient. "Go on, Mimi. What else?"

"You can rely on him to give you the absolute best he has to give."

"Is that it?"

"No. Two things more. He will give you trust for trust."

Peter's exhale was strong enough to rattle her speaker. "And second?"

It was Mimi's turn to release a hard breath. "He knows that you have asked me about him."

"Mimi, wait, what?"

"Trust for trust," she repeated. "Billy had to know."

Mimi ended the call and entered into the living room. Billy was standing by the rear doors, cradling a cup of coffee. When she appeared, he turned around and revealed a hollow gaze. "I've been outside."

"I saw."

"That dream woke me again this morning."

"About your mother."

"My mother's song," he corrected, then sighed. "Letting go is very hard."

She wanted to rush to him, but she only got as far as the cabinet by the fridge, where she set down her mug and got a firm hold on her emotions. She said carefully, "I told you I want to help and I will. If there's no response to your questions, you will at least know I'm there. But right now, there is something else."

"Your sister," Billy said, nodding. "Or whoever it is."

"Yes." She walked over and seated herself at the dining table. "Will you tell me what you think I should do?"

Only when he was done, and they had talked through what he thought the necessary next steps should be, did Mimi allow herself to do what she had wanted from the very instant she had opened the bedroom door. She rose and walked over and molded herself to him.

Billy embraced her, still holding his mug. "Is that a yes?"

She could smell the sea in his shirt. And the coffee. And

the male scent of his body. She rubbed her face back and forth across his chest. Gradually accepting this was real. Her emotions. The day. Her needs.

"Mimi?"

The answer was that she had no idea whether he was right or not. But she was absolutely certain that she could not move forward alone. Nor did she want to. For the first time in her life, being private and safe behind her walls was not enough. She needed to trust him to do this for her. Then she corrected herself, *with* her.

Mimi said to his chest, "Let's do this."

What she thought was, *Together.*

CHAPTER 45

❧

They did not leave Miramar until almost eleven. Once Mimi phoned Peter Veer back and set up the meeting, there was no rush. Peter's afternoon was already booked solid with a preview of the studio's latest film. Peter suggested they meet that evening at the Hyatt in Westlake, a town in north Los Angeles County, about forty-five minutes from the studio.

Billy packed his one case, stored the scripts back in their original two boxes, then locked the cottage and set the alarms. He locked the empty garage, then followed Mimi as she drove her own car back to town. Billy watched the cottage vanish in his rearview mirror. It had certainly not been the stay he had expected. Or come close to what he would have described as a good time away. Just the same, when he joined the main road into Miramar, he was filled with a certainty of new beginnings. Good ones.

When they arrived at Mimi's condo, he told her, "You might want to think medium term."

"What does that mean?"

"Pack for winter and bring your passport," he said. "Just in case."

She stood there a long moment, then said, "I need to let the school know I could be away next week. And the studio."

"Probably best not to tell Yolinda I'm involved." Billy thought it was a poor excuse for a joke, but all he could come up with at the moment.

Even so, she rewarded him with a tiny smile. "Why don't you come inside and make us lunch."

While she was in the bedroom, Billy connected with Expedia on his phone and booked them two rooms at the Hyatt Regency Westlake. He then prepared a just-in-case meal of everything that might spoil, laying out all the ingredients on the counter, for her to mix and match. He boiled the three eggs he found in the fridge, and sliced a block of aged cheddar. He rinsed and chopped lettuce and tomato and olives. Blackberries and strawberries and one lone pear went into a separate bowl. He found no bread, so he spread three different kinds of crackers on a plate. Mimi came in wearing a midnight-blue skirt and gray silk blouse. Both bore the creases of having spent a long time on a shelf. "You look lovely."

They ate in companionable silence. Mimi spoke only twice. Once to compliment him on the meal, then to ask if she should respond to the message board.

Billy asked, "What have you said so far?"

"Nothing. But an automatic alert will have told her I've seen the message."

"Have you heard anything more?"

She nodded. "Twice she has asked me to respond."

"Then it's probably time."

"What should I say?"

"Keep it simple. It's good to hear from her. You will be in touch very soon. Like that."

Billy filled the dishwasher and wiped down the counter. He watched her type, then shake her head, swipe her message away, then type again. "It's done."

He carried her case out to the Land Rover and headed south. Five miles outside Miramar, her phone buzzed. Mimi read the screen, then spent a long time staring out her side window. Billy did not press. Whatever she had read stained her features.

They were almost to Santa Barbara when she said, "Zofia has responded. She says she is very sick. Leukemia."

Billy saw no need to respond.

When they joined the oceanfront highway south of Rincon Point, Mimi said, "You think this confirms that it's not her, don't you?"

"It could be just a coincidence. But, yeah, I think it's looking like a scam." Billy liked the pauses inserted into this discussion. He could feel her tension. But none of this was directed at him. Billy sensed she was moving slowly in his direction. Coming to terms with what he suspected was a lie. So he waited until they had left the coastal route and were passing the Long Beach port to say, "Anyone with a public face these days is hit pretty constantly with frauds. I'm not all that well known, and still it happens to me at least once a month. Sometimes it's a video of me saying things I've never spoken. Usually, I'm spouting politics or bad-mouthing somebody. Others show a shot of my face wearing someone else's body, usually nude. But the most frequent are people requesting money for an urgent operation. And invitations to appear in films being shot in Nigeria, promising huge sums, if only I'll first make a small investment in the project."

They passed the first Oxnard exit before she said, "But I'm nobody. I have no, repeat *no*, fame whatsoever. I live an extremely private life. My case is totally different."

Billy waited until they were climbing the ridgeline marking the LA county boundary to reply, "You could be right."

The Los Angeles sprawl was viscerally connected to all the northern county's satellite towns. But as far as the occupants were concerned, Thousand Oaks and Westlake Village were a universe apart. The two cities had merged into one, and shared a very distinct vibe. They were landlocked, separated from Malibu on the coast by a state park and some very rugged hills. Only three roads cut through to the beaches, none of them particularly good. Billy had visited the towns on a number of occasions. A lot of the behind-the-camera crew lived in one or the other. Housing was reasonable, the streets were safe, people were a lot friendlier than farther south. Billy had often thought of living there, once he was not on permanent call for last-minute auditions. Rush-hour traffic could turn the commute into a nightmare journey lasting up to three hours. Which was another reason why house prices stayed relatively low. For film technicians whose world was not dictated by the nine-to-five clock, the Oaks was a great place to call home.

The Hyatt Regency was a relatively new hotel, adjacent to the upscale Westlake Plaza and built to service the burgeoning high-tech industries growing north of LA. The lobby was enormous, with vaguely suggested divisions where the reception area ended and the bar began, and beyond that the restaurant. They arrived forty-five minutes before the meeting was scheduled to begin. They checked in and were assigned rooms on the tenth floor. Mimi insisted on paying for her room. As they walked to the elevators, Mimi asked, "How should we do this?"

"It's your sister," Billy said. "I need to be careful not to overstep my boundaries."

She watched the light ping up the floors. "I have no idea what to do or say. This is so far from anything I would ever expect . . . Tell me how you think this should go."

"Then I'd suggest you let me meet with Peter alone. Give him a chance to vent. Once he's done, I'll share a quick overview of your situation. Let him decide whether or not he wants to help. If he says no, there's no need for you to be involved. You and I can have a nice meal somewhere, go home tomorrow, and work up a different plan."

"Together."

"I'm not leaving you alone, unless you want me to."

"I don't. Not now, not . . ."

She didn't finish the thought, but it was still enough to have him smiling as the elevator doors opened. Billy checked the numbers. "I'm down to the right."

"Ten eleven. I'm the other way." But she remained where she was. "Peter has come to me for help any number of times. I've never asked him for anything. Well, unless . . ."

"What?"

"I suspect Anastasia charged all the high-powered people she brought to me. I don't know. I've never asked. But all my student debts were paid off, no explanation or even where the money came from. Same for the deposit on my condominium."

"I'm sorry, who?"

"Anastasia was my closest friend through my teenage years."

"Well, if it wasn't her, then you might have a mystery financier."

"Maybe. Both payments came through the same lawyer who's arranged all these meetings . . ." Mimi used the hand not holding her case and waved that away. Later. "Peter can't refuse."

"He can, and he very well might. What I'm suggesting means taking this to a completely different level. For my plan to work, he'll need to involve the studio. There are a dozen different reasons why he could say it's not possible for him to do what we want." He could see the news worried her. "Meet you downstairs in half an hour?"

CHAPTER 46

⥈

Billy stood just outside the hotel entrance, watching the evening crowd come and go. The air carried a heavy burden of city smells. It was nowhere as intense as in the summer months. But just the same, each breath reminded him that he was no longer in Miramar. He watched a stretch limo arrive, then six young women piled out, all of them wearing little gold crowns and screaming their laughter and carrying empty champagne glasses. Then a dark gray Porsche Panamera pulled up with Peter Veer behind the wheel. Billy thought the car perfectly suited the studio exec. Expensive and powerful, but very discreet by LA standards. Peter handed the bellhop his keys and a bill and walked over. Stopped about ten feet away. Stern to the point of very real anger. "Mimi should not have told you."

Billy nodded. "If I was in your position, I'd feel the same. But I'm glad she did."

"Why did she?"

"It's hard to explain."

"You understand, though."

"I think I do."

Peter studied him a long moment. Finally he said, "Trust for trust."

"That's it exactly."

Peter remained where he was a while longer. Then he seemed to reach a decision, and said, "Let's go inside."

They found a table in the bar's far corner, a quiet alcove between the main area and the hotel's restaurant. Peter ordered an espresso and mineral water. Billy said he'd take the same. And waited. Finally Peter said, "Did Mimi tell you about this morning's conversation?"

"Only that she called you."

"Nothing else?"

"No, Peter. That's all I needed to know."

"You didn't *need* to know *anything*."

Billy saw no need to respond. The waitress returned with their coffees. When she departed, Peter asked, "Is she here?"

"Yes. I asked her to let me speak with you alone first."

Peter did not strike Billy as a nervous man. Even so, he fiddled with his spoon, twisted the little cup on its saucer, adjusted the mineral water on its coaster. "All right. I'm listening."

"Mimi has a problem. It's serious. She needs our help. Yours and mine."

Peter tasted his coffee. "I had hoped today's meeting was about future projects."

"That's part of why I wanted to speak with you first. I agree to whatever you want me to do next. Your terms."

"What's that supposed to mean?"

"Whatever it takes for us to shake on this and move on." Billy liked how his words caused Peter to become utterly still. Showing the same intent and focus the executive had revealed on set. "There are a couple of the scripts I like a lot.

And three others I really don't want to do. But none of that matters. Well, it does, but . . ."

"You love her."

Billy shook his head. Not at Peter's words. At discussing that first with the studio executive. "That's for later. First things first."

"Mimi's problem is that serious?"

"It could be. If I'm right. And if we don't help her."

Peter nodded. "All right. I'm listening."

"Thank you, Peter." Billy rose from the table. "It's time for Mimi to join us."

A hotel conference finished as Billy brought Mimi over to their table. Peter's greeting was muted, reserved, very European. Mimi responded in kind. The rising din that filled the bar kept him from hearing everything they said, but Billy could see Peter was not at all pleased. Billy stood apart until Peter resumed his seat and gestured for Billy to join them.

The noise and laughter did not touch their table. Neither Mimi nor Peter showed any awareness of the others now crowded into the bar and spilling into the main lobby area. Billy talked because Mimi asked him to. She did not shrink away, nor did she show any remorse. Gradually her resigned silence eased Peter away from his irritation. When Billy finished relating what he knew about Mimi's early years, which was very little, and the new alert on the missing-persons website, Peter declared, "It's not your sister."

"I agree," Billy said.

"How long has it been since you last heard from her?"

"Almost twenty years," Mimi replied. "I was nine, almost ten. Zofia was four."

"The odds that it's her are infinitesimal," Peter said.

"Plus, there is the risk of criminal involvement," Billy said.

"In Ukraine?" Peter shook his head. "It's a near certainty. Hackers have most likely infiltrated the missing-persons site and are trolling for victims. Give them half a chance and they would drain your resources down to the last penny."

Billy could see how Peter's flat certainty pained her. He reached over and took Mimi's hand. Her fingers were limp, icy.

Peter studied their linked hands, and much of the strain he had brought with him eased from his features. "It looks like we're going to be here awhile. Let's move into the restaurant, I haven't eaten since breakfast. You two go ahead, I need to make a couple of calls."

It was after ten before the planning session ended. That was how Peter referred to their time in the restaurant. An executive-level strategy session that required coordinating with international allies.

Mimi was mildly surprised at her own reaction. She spoke little and ate less, and mostly observed as these two men became intimately involved in her lifetime secrets. It was clear from the outset they saw this as an operation intended to keep her safe, to protect her from becoming a victim of online predators. Several times Billy stopped and tried to reassure her that if they were wrong—if it was her sister—nothing they set in motion would harm her or get in the way of their reunion. Peter simply sat through these exchanges, impatiently waiting to get back to the matters at hand.

After their plates had been cleared away, Billy bought three pads in the hotel gift-shop, and they became busy making lists and structuring a timeline. At one point Mimi objected, "I don't like how fast everything is going."

Both men stopped instantly. She studied their faces for any sign of impatience or irritation. What she found was . . .

Peter halted in the middle of a text and set the phone face-down on the table. Billy stopped writing, leaned back, and said, "Timing could be important."

"Crucial," Peter said.

"That is, if we're right and this is a scam."

"It is," Peter said. "It has to be."

Billy went on, "If we give them time to identify you, and they learn you have money . . ."

"A home, a good job, a car," Peter said. "To them, you're rich."

"They would start working on a strategy to milk you for every dollar they can possibly get from you," Billy said.

"Fake hospital bills, urgent calls for further treatment, the only way they can save your sister's life—"

"Stop, please, both of you. Just stop."

They did not move. Billy and Peter were joined together now, watching her with the same grave expression. Billy told her, "We could be totally wrong, Mimi."

"You don't need to keep saying that, either."

He nodded. "Say we're right. At this point, they've just sent out a feeler. They don't know who you are."

"Once they do," Peter said, "once you respond, then it really starts."

"So our best chance of discovering who they genuinely are is if we move fast."

"What we're planning is all about using Billy to shield you," Peter said. "That was his idea, and I must say it's brilliant. You remain protected. As far as these hackers are concerned, our moves stay hidden. They won't have any idea you're present or involved until it's too late for them to hide."

"But only if we move fast," Billy said. "It gives us a chance to find out the truth. It's the only way I could see to do this safely."

"Billy's idea is a good one," Peter repeated.

She nodded. "All right."

Billy did not move. "You're sure?"

"Yes. What you say . . . Go ahead. Do this."

Friends.

Chapter 47

❧

The evening's lone argument came when Peter started booking their travel. He insisted on doing it, as only he could access the studio's executive portal. Which meant they were traveling on the studio's dime. Billy clearly did not like this. And Peter knew it.

Maybe it was because they were all getting tired. Or maybe it was just Peter's way of getting back at Billy. But he evidently took pleasure in rubbing it in. "You ever flown first-class before?"

"I'm not going first-class."

"Only thing better is a private jet, and we can't spring for that. Yet."

"It's not happening."

"Buckle up, kiddo. It's the only way my people will take you seriously. They have to see you being a star."

"Peter, no."

Peter actually smiled. "You'll get used to it. And then you'll become just another spoiled star we have to pamper so we can watch you act out a role you'd kill for right now."

"Back to the matter at hand," Billy said. "I'll pay. How much will it cost?"

"You don't want to know."

"I don't want any of this. But if I need to, I'm paying."

"Eight grand. Give or take."

Billy was aghast. "Eight thousand dollars?"

"Actually, it's double that. Sixteen thou. Because since we're introducing you to our international team, it's vital that your . . ."

"Associate."

"It will be expected that your so-called associate shares your perks and star status."

Mimi said, "I'll pay."

Both men said, "No."

Peter said, "This is all going to be viewed and expensed out as a promotional exercise. If anyone at this end asks, which they probably won't, I'll say we're using this relatively small market as a test of Billy's ability. Not to mention how Billy's latest release made Ukraine's top ten money-making films for the year. We have to keep this in the framework they'll expect. Which means first-class all the way."

"But not me," Mimi protested.

"I'm paying your way," Peter said. "Personally."

They both said, "No."

"You can't," Mimi said.

"That's the price of my assistance," Peter replied. "Do we have a deal?" He halted further protest with an upraised hand. "In all the time we've known one another, you have never asked for anything."

"I've never *wanted* anything."

"Let me do this, Mimi. Please." When he saw she was weakening, he signed the bill and said to Billy, "I can't believe I've just had this conversation with an actor. I should have everything arranged by ten. You'll need to come into the studio for a final prep tomorrow morning. Just Billy. Mimi, it's best you stay out of sight for the moment."

"Whatever you say."

He rose from the table. "Walk me out, Mimi."

The temperature had dropped twenty degrees while they were inside. The night carried a wintry edge, sharpened by a strong wind blowing from the north. A dozen or so other people stood in three distinct groups, all of them sheltering as close to the hotel entrance as possible. Mimi waited while Peter asked for his car to be brought around. She stepped out far enough to be exposed to the wind and could no longer hear the other conversations. Whatever Peter had to say, she wanted it to remain private. She expected some form of final condemnation, how she was still wrong to have told Billy. How she had breached a very important confidentiality. Just because the rules were unspoken and unwritten did not make them any less vital. She certainly deserved whatever he intended to say. Even if it was the right thing to have done, she had broken Peter's trust. Mimi watched his approach, determined to accept whatever he felt needed saying.

Peter stopped beside her and turned to the night. "I don't like what you did, but I understand why you did it."

"Peter . . . really?"

"Partly, at least." He gave that a beat, then said, "What you told me over the phone. About being able to rely on Billy. This was real?"

"Yes. Peter. As real as real can be."

"Personal feelings and bias do not enter into this."

She liked how he did not pose it as a question. Instead, he simply asked for her to confirm what he had already accepted. "I am coming to know him at least a little. And I can say this with utter conviction. You can trust him with your professional future. With your projects. And with more, besides."

He looked at her then. The cool gray gaze had a pro's ability to probe deep. "As in, with your heart?"

She nodded.

His car pulled up and the attendant got out, holding Peter's door. He walked over, tipped the attendant, then slipped behind the wheel. "I'm glad you two have found each other."

"Thank you, Peter. So am I. Very glad."

He tapped the wheel twice. Thinking. He must have reached a decision, because he looked up and said, "Tell Billy that according to his present contract, he owes us a sequel to our current project, and his payment is peanuts. I'm shredding that deal. While he's away, my team will prepare a new three-film contract."

Mimi found herself unable to respond.

Peter liked her silence enough to smile. He started the car, then added, "Tell him my intention will be to make our newest star very happy."

CHAPTER 48

❧

They flew Lufthansa to Frankfurt the next day.

The LAX first-class lounge was very nice, a large area shared by half-a-dozen international carriers, quiet and nicely appointed and sectioned into semiprivate spaces. Mimi followed Billy to a window alcove, dropped her jacket and carry-on, then returned to the front room for coffee and a sandwich she probably would not eat. She had not seen him since breakfast that morning. Billy had been collected by a studio limo at half past eight, the same limo that brought her to the airport four hours later. Billy was there at the check-in, waiting for her, wearing an expression that said the morning had left him exhausted and somewhat stressed. She wanted to know what happened. She wanted to offer him the sort of thanks a man deserved for doing everything he could to help her. But just then, she was simply too over-whelmed by everything that waited for her. Tomorrow.

Their window overlooked departure gates and six waiting planes. Down below, airport staff pulled luggage out of one carrier and loaded baggage into another. Metal containers holding meals and supplies were elevated up and slipped into side doors. The sun was trapped behind a brownish veil of smog. She watched the silent scene and wondered at how little it had mattered, returning to Los Angeles. As if she had not spent almost a decade vowing never to set foot in the city again. She still disliked the place. But . . . what? Mimi sipped her coffee and tried to sort through her confusion. The city was the same. The smog, the stressed people, the glitz rubbing shoulders with the blue-collar workers who serviced their make-believe world. Nothing had changed. Except for Mimi herself. She was not different so much as immune.

Billy shifted in his chair. "Can I ask you something?"

"Of course."

He set down his mug. "It's about your . . . I don't know what to call it."

"Anastasia wanted to call it my 'gift.' I hated that word."

"What about calling it your 'ability'?"

She shrugged. "That works as well as any, I suppose."

"Okay. Have you tried to use this ability of yours to determine whether it's really your sister?"

She shook her head. "In all the years I've only had two times when a question of my own was actually answered."

"So, what if I asked?"

"It's still a question about me, Billy."

"Can we at least try?"

"I suppose. If you want."

"What do I do?"

"Ask your question."

"Just like that?"

"If there is an answer, that's all it usually takes."

"Okay." He took a breath. "This person who contacted you. Is it . . . I can't remember her name."

"Zofia."

"Right. Is it your sister, Zofia, who sent you the alert on the message board?"

"Give me your hand." It was nice taking hold. Nicer still to see the tense concern on his face. For her. Still, "No, Billy. Nothing."

"Sorry." Reluctantly he released her hand and rose to his feet. "They just called our flight."

The Lufthansa first-class seats were angled slightly and sectioned off by carpeted partitions that divided each place into a miniature cubby. She liked the privacy, but she was sorry not to be able to speak with Billy. Even though he was seated directly to her right, she had to rise from her seat and sort of hang her chin on the partition to be close to him. Which she wanted. Very much. And clearly he felt the same. Because following a delicious meal of lamb and various fresh vegetables, he rose up high enough to ask, "Are you sleepy?"

"Tired. But not ready to close my eyes."

"Same here. Why don't we take our coffee at the bar?"

It was such a civilized way to fly, seated on a stool facing a small curved bar with a polished granite surface. There were open bottles of white wine and champagne in a glistening bucket, a line of liquors behind the bar. A flight hostess brought their coffees and then departed. The jet's constant rush formed a perfect baffle. Even when another couple claimed the bar's opposite corner, everything she said to Billy remained private. This was very good, because soon as the flight attendant left, she said, "I want to tell you something."

"All right."

Actually, the truth was, she needed to tell him. The words came in what probably was a confusing rush. The question she had posed in the church, the utter silence, then that night, the image of her daughter, the sensation . . .

The questions.

Billy was utterly unmoved. He waited until he was certain

she had finished, then said, "I'm going to get another coffee. You want anything?"

She shook her head. When he returned, he took up station around the bar's corner, so as to watch her over the rim of his cup. "I wonder if this will someday get boring. If I'll take first class for granted."

"Is that all you have to say?"

"No." He set down his cup very deliberately. "But I'm not sure now is the time to take this further."

"I need to know what you're thinking."

"Do you? Are you certain? You've already got so much on your plate—"

"Billy. Tell me. Please."

"Okay." But he was smiling. Both serious and holding a real spark in his gaze at the same time. "Because if you're sure you want to know . . ."

"I'm not going to beg."

"You don't need to. But, Mimi, what you're saying is, we have a baby."

"*But* you're *not there.*"

"So? Mimi, were you sad?"

"No. The opposite. I was complete."

He shrugged his utter lack of concern. "There's your answer."

"I have no idea what you are talking about."

"If it was bad, you know, the reason why I wasn't with you, how would you feel?"

The answer was, she'd be devastated. Already she knew that much—even when the word "love" remained this unspoken whisper at the back of her head, hidden in the recesses of her heart. "I'd be sad."

"You see? So I wasn't there, and you were with our daughter." His smile grew broader still. "Man, you don't know, you can't imagine what that feels like."

She could. But she didn't want to have that force bind them together even more. Not yet. "Tell me."

"Say we're still in Miramar. Together. Say this change in my career is real. So, what does that mean? Not for us. For our future. You understand what I'm saying?"

"Not really, no."

"You can't travel and be on set when you're pregnant. I mean, you could, but why bother? I work fourteen-hour days, it's a totally disrupted schedule depending on whether we're shooting day or night scenes. I get up. I work out. I do my takes. I come back. I eat and I crash. Those are my days during a shoot. It's boring and exasperating and exciting and wonderful, all those things. But the last thing I'd ever want, the very last thing, is to have to worry about you and our baby being there with me."

The way he said it, "our baby," so matter-of-fact, brought shivers. "I think I understand."

"You know what I've been thinking about since we met Peter? How I've never had a home of my own. I was raised by my grandmother. After university I traveled around for three years, crashed on a Brooklyn floor for nine months, shared an apartment in Queens with seven other actors. Then, once I started getting gigs, I moved out to LA and started all over again. And then I landed in Miramar."

The shivers made it hard to say: "We were talking about my baby. And me being alone."

"We still are. And it's not alone *permanently*. It's you being alone for *that night*. You said it yourself. You felt 'complete.' That word is so beautiful, Mimi, it makes me want . . . I wish I could hold you."

She watched her hand reach over and settle on his. Wondering if he could feel the tremors, little quakes that were mostly down below the surface. Where it mattered most.

* * *

They landed in Frankfurt to a dismal gray late afternoon. They collected their luggage and followed the signs to the Hilton. Every exit they passed blasted Billy with frigid air that tasted metallic.

The hotel receptionist accepted their passports, zipped them through her little machine, then handed them back with two mini-folders holding their keys. "You are already signed in, Mr. Walker. Unfortunately, we were unable to follow your instructions exactly. Our hotel does not have suites with two bedrooms."

"Good grief."

Her smile slipped. *"Bitte?"*

Mimi stepped up beside him. "Please excuse Mr. Walker. We're both exhausted."

"But of course." She wrote the room numbers on their card holders. "Mr. Walker, your gold key opens the doors to your living room, the white key unlocks your bedroom door from the hall. Ms. Janic, your room is adjacent. You would perhaps like a suite key as well, Ms. Janic?"

"Please. Living room only."

"Certainly." She ran off another plastic key. Then she reached below the counter and came up with two thick manila envelopes. "These were left for you."

One envelope bore Billy's name, the other hers. Underneath both names was the handwritten word, *Itinerary.* "Thank you."

He followed Mimi to the elevators. They did not speak again until Billy unlocked the suite's door and he said, "Would you get a load of this."

The living room was large and functional. Two sofas, chairs, coffee table, huge flat-screen TV, dining table, kitchenette, counter stools. And flowers. Four vases full. And the champagne in an ice bucket. And the trays. One of sliced fruit, another of cheese, and a third of sandwiches.

Mimi pulled her suitcase inside, dropped her purse on the coffee table, opened her file, then read its contents. "We are booked out on a flight tomorrow evening at six."

"We already knew that."

She leafed through the other pages, then dropped the sheets onto the table by her purse. Mimi walked to the windows flanking the opposite wall and stood staring out at the bustling airport.

Billy watched her take a double-armed grip of her middle and knew it was time to remain where he was, silent and waiting for whatever came next. It did not take a genius-level intellect to say the woman had something on her mind.

After a time she said, "It is so hard to let go."

He recognized his own words. Billy rubbed his face, trying to clear away the jet lag and pay attention. "Who are we talking about here?"

"Me. You said the words about your own mother, I know. But they were meant for me, too." She shook her head, her gaze locked on the window as a jetliner rushed in for a landing. "This is another element binding us together. You and I. A most unwelcome element, Billy. A portion of my most secret life. Something from the darkest corner of my past."

Billy pulled out one of the counter stools and seated himself. He waited.

"So very hard," she murmured. Billy had the sensation of watching Mimi untie a knot inside herself. Trembling slightly from the strain. "After my father died, my mother spent every waking hour searching for him. She drove to Pervomaisk, day after day after day, pestering the hospital and the police and the city officials. Anyone and everyone. She demanded answers. She screamed in their faces. I know, because when she could not find someone to mind us, she took us along. Locking us in the car. Making us sit there for hours while she rushed from one building to another. Waiting outside the hospital and police station. Then pouncing. People reached the point of knowing her car and running away as fast as they could whenever they spotted her parked outside their building."

She took a long breath. Billy watched her shut her eyes. Lost now to the telling. "When I tasted the air here, I remembered something that hasn't been part of me, not for years and years. I remember the taste of snow, bitter and tight and burning my hands and face. Mama dragging us out to the car. Both of us pleading for her not to take us. But she wasn't listening. We would drive and drive, and then she would leave us. For hours and hours, long enough for the air in the car to become frigid, the windows frosting over from our breaths. Zofia was three and didn't understand. I tried to keep her warm all through that winter. It was so cold, waiting there while my mother ran back and forth in the snow. I remember the sound of her footsteps, scrunching through the ice. Zofia was not a child who cried. I think even at three she knew it would make no difference. But she whimpered when the cold bit her face and her fingers. I would take off her shoes and her gloves and rub them. I remember sticking her toes in my mouth to try and keep them warm. I remember the taste of her. I remember . . ."

The power of her confession robbed him of everything. Even air seemed hard to find. Billy felt the cold that wracked her frame. He heard her say, "There were neighbors, Poles whose son was involved in politics. The division between those in western Ukraine who wanted to bind their nation to the West, and those in the east who were patriotic to Russia, you cannot imagine the hatred, the rage, the danger."

She went quiet for a time, long enough for Billy to think perhaps the telling was over, that it was time for him to rise and walk over and try to find some way to show her what it meant that she would be so open. So trusting. Then she said, "I have dreams, too. One in particular. It still comes to me from that time. I dream of a house on fire. I remember it now, like I have fallen asleep and I'm seeing it anew, the memory is so clear. That winter the paramilitary forces burned down our neighbors' house at night and killed everyone inside. People said it was because of the son being involved in politics. Five children, the youngest was my very best friend. I slept through it all. When I learned about their deaths, I felt so guilty. Everyone who came to the funeral, they told my mother she should take it as a warning. If she kept searching for her husband, if she kept demanding answers that would never come, they would burn down our house as well. But they didn't. They simply made her disappear. Just like Papa."

"Oh, Mimi."

"We were alone for three days, trapped inside by a terrible storm. When the snows passed, I walked to people who had remained my mother's friends even when most everyone else had given up on her. It was too dangerous for the others to stay in touch. They, too, had families." She turned toward him, but Billy doubted she saw much of anything. "I have spent years hating her for leaving us alone. Treating the man who was already dead as more important than her two daughters. She abandoned us. She . . ."

"I'm so sorry."

"She wasn't looking for my father. I know that now. She was searching for a way to join him. Her life was over. She just wanted to find someone who would finish the deed."

Billy walked over and took her in his arms. He felt her great wracking tremors, like she was sobbing. But she made no sound and there were no tears. Billy held her so tight it felt as if he was doing his best to breathe for her.

"I can't be crying. Shed tears for my mother? Impossible. For my sister, for myself, yes, all right. I will cry for us. I've spent years secretly weeping over what happened to us. Perhaps I should let them out now. Perhaps . . ." Mimi broke free of his arms and made her way around the sofa. "I must sleep. Tomorrow . . ." She seemed to have trouble taking hold of her purse and case. "Good night, Billy. Sleep for both of us."

He was still standing there long after the door clicked shut.

CHAPTER 49

❧

Billy was brought to full alert by yet another dream of his mother's voice. Singing some song he actually didn't remember. At least, not until he was up and dressed in gym shorts and sleeveless sweatshirt and running shoes, taking the concrete stairs down nine flights, getting the blood flowing nicely. Then it hit him. The song was "Hard to Say I'm Sorry," which took Chicago to number one in 1982. This was interesting for a lot of reasons, mostly how his mother had never sung rock and roll. Jazz, blues, swing crossover. Never rock. Billy stopped for a coffee from the urn set up in the hotel lobby and drank it while watching a sleety snow fall outside the front windows. He entered the gym and pushed through a workout hard enough to banish the morning's melody.

When he returned upstairs, a white-jacketed waiter was knocking on his suite's main doors. Billy hung back as a woman he did not recognize opened the door. Inside, he saw three or four people moving around and speaking in what sounded like at least a couple of different languages, neither of them English. When the living-room door shut again, he used the white key to open his bedroom door. After he took a shower, he heard his phone ring. "Hello?"

"Mr. Walker, a very good morning to you. I am Darek, your director."

"Where are you calling from?"

When Darek laughed, the director sounded about fourteen years old. "I am next door, of course. Miss Janic has ordered you a breakfast. Are you ready to begin?"

What he thought was, maybe he should have given the itinerary a closer look. "Give me five minutes."

Billy had always made a point of dressing nicely for his auditions, unless the role clearly required him to play down on his luck. Clothes were the one component of his life where he had spent beyond the minimal—he shopped sales and took semiregular trips to the outlet malls. His other primary expense was a studio apartment that was his and his alone. The north Hollywood apartment was smaller than this hotel suite's parlor. But it had allowed him to live on his own and still meet expenses even during his really bad months. As Billy dressed in his least wrinkled audition clothes, he wondered he really was about to leave all that behind.

Then he entered the suite's living room, and was greeted by the sight of a full set of lights and professional-grade digital camera and four gaffers and a soundman and recording equipment. Mimi smiled from her position at the dining-room table and said, "They just sent down for fresh coffee."

Billy made himself a plate of fruit and yogurt, added a croissant, then allowed the slender director to introduce him to the team. Other than Darek, only Ivan, the soundman, spoke English. Darek was slender and floppy-haired and wore a vintage Led Zeppelin T-shirt and low-rider jeans and motorcycle boots. At least in that regard he looked the part.

LA directors were known to be the worst-dressed people on earth.

Darek personally answered the door when the waiter knocked. He poured Billy a mug of fresh coffee and pushed the milk pitcher and sugar his way. "There is also cream, if you like."

"Just milk is fine, thank you."

Darek watched him spoon up the yogurt and fruit. "Ms. Janic says you were in the gym."

"Is that a problem?"

"No, of course not. We just . . ." Darek turned and said something to his crew, who smiled in unison.

Mimi translated, "They are not used to American actors who hold to a healthy lifestyle."

"Ask your team not to tell," Billy said. "I don't want to spoil anybody's reputation."

Mimi said, "They want to interview me. About my childhood."

Darek said, "We were overjoyed to learn Ms. Janic speaks Ukrainian."

"I used to speak it," Mimi said. "Not anymore."

"Ms. Janic, believe me, your story and your accent and your . . ." Darek showed her two open palms. "How you look, it will be . . . *mahiya*."

"Magic," she translated.

"There, you see?"

"You don't know anything about my story."

"No? You were born in the East, yes? You emigrated because of the troubles. To the United States. Now you are here because of the sister you lost."

Mimi showed very real alarm. "How are you knowing these things?"

"Of course we know because of Mr. Walker's people."

"Call me Billy."

"It is also a story known to so many. But you have come

back and it is the perfect time to reveal this scam." Darek was no longer smiling. "So many scams, this is what our country is known for. Your story, it will become part of a message of hope."

Billy watched the change come over her. From panic stricken to listening. "What are you talking about?"

"When the call came from Los Angeles, it hit our studio like, how you say, a *bliskavka*."

"Lightning bolt," the sound technician said. Ivan made an explosion with outstretched arms. "Boom."

"Everybody goes crazy. Nobody sleeps." He said to Billy, "Now we have help from so many places. You wait. You will see."

"We don't know it's a scam," Mimi protested.

Darek glanced at his sound man. "Of course."

"I don't want to seem naive. I understand the risk, but . . ."

"But you need to hope. Of course. We *all* need." For the first time Darek actually looked old enough to lead a full crew. "And if it is indeed your sister, this is one hope. But we are now preparing, you understand?" He turned back to Billy. "In case it is the *other* thing. In case it is *not* your sister."

"I thought this was a promotional tour for Billy's new film."

"Of course, yes, but can you imagine what this means?" The chair was no longer capable of holding Darek. The young man rose and paced and shaped images with his hands. Entering into full director mode. "Billy Rose Walker. His film was one of our biggest hits last year."

"Not just Ukraine," Ivan said. "All Baltic states. And Scandinavia. And Poland. Billy Rose is big, big star."

"And here comes his new one," Darek went on. "In three weeks it hits our cinemas. But wait, what is this? Billy Rose has come to *Ukraine*? And why? Because he wants to help his friend! Mimi Janic! She has heard from her sister in, how long?"

"Twenty years."

He did not actually get down on his knees, but Darek came close. "Ms. Janic, we need you to speak. Tell us what you can. Nothing more. Please."

The sound technician said, "For all those who do not hear from their loved ones ever again."

Mimi turned to Billy. "I haven't spoken Ukrainian in a dozen years. Longer."

Billy offered, "They can have a translator work with the tape. Add the words you can't find and speak in English, am I right?"

"But of course. You can say the whole story in English if you like. But to try, even one sentence, it would be . . ."

"Speak for all the mothers whose arms remain empty," the sound technician said.

Mimi held him with her gaze. Finally she nodded. Once.

Still, it was enough for Darek to pump the air. *"Yes."*

She said to Billy, "Will you hold my hand?"

CHAPTER 50

At the prep-work began, Mimi found herself becoming part
of a team. She was the focal point, but still one of seven. It
was a team that included Billy as well. They were respectful
to the star from the West. But they had a job to do. And
what clearly mattered most was that Billy was willing to become part of their real intent, which was not to promote his
upcoming film. That was secondary to telling Mimi's story.

Darek clearly did not approve of her travel outfit of navy
linen jacket and charcoal sweater with matching pants. He
spoke at length with the cameraman, the two of them standing at a distance and eyeing her in a totally new manner.
Studying her clothes as a component of whatever they already envisioned. When Billy asked what was going on, she
replied, "They want me to change."

Darek said, "It is fine, what you have." But Darek's words
said one thing, while their mutual expression said something
else entirely.

Billy asked, "Would you mind if I had a look at what else
you've brought?"

Soon as they entered her bedroom and she opened her case, he pounced on a formfitting russet turtleneck, one shade darker than her hair. This led almost naturally to him suggesting a paler lipstick, a bit more blush, and suddenly he was the one holding the cosmetic brush, smoothing the color on her cheeks, then applying a hint more base to the lower rims of her eyes. He made some joke about them both being stained by jet lag, spoken like an apology. But he was so calm, so professionally detached, Mimi found she actually welcomed his help.

As they started back, Billy halted with the door slightly opened and studied her.

"What is it?"

He worked up a smile. "You look lovely, Mimi."

"That's not what you were thinking."

"How would you feel about taking out your hair band and letting your hair fall loose over your shoulders?"

The answer was, she had worn her long hair in a ponytail so long, it was part of her identity. Something she never even thought about. Brushing her hair, then pulling it through the band and doubling it and pulling it through a second time, she did it without conscious awareness. Like putting on shoes before walking outside.

Mimi moved back to the cosmetics bag still open on the little table. Billy let the door click shut. She pulled the hair band down the length of her hair, which allowed it to spill over one shoulder. "Like this?"

"Turn this way." He studied her with that same clinically detached expression. "Now let it go down your back. Okay. That way will photograph better."

She turned to the mirror and brushed her hair until the dimple caused by the hair band was erased. She had not worn her hair loose and flowing like this since childhood. "All right?"

"Better than all right. *A lot* better."

He held the door for her, and followed her back into the suite's parlor. When she reappeared, Darek did not actually swoon, but he and the cameraman both offered them a smile of approval. The cameraman said in heavily accented English, "Super-duper A-OK."

Ivan wired them both with collar mikes and battery packs. They positioned her on the sofa's right side. The drapes were tightly shut, meaning the room's only light remained totally under their control. They put two spots directly on her face, a third behind her and to the right, then aimed a fourth at the ceiling. When they were satisfied with her, they positioned a fifth light at Billy. The director remained polite, but he dictated now. Very intent. Very professional. Billy allowed himself to be positioned, folded, shifted, positioned again. Finally Darek and the cameraman were satisfied, and Ivan stepped forward to adjust a third mike suspended above their heads. Billy explained, "This adds a three-dimensional depth to the sound."

Mimi nodded. Despite the alien situation, or perhaps because of it, she found herself drawn tightly to Billy. His magnetic appeal had a purpose now. She was seeing his world from a totally different perspective. She did not particularly like it. She had no real interest in ever being part of it again. Just the same, it felt better than good, being intimately connected to his professional life.

And that was the moment she realized she was in love with this man.

She heard the quiet tapping of sleet against the hotel windows. She heard the five crew members talk softly as Darek and the cameraman studied her through the viewfinder. Billy had retreated inside himself, his calm as total as a windless Pacific dawn. She had no desire to reach over and touch him. She already rested easy in their closeness. Of course she was still afraid. At some level, almost beyond reach in this moment, she could feel the faint whisper of terror: about Billy, about her sister, about her own future, about this entire strange episode here in the airport hotel. But the man's calm and his resolve and his strength were there for her to use. And his love. She knew this was the truth, a definite fact. Wanting to hear him say it was like waiting for the first taste of a kiss they would soon share. She felt the intimacy and the knowledge surround her. Shielding her totally. Even from this moment, as Darek said, "We are going to shoot a few stills. For promotion. Later."

The lights flashed in unison as the photographs were taken. Mimi asked, "Why are we doing all this now?"

It was Billy who responded, "Because they are in control here."

"Yes," Darek said. "Is exactly this."

"Once we land in Lviv, did I say that right?"

"No," Darek replied. "But it does not matter."

"There will be other voices talking at us," Billy said. "A lot of them. And confusion. Here, it's just us."

Darek stepped in close to the cameraman and scrolled through the stills. Then, "All right, are we ready to begin?"

"Yes," Mimi said.

And she was.

CHAPTER 51

❦

Billy's presence made all the difference.

He maintained that same clinically detached air as Darek said, "I will ask whatever you need. But if you can, please just speak. You understand?"

"Not really, no."

Billy explained, "This isn't an interview. Darek will be off camera. The less his voice is heard, the more the audience can connect with you directly."

"Is so," Darek agreed.

"Plus, they may decide to cut away from you and show different scenes as you talk. This works best when your story isn't interrupted by an unseen outsider."

Darek asked, "You have worked on documentaries?"

Billy shook his head. "This isn't about me."

Darek and Ivan exchanged a look, but all he said was, "Mimi, speak, please, for the sound check."

"You want me to begin where?"

"Check," Ivan said. "We are good to go."

Darek took a step farther away, moving outside the lights' reach. "Camera."

The cameraman replied in Ukrainian, "Rolling."

"Talk with me." Darek addressed her in the language of her first home. "Tell me what you think I should know about your early days."

Mimi found a very distinct pleasure in Billy's presence. Even now, when she was being asked to divulge her darkest secrets. On television.

Having told Billy the previous evening definitely made it easier. As Mimi recounted her early years, she wondered if she had known this would happen. Not at the level of conscious thought, of course. But so much of her life contained elements that defied logical explanation. Perhaps this was another such event. Like viewing her baby girl. Time after time, as she paused for breath, or to steady herself after a difficult sentence, the image flashed briefly into her mind and heart. As powerful a calming force as Billy seated there next to her.

He remained perfectly still, curved slightly so one knee was pointed at her and his right hand rested on the sofa's back. Close as possible to her without actually touching. He shifted position only when the director called for a break. Which Darek did five times. After her childhood, her father's disappearance, her mother, then her sister's illness and Mimi's departure for America. Otherwise Billy might as well have stopped breathing, he was so motionless.

Mimi heard herself speak Ukrainian, knowing she made numerous mistakes as she recounted the early days. Her voice sounded lighter, a bit higher, as if her childhood self had somehow emerged to take over the telling. She dropped in a number of English words when the Ukrainian vocabulary wasn't there. But no one objected. It must have worked, for twice she noticed Ivan bending over his sound apparatus, wiping his eyes.

She was vaguely aware of time's passage, but she could not have said how long they went on. Darek asked then if she wanted to break, have a bite to eat, something. Mimi replied that she would prefer to get it all over with. Billy simply sat there, watching her with that gaze, making it possible to look over anytime she needed and draw from his strength. And his love.

She moved faster through her early life in LA, university in San Lu, and finally the move to Miramar. This time, when Darek stopped them, he said, "Enough."

Ivan said softly, "Wow."

Darek switched back to English. "Ms. Janic, you are a natural."

"Mimi. Please. It was really okay?"

Darek kissed the tips of his fingers. "We have spun a cloth of gold."

"I wept," Ivan said. "For you and your sister. For all the others who will never find their way home. Yes. I wept."

"Millions will weep," Darek said. Then to Billy, "Thirty-minute break for sandwiches and coffee, then you, yes?"

Billy's interview astonished them all.

Clearly the director expected something about friendship, maybe even romance. A few words about concern and indignation over Mimi's story, a desire to help a friend or lover. The kind American star who decided to use his influence and help Mimi out. Like that.

Instead, Billy told them about dying.

The news was so astonishing Darek and Ivan exclaimed aloud, which probably should have halted the shoot, except Darek translated for the crew how Danny had been electrocuted on the set of his latest film.

Darek halted the filming long enough to reposition Carl, the cameraman, and one of the lights. Then Billy stood and lifted his sweater, or tried to. He winced at how the motion pulled at his injury, so Mimi rose and helped him. Even now, fifteen days after the incident, his entire side remained laced with blue-black striations.

They filmed him working back into his clothes, wincing and moving slowly and telling Mimi that he needed another session. Which was when Darek asked what he was talking about. So Billy explained how Mimi had, as he put it, brought his body back to working order.

The director said to Mimi, "But you told us you now teach school."

The camera shifted slightly as she replied, "I also teach Pilates."

Billy said, "She is the absolute best." He explained how a friendship flowed from that, and how they were now talking about a new future. But because it was all so new, he did not want to say anything more. For the moment he simply wanted to be there for her. As she had been for him.

There was a long silence as Billy turned and looked at her. Giving her more of that deep and caring gaze.

Finally the director said, "Cut."

CHAPTER 52

❧

Only Darek and Ivan and Carl joined them on the Lufthansa flight to Lviv. The gaffers and junior techies were booked on the midnight Ukraine Airlines flight. The split-up was necessary because they continued working until the very last possible moment. Darek's crew remained in Frankfurt to pack up.

Once they finished Billy's interview, they started back with Mimi. Asking follow-up questions about her father. About what she remembered from her earliest days. At one point Mimi heard herself describing the fire that had consumed her best friend and all his family, and the warning that had followed. The ease of her conversation astonished her almost as much as the constant sense of separation. Mimi felt as though she listened to someone else. When time ran out and they finally left for the terminal, Mimi rode the elevator wondering if she would soon wake up to terror and regret over shattering her lifetime cloak of secrecy. Just then, however, it was enough to listen to Darek and Ivan talk with quiet satisfaction about all they had accomplished. That and holding Billy's hand, leaning her head briefly on his shoulder, feeling his lips touch the crown of her head. Enough.

They picked up their tickets and dropped off their luggage and were informed their flight was delayed half an hour. Darek shared a smile with Ivan over the news, then translated for Carl, who laughed out loud. When Billy asked what was so funny, Mimi explained, "Only the Germans would apologize for a flight to the Ukraine being half an hour late."

"Half an hour late on Ukraine Airlines, they would make you pay double," Darek said.

"They would brag," Ivan said. "Look at us. It's a good day to fly."

After they passed through customs, Darek asked, "Do you want to go to the first-class lounge?"

Billy shook his head. Mimi said, "No, thank you."

When they arrived at the gate, Mimi settled into a seat next to Billy. Darek indicated the seat on her other side and asked, "May I?"

"Of course." When Ivan took his place next to Darek, she asked, "Why are you here at all?"

"Excellent question," Billy said.

She turned to him. "But you know, don't you?"

"It's like I said back in the suite." Billy leaned forward, as to look at Darek on her other side. "This whole thing has been kicked up a level."

"Five levels," Darek corrected. "Perhaps ten. Or a dozen. More."

"Our director wanted to get us on tape while he was still in control of the situation," Billy said. "When we arrive, things accelerate."

"If everything goes smoothly, acceleration," Darek replied. "Otherwise, chaos."

"Welcome to Ukraine," Ivan said. "We do chaos better than anybody."

"Only not on this shoot," Darek said. "I hope."

Ivan snorted, but did not contradict the director. He translated for the cameraman, Carl, who stood between them and the window. Carl spread his arms up high and wide, and said, "Boom."

"This acceleration, it is a very good thing," Darek said. "We are now speaking about more than just a news piece."

"Which is why others have become involved," Billy said.

Mimi protested, "All I want is to find my sister."

Billy remained beyond patient. "If it is your sister, and if she is really sick, having all these people involved will assure she gets the absolute best possible care."

"Is exactly as he says," Darek confirmed.

"And if it's not, they will keep us safe." Billy remained bent over, his gaze on Darek. "But it's a lot more than that now, isn't it?"

"So many peoples and nations are worried about Russia," Darek confirmed. "They see what is happening in eastern Ukraine, and they worry, are we next?"

"Lithuania," Ivan said. "Estonia. Latvia."

"Scandinavia," Darek said. "They already see Russia jets invading airspace, the navy destroyers patrolling their waters, submarines outside their harbors. They are right to be afraid."

"So here is a famous American star coming to Ukraine with his friend, who fled Donetsk because the fighting," Darek went on. "Looking for her sister."

Ivan said, "And if not sister, is criminal hackers."

"Ukrainian hackers," Billy said.

"Exactly," Darek said. "Ukrainian hackers who invade all countries." He mimicked his team's action, lifting and spreading his arms. "Boom."

CHAPTER 53

A̶s they stood waiting to board, Darek received a phone call. Three minutes later, he slipped next to Mimi and touched her elbow. When she looked over, he gestured for her to step away.

Darek led her from the crowd gathered by the gate. He kept his back to the boarding process as he said, "My producer thinks we must focus on Billy Rose."

The words were enough for her to understand his sudden nerves. "The star."

Darek nodded. "My television station was once part of the national government communications bureau. Now it belongs to a new private corporation. You understand? This same company also licenses films from the Americans."

"I understand."

"If Billy Rose is upset with his treatment, we could have problems with the American studio. Not this film. The next one."

"Billy doesn't care."

"You are certain? If Mr. Rose becomes angry, I am the one who also pays."

"Billy is here for me." When Darek remained worried, she said, "You should have your people ask him when we arrive."

"You will speak with Billy about this?"

"Of course I will."

"Thank you, Mimi." Darek led her back toward the gate. "He is very special, your Billy."

She nodded, thinking, *My Billy.* "Yes. He is."

They were given the first two seats on the plane's left side, just back from the jet's entryway. Mimi took the seat by the window and waited as they pulled back from the gate, and the engines were powering up, to say, "We need to talk about what we both don't want to talk about."

Billy's only response was to shake his head when the flight attendant offered him a glass of champagne. Mimi did not even glance over. She tightened her grip on Billy's hand and said, "This could be our last chance for a while. Do you want to wait?"

"Absolutely. I'd be happy to put it off forever if I could."

"So would I. Absolutely. But can we?"

Billy watched her and did not speak.

"It's been with me since I listened to you talk for the cameras," Mimi said. "You love me."

His gaze opened. "I do."

"And I love you. And this is a quiet moment. Perhaps our last for a while. And I don't want our past to shape our future."

"Strange thing to say," Billy pointed out. "Here we are, flying to meet your past."

"You are helping me, and I am hoping to help my sister. This other thing is different, and you know it."

"It terrifies me," Billy said. "This other thing."

The words were there, so clearly she might have been reading a script planted in the air before her face. The plane surged into takeoff, so Mimi leaned closer still. "Ever since I told you about my mother, I've known we need to do this. Before then. Since I saw you standing alone on the point."

"Cape Farewell," Billy said. "If only I could do it. Say farewell."

"We both need to find a way to move beyond everything we've carried with us," she said. " We've spent a lifetime pretending it didn't stain our world. And we've been lying. And now . . ."

He nodded slowly. "You're right. It's time."

She turned slightly, so that there was no room for anything besides his face. His gaze. His heart. "Ask your question. For both of us and all we carry."

CHAPTER 54

~≈~

When they landed ninety-seven minutes later, Mimi had still not received any sort of answer. Just the same, there was a very distinct and very positive element to the silence.

After Billy asked his question and there was no response, the intimacy and tight focus that bound them together remained. They had entered into something new, and they both knew it. They were sharing the dark components of their memories, opening to one another with a new level of trust and closeness. After she apologized for not having anything to offer him, after he thanked her for trying, Mimi settled into her seat, cradled Billy's hand in both of hers, and closed her eyes.

Mimi doubted she would be able to reach any sense of clarity over what had just happened. Not with everything else that was going on. That was not what she was after here. She simply wanted to absorb this. Work it into every fiber of her being. Become firmly wedded to this incredible space. When there was absolutely no divide between her and this man. She and he were one. She breathed the jet's cold filtered air, and felt as if they shared the same set of lungs. It would pass, she knew. They would land and become surrounded by tension and risk and people. But just now, this was hers. This was *theirs*. She wanted to be able to draw on it with the same intense recollection as she did the image of her baby. Which was the instant she realized the two moments shared something very special. Lifting her future child, holding Billy's hand, they both left her . . .

Complete.

Mimi must have drifted off, because the next thing she knew, the flight attendant was picking up an empty coffee cup from the armrest she shared with Billy.

Billy smiled when he saw her opened eyes and said, "We're ten minutes out."

They landed and taxied through a blinding snowstorm. Mimi stared out her side window and remembered other snowstorms and other windows. As soon as the Jetway reached them and the plane's door opened, a trio of officers stepped through. They wore the dark blue uniforms and stern confidence of Special Forces. Three seconds later, the flight attendant came on the intercom. Mimi translated, "They're asking everyone to stay seated."

"Everyone but us, right?"

She nodded as Darek and Ivan and Carl stepped forward. Darek spoke briefly with the lead officer, then smiled nervously at Billy and Mimi and said, "This is our welcoming committee."

Mimi followed Billy off the plane and past the gate and through a crowd of people who watched them with open curiosity. When they reached the customs booth, the officer spoke through the glass barrier, and the customs officer waved them all through. A portly, nervous gentleman in a rumpled gray suit and a bad comb-over stepped forward. He shook Billy's hand, then Mimi's. His hand was limp, moist.

It felt to Mimi like she grasped wet dough. She waited until the producer greeted Darek to wipe her hand on her trousers. The lead officer spotted her action and offered a tight smile. Billy listened to what Darek was saying, and shook his head. The producer spoke faster and Darek rushed to keep up.

A woman stepped to Mimi's right and said, "You understand what they are talking about, yes?" She was a slender woman, perhaps ten years older than Mimi, with gray streaks to her dark hair. She wore a navy suit and gray blouse and a lanyard with a photo ID around her neck. "I am Galyna. Your translator."

There was an edge to this woman, a confident strength she shared with the officers. "You are police?"

"State security. I am attached to the anticorruption bureau. My boss waits for you at the hotel."

"Really?"

Galyna clearly approved of Mimi's surprise. "We are hoping your arrival may be a break for us."

Billy chose that moment to chop the air between himself and the producer. Cutting off the older man's oily flow. He spoke tersely, then turned away. Galyna asked a second time, "You know what they are speaking about?"

"The producer is concerned that Billy will be upset with not having everyone treating him like the star of the hour," Mimi replied. "Billy just told them to forget it."

Galyna smirked. "I am liking your Billy."

"That makes two of us."

Galyna signaled to the senior officer and said, "A subordinate will bring your luggage. We should hurry now."

A phalanx of four cars waited outside the terminal. Two dark Mercedes S-Class vehicles were flanked by police cars. Mimi watched the producer hustle Billy toward the first vehicle. Galyna asked, "You want to travel with them?"

Galyna was sporty and tight and had a cop's humor. Mimi heard the smirk in her voice. "No, thank you."

Darek stood by the first car's open front door and pointed Ivan and Carl toward Mimi's car. Ivan walked over and said, "My thumb is out."

"You are most welcome to join us," Mimi said.

The trip to the center of old-town Lviv took less than half an hour. The snow swirled in clouds so heavy it completely blocked Mimi's vision. Police lights atop the cars ahead and behind turned the scene a flickering blue. Their driver was highly professional and completely ignored the white blanketing the road. Mimi sat behind the driver, with Galyna in the middle and Ivan by the opposite window. The cameraman spoke from the front passenger seat, and Ivan translated, "Carl wishes to know if he should wave to the crowds."

"No crowds, no waves," Galyna said. "Waving is a shooting offense."

Ivan asked Mimi, "You have visited Lviv before?"

"When I was nine," Mimi replied. "In by train, out by plane. Three days here. Maybe four."

"With your sister."

"She had pneumonia." Mimi recalled the constant coughing, the weak wails when she learned Mimi was leaving without her. But even this could not touch her at the deepest level. Down where it mattered most, she remained separate. Immune from all the swirling clouds of icy regret. "She was often very ill."

They pulled up in front of a massive edifice, built in the heyday between the World Wars. "The Grand Palace Hotel," Galyna said.

"I have passed by a hundred times," Ivan said, "and never been inside."

"We go straight through the lobby and up the stairs," Galyna said. "We have already checked you in."

Mimi watched as the police rose from the two cars and took up stations by the Mercedes. "Why all the fuss and bother? No one knows we're here, yes?"

"And that is how we keep it," Galyna replied. "No one sees you, no one knows what is happening until the net falls. Ready?"

As far as Billy was concerned, the ride into town could not have ended soon enough.

He was seated directly behind the female driver, a professional security agent right down to her earpiece and the bulge under her jacket. Darek was in the front passenger seat. The producer, Ilya, shared the back seat with Billy. The guy talked non-stop. Now and then, Ilya leaned forward and poked Darek in the shoulder. Darek translated in a voice as flat as a deflated balloon.

When the producer's phone rang, Billy leaned forward and ask Darek, "What is this guy's story?"

Darek continued to address the front windshield. "He was a senior executive under the last regime. Which was very pro-Russian. You understand?"

"He's scared for his job."

"Like a rabbit, this one," Darek agreed.

"Plugging away at me won't do him any good."

"Today, everyone talks about stopping corruption. He shows he is a part of this. You are here to help. Big people from our new regime are watching. He insists on being involved."

Billy flashed back to enduring a director who wanted him gone. "You spend your days holding your breath."

"Exactly."

Billy hurt for the guy. "What would be your ideal situation here?"

Darek turned around and glanced at Ilya, who was leaning over now, cupping his phone and talking softly. Darek said,

"In the hotel is a very good woman. Her name is Greta. She is deputy head of the government's new anticorruption bureau. She wants to use this news special as a way to show the nation that she is involved, that the fight against corruption is very real."

Snow blanketed the world beyond their car. Billy caught brief glimpses of passing headlights, a few buildings, a white world. "You want more."

"If this is as good as I hope, I want to make a documentary." The words came in a rush now. "You heard what I said before the flight. All the region is watching."

Billy saw a question in Darek's gaze. "We don't have much time. Get to the issue."

"To do this, I must have written consent. From you and Mimi. There would be the issue of payment."

"Not an issue," Billy replied.

"It is an issue until it is not, you understand?" Darek spoke in a whispered rush. "Our legal department must be involved."

"Which means this guy here."

"Exactly. The documentary I want to make only *starts* with Mimi." Darek's words were a rapid-fire murmur. "It grows into something that represents the corruption we face as a nation. And that risks uncovering . . ."

Ilya tapped his phone, leaned back, and snapped a question at Darek. Instantly the director resumed his blank-faced role. "Ilya asks what we are speaking about."

"I am so very interested in your country and its struggles," Billy replied. To his ears, his voice had become almost as bland as Darek's. "I am grateful for anything more your boss can tell me."

He turned to the window and blanked out the man, his words, Darek's translations, everything except the snow. An endless ten minutes later, Darek broke through, saying, "We have arrived."

The doors to both cars opened in unison. Billy allowed himself to be swept across the entryway and up the stairs and through the ornate lobby at one pace below a run. Faces turned their way, but they were in and through so fast, with people tight to Mimi's sides, Billy doubted anyone could identify her as anything more than female. They climbed the grand central staircase, up to where another security man with an earpiece and military-grade expression held open the double doors. A brass plaque on the left-hand wall declared this was the PRESIDENTIAL SUITE.

The living room was vast and very crowded. Billy spotted two separate camera crews, one operating a standard device on a tripod, the other prepping a Steadicam. Six gaffers set up a variety of lights and taped sound and light cables to the parquet floor. A technician was preparing what Billy recognized as a radio-phone connection. Uniformed officers stood around the perimeter. A trio of dark-suited individuals huddled by the rear doors. Despite the movement and people and hushed conversations and tension, Billy instantly recognized the prime target. The boss. There was no question. None at all.

Greta was a very small woman, scarcely five feet tall and dressed in a smoky blue suit that seemed intentionally chosen to make her look even smaller. Her hair was perfectly coiffed, her features as finely carved as a timeless ivory statue. She was impossibly erect, very calm. Her crystal blue eyes swiveled Billy's way and took his measure, heels to hairline, all in about half a second.

Billy walked straight over. "I have a favor to ask."

"Which is hardly what I would expect," she replied. The producer started hustling toward them, but Greta halted him with a single upraised finger. "My experience with Western powers is, they demand. Is that what you intend, Mr. Rose? Or should I call you Mr. Walker?"

"Billy works just fine."

"So, what is it?" Her English was as precise as cut crystal, her voice very refined. "A polite demand, or a genuine request. Which, of course, means I can turn you down flat, and we still remain on polite terms."

"I hope what I want to ask is in everyone's best interests," Billy replied.

"What do you know, a star who is also a diplomat." Greta did not smile. Her features did not crease at all. Even so, Billy had the distinct impression that she found him mildly hilarious. "So I am all ears. Make your request."

"I was hoping you could make Ilya disappear."

"Ah. An understandable request." Greta watched as a woman carrying a professional cosmetics case led Mimi toward the rear door. Two other women followed. Mimi cast Billy a swift glance, then stepped inside and the door closed. The woman said, "I must apologize in advance. It is illegal to shoot irritating people in Ukraine. Even for visiting Hollywood stars."

Billy found himself liking this woman just fine. "The director responsible for this show is standing over there with his soundman."

"I am very familiar with Darek. I agreed to participate because he was in charge. Not only does Darek do excellent work. He is also a strong supporter of my cause."

The news made Billy's pitch a whole lot easier. "Darek wants to turn this into a full-on documentary. Which means major international publicity for your anticorruption drive."

Greta's attention now held a laser quality, a burning intensity. "Go on."

"You're not here because this is some major break in your work. This circus isn't just about one woman and her search for her sister. That's too small for the sort of action we're seeing here. You're here because this might show the Ukrainian public you're serious about helping them. Your work can touch all their lives."

"Not just Ukraine," Greta said. "This scam reaches all the way to California, no?"

"Which makes the documentary even more important," Billy said. "Darek is concerned that his work will be tainted. Or destroyed."

"It is a valid concern." She made a subtle gesture in Ilya's direction. "There are new corruption laws in place now. Laws with teeth. Our producer friend has been careful since the new administration came to power. We have not bothered to look into his past because he is too minor. A small irritating fly."

"Not as far as Darek is concerned."

"No, perhaps not. But this fly still has connections. We have kept him in place because we also need the support of his political allies. And with all of us watching, we can be fairly certain he will not make the wrong call and taint our work. As you say, this is not a huge operation. Even so, we have tapped his phones and put him under surveillance. And we have let him know he is on a very tight leash."

"That's great, but it's also not the point." Billy shifted so his back was to the room. "We've moved from simple news to a commercial release. Darek needs contracts with me and Mimi before he can use us in a documentary. Put Darek in full control. Give him full say. Sole producer credit. Do this and we will both sign the release."

"What you are asking does not come under the authority of my department."

Billy just waited.

She liked that enough to smile. "Is that all?"

"Do this, and all payments due to me will go into a missing persons fund and relocation program. I can't say for certain, but my guess is, Mimi will agree to this also. Your department and Darek will handle these funds."

She spared him another thirty seconds of her intensity. Then, "Excuse me, Mr. Rose."

"Billy."

"I must make a few calls." She pointed to a young man who had just entered the parlor. "Go introduce yourself. There is someone who needs a friend."

Darek was already moving toward the guy. Ilya frowned and started to intercept the director, but Greta barked a single word, halting the producer in his tracks. Ilya shot Billy a venomous look and changed course. Darek asked, "What did you say to the czarina?"

"You actually call her that?"

"A woman that powerful, it works as well as anything."

"It's probably best if I wait and let her tell you."

"That sounds positively Ukrainian." Darek halted before the tallest man in the room. Early forties, balding, at least six feet seven, and unattractive in a distinctly techno-geek manner. Rumpled denim trousers, frizzy hair, stained Miami Heat sweatshirt stretched over a bulging gut, ancient mushroom shoes, spine bent in a perpetual attempt to bring himself down to everyone else's height. "This is Avel. The website Mimi used is his work."

Billy showed his surprise. "I guess if you're here, it means nobody thinks you're part of the scam."

"Avel very much wears the white hat," Darek said.

"Works for me." Billy offered his hand. Avel's grin carried the same nerves as his sweaty hand. "He doesn't speak English?"

"I am biggest number one fan," Avel said, his accent mangling the words. "This very huge deal, meeting Mr. Superstar Hollywood."

"I actually don't know what to say to that," Billy said.

Darek asked, "Can we shoot the two of you talking?"

CHAPTER 55

Of the three local women in the bedroom with Mimi, only the senior cosmetician spoke any English. A second woman stood with hands tucked together by her middle, head cocked to one side, and asked through the cosmetician if madam had anything else she might wear. When Mimi replied in Ukrainian, saying their baggage was coming from the airport, all three faces lit up.

Mimi then apologized for making so many mistakes in everything she said, and all three became her allies. Perhaps even friends. They made a few minutes polite conversation, apologizing for the weather, asking if Mimi wished for tea or something to eat. Three minutes later, a knock on the outer door announced the arrival of her luggage.

While the makeup ladies worked on her face and hair, the third lady went through Mimi's clothes. Without being asked she selected the same outfit that Billy had suggest she wear. The seamstress hung her clothes on a trio of hangers and gave them a very careful going-over. First she sponged off travel stains that only she could see. Then she took a hand steamer from the cosmetician's case and went over the blouse and jacket and slacks. Then she pulled an ironing board from the side cupboard and pressed her clothes. When Mimi tried to tell her not to take so much trouble, the seamstress replied, "You must look your best. You speak for all of us who have such stories, but no voice."

The cosmetician's fingers smelled of old smoke. But her touch was gentle, and her eyes held a wealth of experience. "They will want to see a successful American who has not forgotten her family. Or her heritage."

"I wish I spoke Ukrainian better."

"You left when you were still a child, yes? That you even try is enough."

"My accent is terrible, I know."

"It is like music, your voice. The hint of America will touch the heart of everyone who watches."

The youngest of the trio stopped brushing Mimi's hair long enough to come around and smile, where Mimi could see. "Hollywood is so special like they show?"

"Some of it. Other parts are very ugly."

"We leave your hair loose, yes?"

"Whatever you think is best." She let the cosmetician and seamstress ease her back into her clothes, taking care so as to keep her face from smearing. As they checked her hair and adjusted her jacket, she asked, "Will you be doing Billy?"

"Darek wants him to stay as he is. Show the strain that you do not." The cosmetician nodded approval. "A smart one, that director. He will go far."

The youngest lady pretended to swoon. "Your star is such a handsome man. Is he nice as he looks?"

"Enough with your dreamy talk." The cosmetician smiled and steered Mimi to the door. "Now go and steal the heart of our nation."

CHAPTER 56

᷿

As soon as Mimi reentered the parlor, she thought every face carried the same message.

Her sister was not there.

Mimi found she was neither surprised nor very disappointed. She realized she had known this was probably true all along. Even seated back there on Cape Farewell.

Mimi did not feel any sense of the tragic. Her sister was in some respects closer now than she had been since the day they were split apart.

As Mimi studied the people and the room, her gaze repeatedly settled back on Billy. He stood to one side, next to an unattractive man as rumpled as his clothes. While the Steadicam operator filmed the two of them, Billy remained positioned inside Mimi's field of vision. Soon as she entered the room, there he was. Waiting to see if she needed him.

She met his gaze and felt the rest of the room and the people and the tumult fade into the background. Mimi found herself thinking that perhaps this journey of theirs had never been about finding her sister. Perhaps the true purpose was to strip away her secrecy. To force her to accept that she *needed* him. To bring her to the point where she would willingly join with him. In love.

Darek stepped up. "You look very beautiful, Mimi."

She resisted the urge to step to one side, so as to maintain her focus on Billy. He was still there. Waiting. "Thank you."

Darek fitted a microphone to her lapel, then offered her the battery pack and a nervous smile. "We are ready whenever you are."

"We have continued to send short messages while you traveled here," Galyna said. She was seated to Mimi's right, Billy to her left. The three chairs were pulled up to a desk holding a laptop computer and microphone and cell phone and multiple cables. Galyna touched her tablet's screen with an electronic pen. "Here are the communications, all in English. We have written just enough to keep them aware of your concern. We ask about your sister, can we speak, and so forth. They have supplied a phone number."

Mimi scanned the dozen or so messages, short as phone texts. All the incoming messages spoke about her sister's urgent need for money. Mimi handed back the tablet. "What happens now?"

"We suggest you place your call. This is your connection, you understand? We have ideas, how this can go. But you must decide."

The room had been mostly emptied. Darek stood in front of her and slightly to Mimi's left, next to Carl and his tripod. Behind them stood Ivan and Greta, the woman Darek had introduced as the anticorruption czarina. Two gaffers stood in the corner, in case they were needed. The Steadicam operator hovered to her right, so as to shoot Mimi's face over Galyna's shoulder. All the others had been ordered outside into the hall. Mimi was surrounded by a forest of lights.

None of this touched her. Not down deep, where it mattered.

"Tell me what you want to have happen," Mimi said.

"Speak a few words," Galyna replied. "But do not tell them you are here."

"Tell *them*."

Galyna nodded. "If we are correct, someone will answer, and soon as they hear it is you, they will put on someone else."

Mimi felt an internal prompt, as if she needed to continue to play the role of concerned relative. Even though everyone else knew it was a false hope. She said, "Not my sister."

"Again, if we are correct." Galyna was the professional here, in her medium, even under the lights. Stern and hard and precise. "This second person will claim to be your sister's friend. Perhaps her lover. He or she will say that your sister is very sick and needs your help. Immediately. Desperately. Time will be a crucial factor."

Mimi nodded. "Time."

"Precisely. They will use time as a weapon to keep you off balance. You must send money or your sister will die." Galyna hesitated, as if it was necessary to ensure Mimi did not fall apart at the callous nature of her scenario.

Instead, Mimi said, "This is when I tell them I am here."

"It will come as a shock. A huge one, if we are correct." Galyna continued to inspect her with that tight cop's gaze. "If at any point you feel that you are losing control, you simply say you have hired me as your guide and translator. I will take over."

Mimi decided there was no need to tell them she had never felt more in control of herself. "Make the call."

CHAPTER 57

A male voice answered on the second ring with a single Polish word, "Mówi." Speak. The Ukrainian and Polish languages were intimately linked, and most citizens of western Ukraine used the two daily.

"Ah, hello, do you speak English?"

"Yes. What you want?"

"My name is Mimi Janic. I am calling about—"

"Sister. Yes. I am just operator. One minute."

"No, wait, I need . . ." She stopped speaking when the line clicked.

Mimi almost lost it then. She could not say precisely what impacted her so deeply, shaking her world. The intensity mirrored on all the faces. The lights. The two cameras watching her with their bulbous glass eyes. Whatever the reason, in that instant the calm that had held her so intimately was fractured. The fear and confusion and sorrow all crowded in. Then Billy shifted slightly, as if he sensed her need. A gentle touch to her arm. Mimi turned in her seat, and there he was. Resolute. Strong. Caring.

When the second voice came over the speaker, she was ready.

"Hello, this is Petro, Zofia's special friend. Do I speak with Ms. Janic?"

"Please. I am Mimi."

"*Zdravstvuyte.* I wish I could say it is a pleasure, Mimi. But your sister, Zofia, she is so very sick."

"That is why I am calling."

"Yes, it is so good you reach out to her." The man's voice was smooth, almost delicate. "When can you send the money?"

"Can I speak with her?"

"Unfortunately, no. We can arrange a video link. Tomorrow. Yes? Today she receives treatment. Speech is so very difficult. You understand?"

Mimi glanced at Galyna. The agent nodded and mouthed one word. *Now.*

Mimi replied, "Actually, that won't be necessary."

"Excuse me?"

"I am in Lviv."

"You . . . What?"

"You said it was urgent. I dropped everything and came."

His voice hardened. "You are here."

"At the Grand Palace Hotel. Give me her address. I will come immediately."

"No, no, I told you already. Today is impossible. Next week, perhaps."

Galyna used her electronic pen and wrote on the tablet's screen.

"Hello, Mimi, are you there?"

Mimi read off the screen: " 'It has to be tomorrow morning. I leave on the afternoon flight to Frankfurt. If I can't see my sister, I . . . can't be involved. Do *you* understand?' "

Another pause, then, "I will come and fetch you."

"That won't be necessary." Mimi read off Galyna's screen: " 'I have arranged a translator and guide. And a friend is also here with me. From America.' "

"You should come alone, Mimi, your sister . . ."

"I am coming with my associates. And it must be tomorrow morning. Or not at all." Mimi heard her own voice take on the same hard note as the man's. "Now please give me her address."

CHAPTER 58

~⚘~

Billy woke and said to the darkened room, "Enough."

The clock on his bedside table said it was a quarter to five, an hour and a half before he needed to wake Mimi. He turned on the light and swung his feet to the floor and walked to the bathroom. When he emerged, he drank a bottle of water and pulled gym shorts and sweatshirt and sneakers from his case. Something had woken him before his mother's song could take hold. He was fairly certain he knew what it was, and why.

When he emerged from the bedroom, the security guard rose from his chair, checked Billy's clothes, and said, "Gym?"

"You got it."

"Please to wait." He signaled to another guard seated in front of the elevators. The woman approached, nodded to whatever the first guard said, and told Billy, "Come."

The guard took up station just outside the gym's glass door. Billy felt the tension and overall weariness at a bone-deep level. But another hour's sleep would not change anything, and he knew from experience that a low-key workout would help him through the stressful day ahead.

He set the StairMaster's level just a couple of notches above flat walking and climbed on board. He was not after pushing himself. This was a time for taking it easy, just working the heart and his muscles at a steady pace. It granted him the perfect opportunity to look at his silent dawn with a fresh perspective.

The dream had not been granted the chance to inject more fear and pressure into an already overfull day. The result was, Billy had a chance to view it at a double distance: nine thousand miles, a stranger's snowy city, and a frigid hotel gym. Not to mention the silence in his mind. Perfect.

It had never been his mother.

The chance at success, the near-death experience, the stress of a film directed by a man who wanted him to fail. All this had squeezed his mind and emotions to where his younger self had woken up.

It was scary and glorious in equal measure, facing the fact that his greatest terrors had been given a voice in his dream time. Billy Rose Walker, the man abandoned by parents who did not consider him worth taking along.

If anyone did not deserve stardom, it was Billy.

If anyone should spend his entire life scrambling for a chance that would never come . . .

Billy stepped off the machine, toweled his face, and grabbed a couple of free weights. He started on slow and easy repetitions. The workout that had carried him through so many hard and seemingly hopeless days. Even now, when the crisis was not his, but rather belonged to the woman he loved.

It was so easy to confess these feelings. As if Mimi had been part of his life for years. Amazing.

He stared at his reflection in the wall-sized mirror, recalling her conversation on the flight. Traveling toward the nightmares she had carried all her own life. Setting aside everything she faced. Taking his hand. Saying it was time to take his problem for a spin.

Amazing.

He suspected Mimi's lack of any response and what he had woken to this morning were linked. This was not a single problem. It was not merely letting go to the rage over how his mother had treated him.

Billy needed to let go of his own past. Release the child he no longer was. Free himself from the cage of his early days.

And Mimi would help.

When the security guard knocked on the door and touched her watch, Billy replaced the weights, wiped his face again, then headed for the door.

It was time to go be strong for Mimi.

CHAPTER 59

❧

Mimi slept in fitful snatches. She wrestled through any number of troubling dreams that often jerked her awake. She knew the bad elements of her past were trying to crowd in, and still she managed to settle back and breathe once or twice, then return to sleep.

A knock on the door woke her when it was still dark. Too soon. "Come in."

Billy appeared bearing a steaming mug. "The troops are gathering."

She pushed the pillows behind her and sat up. She watched him shut the door and cross the room and settle down beside her. She accepted the mug and asked, "How can you be so awake?"

"Disrupted schedules are part of every shoot." He watched her sip her coffee. "Did you sleep?"

"Some." She finished her mug and set it on the side table. "Thank you, Billy."

"More?"

"In a minute." She reached for him. "First come hold me."

* * *

Galyna knocked on Mimi's door while the cosmetics and hair and clothes trio were still working on her. "It's time."

Mimi stared at the agent. Galyna looked like what Mimi's younger students would call a total frump burger. Her hair was a barely controlled rat's nest. She wore pale octagonal glasses, a cheap gray-checked jacket and skirt, and square-toed lace-up shoes. "You look like the evil librarian."

Galyna smiled. "They see me, they think you have hired a local guide through a website and overpaid. They won't be looking for the twelve-man specialist team stationed around the perimeter." Galyna handed her a black device, slightly thicker than her hand. "You know this?"

"It looks like an oversized phone."

"Is a disguised weapon." Galyna might as well have been discussing the snowfall. She pointed to a silver button embedded in the side. "You push this so." The top popped back and two steel needles slid out. "You touch this to your attacker. Press button a second time." She did so, and a spark flew between the points. "Bad guys go away double time."

"Are you sure . . ."

"Just in case." Galyna pressed and held a gold button on the device's opposite side. The needles retreated. "First they must go through me. And Billy, he has another."

Snow drifted in a fitful wind as they emerged from the hotel. Galyna led them past a line of Western automobiles, Mercedes, Citroëns, one BMW, a pair of Audis. Out on the street she directed them to a boxy four-door vehicle with rusting fenders and a cracked windshield. Mimi asked, "What is this?"

"A Škoda Superb," Galyna replied. "The name is a lie."

Billy asked, "Is it safe?"

"Not really. But I am a very safe driver. And this is what a local guide and translator would be driving," Galyna replied. "A cheap one. Mimi, you are in front seat with me."

Lviv's central old town held a fairy-tale air. The snow fell in a soft, constant silence. The cars along the white-ribbon streets moved at a respectful pace. The ancient buildings shone soft and mystic and timeless. Behind the hotel and to Mimi's left rose the great central hill, topped by the ruins of an ancient royal castle.

Six blocks later, everything changed.

The shift could not have been more drastic. The street widened to ten lanes, lined on both sides by Soviet-era structures. Big concrete high-rises, one after the other, all of them adorned with violently colored graffiti. From his position in the rear seat, Billy said, "Wow."

Galyna said, "No one does ugly like the Soviets."

Gradually the space between the horrid cell-like towers broadened. A few older structures began to appear, little more than rustic hovels, their roofs bowed and their walls uneven, as if their blankets of white were ready to send them crashing to the earth.

Forty-five minutes later, Galyna pulled down a farm lane, following tire tracks plowed recently through the snow. She entered a thick forest glade. Mimi thought they were silver birches, but could not be certain. A number of heavily armed troops in snow-camouflaged garb drifted among the trees. The rear doors of a paneled truck opened and Darek dropped to the earth. He and the cameraman both wore the same white one-piece as the soldiers. He greeted Mimi and pointed her into the truck, then pulled Billy to one side. Mimi remained standing by the van's rear doors, and heard Darek say, "I don't know what a Ukrainian director could ever do for a big Hollywood star."

"Next time I meet one, I'll ask," Billy replied.

Darek would not be deflected. "What you have done, you cannot imagine."

"I've worked for my share of bad bosses. I have a pretty good idea."

Darek pressed a card into Billy's hand. "One call, one text, one e-mail. Wherever you are. I come."

Mimi and Billy were all fitted out with radio mikes hidden inside their hair. Billy was given a knitted wool cap and ordered not to take it off. Tiny button-sized cameras were attached to Mimi and Billy's outer jackets. When Mimi asked about wiring Galyna, the agent pointed to her glasses and said, "You think I wear these for their beauty?"

They returned to the car and rejoined the rural road. Ten minutes later, they pulled through a pair of iron gates adorned with half-a-dozen rusting signs. Galyna said in Ukrainian, "We have arrived."

CHAPTER 60

They pulled into a semicircle of wooden structures, so decrepit the snow only magnified their feeble state. The main farmhouse rose to Mimi's left. Directly ahead of them was a long, low building that could have once held rooms for farmworkers. To their right were a trio of low barns containing a repair shop for tractors. Their front yard held a haphazard mess of dismantled vehicles, engine parts, rusting plows, harvest machinery, several trailers, and stacks of tires.

"Is perfect," Galyna said. She beeped her horn once and left the motor running. The heat fan rattled softly, as if the car was chattering in fear. "What you see here, it is a mask. Behind the farm machines is a business for tearing apart cars."

"Chop shop," Billy said.

"Is so. We knew it was somewhere." She pointed to the shadowy shed inside the open doors. "For any outsider, they are shown farm machines not being repaired. In back everything is stolen. Interpol says cars are coming to Lviv from Germany, France, Belgium, Holland. Now we know where."

Billy said, "Check out the power cables."

Galyna glanced back at him, followed his pointing finger to the overhead lines. "Greta is doing flips."

"That I would like to see," Billy said.

"Forward, backward, side to side." She noticed Mimi's confusion and said, "See how the three thickest all go to that shed by the main house? So much power means only one thing."

Billy said, "That shed, see the white metal brace coming up out of the snow? It could be a backup generator."

Galyna checked him out in the rearview mirror. "You know this how?"

"Film sets. When we're shooting on location, a secondary power supply is always on standby."

"Here is only one reason."

"Servers. A lot of them."

Billy reached forward and rested his hand on Mimi's shoulder. He did not speak, which Mimi both liked and appreciated. Any assurance he might have offered just then would have been a lie. Galyna glanced at the two of them and nodded. Then she spoke in Ukrainian. "Alert. Alert. We have company."

An odd-shaped man emerged from the central structure. He was almost as wide as he was tall. He wore boots so large, Mimi wondered if perhaps they had been specially made. The upper laces were undone, because his shins were as broad as his neck, which was almost as wide as Mimi's waist. His face was a blank slab of pale flesh, tiny nose, emotionless eyes, and a slit of a mouth. Blond crew cut. He wore rumpled cords and a checked shirt and appeared indifferent to the snow that fell on his shoulders and bare head.

"This one I know." Galyna's voice and manner underwent a sharp transition.

Billy asked, "He knows you?"

"We have never met, but his work I have seen. He is enforcer for local mob." Galyna said to Mimi, "You speak no Ukrainian. Whatever you need to say, you speak through me. Be direct. First you see your sister."

Mimi heard her voice flutter nervously. "I understand."

"Billy, you stand back. If there is trouble . . ."

"I use the Taser and get Mimi out of there."

"Correct." Galyna pointed to the keys dangling from the ignition. "These stay here. Just in case. And if I speak the word 'attack,' you run for the car. You stop for nothing. Ready?"

"Yes."

"All right." In Ukrainian she said, "We are entering the lair."

The car's radio spoke for the first time. A voice Mimi did not recognize replied in Ukrainian, "We are in position."

Galyna cut the motor. "Here we go."

The man watched them approach, then spoke in a reedy, high-pitched voice, almost a whisper. Galyna translated: "He wants to know if you are Zofia's sister."

"Mimi Janic. Yes."

Another exchange, then, "He says, only you."

"We all come," Mimi replied. "Or I turn around and leave."

His face remained utterly blank. Finally he turned and pushed through the central door.

Galyna said softly in Ukrainian, "Central structure. We enter by main door."

The front door opened into a tight airless alcove, Mimi remembered these from her childhood. People shed their outer coats and shoes before entering the house proper. But the big blond man pushed through the second door, clomping snow and mud onto the parlor carpet. It was a large room, nicely furnished with heavy plush chairs and sofas. Two men were seated at a wooden dining table playing cards. A third man stood by the side window, talking into the phone. He was older and dressed in a jacket and black dress shirt with an open collar. He turned and waved to them, lowered the phone and said in English, "You are Zofia's sister, yes? Welcome to my humble home. You will take tea?"

Mimi recognized his voice as belonging to the man she had spoken with the previous day. "I want to see my sister."

"Of course, of course." He addressed the giant in rapid Ukrainian. Then, "Go, go, we will speak later, yes? Thank you for coming. Your sister, she is so grateful."

They followed the large man down a long side corridor. Bare yellow bulbs dangled from the ceiling. They passed half-a-dozen closed doors before entering a large kitchen with a stone sink and gas Bakelite stove. An old woman kneaded dough on a battered central table. Her hair was gathered beneath a stained headscarf, and her arms were white with flour up past her elbows. She did not give any sign she noticed their passage.

Down a second corridor, then the man entered the last door on the right. He stepped to one side and whispered.

Galyna stepped to where she stood between the man and the figure on the bed. "He says the illness has almost taken her, and you must help."

Mimi walked forward and knelt by the bed. She was already certain this was not her sister. Wrong hair color, wrong age, wrong face, wrong everything. But she sensed the large man's eyes on her. She knew her actions were important for the sake of appearances. Mimi guessed her age at sixteen or seventeen, too young to be Zofia. She was covered by a stained quilt, and watched Mimi with eyes that floated in and out of focus.

Part of her training as a student counselor had been drug-related therapy, and this had required her to spend a semester working in a rehab center. The young woman exhibited all the signs of having been fed a drug cocktail, Mimi suspected it contained both an opiate and a stimulant. She remained there on the frigid stone floor and stroked the woman's cheek. She was grateful for the sense of calm distance that remained in place. Even here.

Finally she rose to her feet, faced their guide, and said simply, "Thank you."

The man offered a reedy response. Galyna translated, "He wants you to come speak to Zofia's friend about paying for treatment."

"Of course."

"You must go straight out the front door, not stopping."

"I understand."

But when they emerged from the kitchen and reentered the front hallway, the two men who had been playing cards in the parlor now stood sentry by the exit. Mimi heard Galyna address the older man in Ukrainian, "My client needs some air."

"Of course, of course!" The older man's Ukrainian was clear, his voice almost jovial. "First we shall have tea, and discuss payments, yes? Then she will have all the air she needs!"

Billy stepped up alongside Mimi and said, "Straight ahead."

She felt him reach into her pocket and saw his hand emerge holding the Taser. He walked up ahead of her, straight at the two men. Galyna said, "My client wants air *now*."

The older man stepped into the doorway and replied in precise English, "Ah, but you and your friend are in no position—"

Billy waited until both sentries were reaching for him, then jammed the two Tasers into their sides.

There was a quick electric hiss, and both men spasmed.

Mimi heard a third click-hiss behind her, and assumed Galyna had taken out the giant.

The older man roared in fury.

Galyna shouted in Ukrainian, *"Attack! Attack!"*

Billy dropped the Tasers, gripped Mimi's arm, and slammed through the doors.

White-suited troops assaulted the compound from all sides, with Darek and two cameramen hot on their heels.

CHAPTER 61

❧

It was, by all accounts, a major bust.

According to both Galyna and Greta, the rear three buildings and the main house together held one of the largest hacker sites ever uncovered. All Billy saw was how the people kept pouring out of the dormitories and kitchens and computer rooms. They filled all three patrol wagons; then more were forced to sit cross-legged in the main house's front room, wrists locked behind them, while a pair of buses were brought up.

Three senior mob bosses.

Stolen luxury sedans whose plates said they had come from as far away as Portugal.

Drugs.

A barn full of cash.

Billy did not actually witness Greta doing handstands, but she bestowed smiles and congratulations on everyone.

Especially Mimi.

Soon as he was able, Billy asked Galyna for transport back to the hotel.

Greta personally saw them off. She showed a cop's ability to stow away her good humor, at least long enough to tell Mimi, "I am sorry it was not your sister that we found."

Billy saw Mimi taste several replies, then simply say, "Thank you."

"I will personally oversee a nationwide DNA search. Galyna will obtain a swab before you leave."

"I . . . appreciate that very much."

Greta turned to where Darek stood by the Steadicam operator. She spoke a word, and the pair stopped filming and walked off. She said to Billy, "The strangest thing. Ilya has disappeared."

"I'm sure Darek misses his producer very much."

"He does not know yet." Greta turned to where Darek was pointing the camera operator to film the chorus line being readied for the arriving bus. "I'll wait until his celebrations don't risk drowning our project in vodka."

"Probably a wise move."

"I told you we kept Ilya under tight supervision. Somehow he managed to slip away from my people. And my people are very good. We suspect he has gone east. There are allies in Donetsk who will welcome him and his stories about maltreatment at the hands of our new regime."

"They can have him."

"You must come again. I rarely say this to an American and mean the words. And now I am speaking to a Hollywood star." Greta offered him and Mimi a frosty smile. "I look forward to showing you both the new Ukraine."

CHAPTER 62

The snow stopped as they pulled in front of the hotel. Billy thought it was probably just a temporary pause. As they climbed from Galyna's car, the sky overhead was one single cloud, bunched and knitted from multiple shades of gloomy cotton.

"Go and pack," Galyna said. "There is no need to check out. I will drive you to the airport." She smiled. "In a nicer car."

Mimi walked up to where Billy stood on the sidewalk. "When does our flight leave?"

Galyna checked her watch. "In four and a half hours."

"Can we please take a walk?"

"At the airport, beyond customs, you are safer. There may be associates on the hunt, you understand?"

But Mimi was firm. She pointed to the snow-covered hill rising above the old town. "I'd like to go there. With Billy. Please."

Galyna inspected her carefully. "You wish to say good-bye."

Mimi nodded. "I have no reason to ever return."

"Greta and Darek and everyone involved, they will hope

you one day change your mind." When Mimi did not respond, she decided, "Go and pack. I will make calls."

"Thank you, Galyna."

"You cannot go alone, you understand?"

"Of course." She tugged on Billy's hand, leading him through the revolving doors and into the hotel's warmth.

Billy remained silent as they rode the elevator upstairs. He had not spoken ten words since they left the compound. He had no idea what to say to Mimi, then or now.

He was standing outside Mimi's door when she appeared with her cases. She had dressed in a fresh outfit of comfortable-looking blue trousers, a thick cotton turtleneck the color of her autumn gaze, and a matching hair band. Billy thought she looked fantastic. She let him take her case and asked, "You'll be warm enough?"

He wore navy cotton cords and dress shoes, the only other pair he had brought. The boots he had worn during the takedown were soaked. "I can warm up at the airport."

As they waited for the elevator, she asked, "You have other dry shoes?"

"Just my gym shoes."

She pressed the button for the lobby and said, "You should pack them in your carryall. And dry socks."

"I hadn't thought of that."

"You can pull them out at check-in." She noticed his smile in the doors' mirrored surface. "What is funny?"

"Oh, nothing." But he carried his smile across the lobby, thinking how they sounded like an old married couple. Instead of like two people who had known each other for a couple of weeks.

Galyna stood beside a new Mercedes E-Class when they emerged. She put their cases in the trunk, then asked them to wait. As she slipped into the car and used the police radio, Mimi said, "All these elements of my childhood, they are with me again. This is the first time I have seen snow in years. It all feels like yesterday."

Galyna emerged and said, "We can go now."

Lviv's Castle Hill towered above the city's old town. The gray sky, dim light, and bare snow-covered trees gave the hillside a brooding menace. It was as if the half-buried giant with his ruined stone crown was mightily displeased by the city he now surveyed. The asphalt paths were sprinkled with salt grit and remained free of snow. Galyna and another officer walked thirty paces back. Billy spotted another pair tracking them from up ahead. His nerves still jangled from the compound's assault. He was grateful for their company.

It was only now as they climbed that he felt some of the day's invisible tension begin to ease. He had used pretend Tasers in several films, but the real thing was something else entirely. Billy flashed on the two enforcers and their calm menace. He pushed the memory aside and focused on what was before him: the yellow streetlights lining the path, the gray day, the frigid air, the warmth of Mimi's hand in his. He found himself very grateful for this chance to walk with her.

Her calm was both wonderful and somewhat disconcerting. Billy had the impression that somehow Mimi remained distanced from everything that had happened. The arrests, the false sister, the cameras, all of it. Nothing could penetrate her shield.

Except him.

Mimi did not just hold his hand. She clung to him. Whenever the path leveled off and the walk grew easier, she molded herself to his side. Billy could almost feel her drawing on his strength. He wanted to tell her how much that meant. And he would. When the time was right, he would tell her exactly how he felt. He willed himself to remember everything about this walk in the gray-shrouded gloom. So that one day soon he could describe this incredible moment.

And thank her for entrusting him with everything this journey represented. In a time when words were again made welcome.

They reached one level below the castle ruins. An empty ledge jutted out from the path like a stone lip. Two streetlights illuminated a snow-dappled railing and the city beyond. Mimi pulled him over to the ledge. Tendrils of smoke rose up from the city, knitting a veil that softened the hard edges and masked some of time's wounds. Lviv would never be beautiful, but here in this wintry light, it shone with a secret luminescence, as if proud of surviving all that had come its way.

Mimi stepped over so that she stood in front of him, then reached around and wrapped both his arms around her. They stood like that for a time, listening to the city's snow-muffled hum. She said, "I think I know why there was no response when you asked your question on the plane."

Billy rested his chin on the top of her head and breathed in her fragrance.

"Like you said, letting go is hard. It is also a process. There is no single act. Not just one answer."

He rubbed his chin up and down on her hair. Nodding.

She turned around and faced him. Her features held the same luminescence as the city below. Only stronger. And far more beautiful. "I want to make a future with you. I want to heal. But I need your help."

"You have it," he replied. "You know that."

"I do know. And I will help you."

She kissed him, a slow, languorous melting together. Then she stepped back, smiled, and said, "Let's go home."

As they started back down the hill, it began to snow.